What the critics are saying:

"Readers looking for romance will find a well-traveled road in DANGEROUS DESIRES. Erotica fans will savor competent sex scenes that will leave them within they'd been doubled in number and uninhibited relish." -*Annabel, Word On Romance*

"Once again, Julia Templeton has delivered a delightful story. Her talent for bringing forth the emotion in her characters is amazing, and I found myself teary-eyed as the characters were faced with difficult challenges and choices. I highly recommend this book. The passion and emotion weaved throughout is so engaging that anyone who loves a good tale of hard choices, sacrifice, and love will not be disappointed." -*Danica Favorite-McDonald*

"I enjoyed reading this story very much. The plot and characters were interesting and the love scenes were very sensual. The heroine was strong and independent, not a fragile flower at all. The hero was sexy, possessive and a little tortured, just the way I like them! The story was very well written and I was immersed in the storyline from page one." -*Sara Andrade, Sensual Romance*

"DANGEROUS DESIRES is an entertaining blend of erotica and historical romance. Ms. Templeton remained true to the time period. All in all, a very satisfying read from the co-author of FORBIDDEN." -*Kristina, Sime-Gen Perspectives*

DANGEROUS DESIRES
An Ellora's Cave Publication, July 2004

Ellora's Cave Publishing, Inc.
PO Box 787
Hudson, OH 44236-0787

ISBN #1-84360-905-3

ISBN MS Reader (LIT) ISBN #1-84360-410-8
Other available formats (no ISBNs are assigned):
Adobe (PDF), Rocketbook (RB), Mobipocket (PRC) & HTML

Originally published in March, 1999 by Kensington under the title *To Honor & Desire*

Edited by *Allie Sawyer*
Cover art by *Scott Carpenter*

DANGEROUS DESIRES

Julia Templeton

To Kip. I love you!

Chapter One
Rochford Manor, 1810

Arlie sat on an uncomfortable settee shivering from both fear and cold. It had been a long ride from her home in Wales to this manor, and now as she sat awaiting her introduction to her guardian, she wished to be anywhere else.

Just days ago she'd been living in her small cottage by the Irish Sea. A home she had shared with her father, until his death. Now her father was gone, her house was gone, and her fate lay in a stranger's hands—Dominic Santrell, the Earl of Rochford. Though she knew little of the man, what she'd heard from others was not exactly flattering. Apparently, he was a womanizer of the worst sorts. A rakehell so sinfully handsome, women had fainted at his feet.

Arlie rolled her eyes. How utterly dramatic the stories were. His appeal most likely came from his title and vast wealth, made obvious by the grandeur of his home. From the moment she'd caught sight of the three-story manor with its numerous archways and columns, she'd been intimidated. And that was before she'd stepped across the threshold of the manor to find extravagance far beyond her expectations. The spotless marble floor of the landing came up against an enormous staircase. The steps led to different wings, one of which would contain her new room.

Her gaze strayed to the walls where gold-framed portraits of Rochford ancestors hung on display. The stern faces that stared back at her made her seriously doubt the earl was as handsome as rumored.

She ran her hands down the worn fabric of her breeches and sighed with impatience. How rude of him to leave her sitting for so long. She tapped her boot on the marble floor. The sound brought a butler out of an adjoining room. His brow lifted as he regarded her.

"Miss Whitman," he said with a curt nod, "his lordship will see you now."

Arlie followed the man, peeking into lavish rooms that confirmed the earl's status of filthy rich. After passing the largest library she'd ever seen, Arlie backtracked. She loved to read. When her father had gone out to sea, she spent nearly every night reading about different adventures, learning about things no school would dare instruct. And when he returned, he would ask her to read for him. It was a ritual, one that both of them had become fond of.

"Miss Whitman?"

Arlie glanced up to find the servant at the end of the hallway before a pair of open doors, motioning for her to enter.

The dark-paneled room was filled with heavy, masculine furniture.

"My lord, I shall return shortly," the butler said from behind her.

"Thank you, Joseph," a deep voice replied from across the room.

As the door closed, Arlie moved toward the man who kept his back to her. Ignoring her, the earl stood staring out the window. *Her guardian.* Swallowing the lump that had formed in her throat, she stopped beside a high-backed chair, but rather than sit, she stood, her fingers digging into the velvet. "My lord," she said, wincing when her voice came out a squeak.

For a moment she thought he didn't hear her. She opened her mouth to repeat herself when he turned to her, his gaze sweeping her length. Her pulse skittered. She knew this man. Her mind scrambled thinking of when she had last seen him, and then it hit her with a force that nearly stole the breath from her lungs. The stranger with the ring—the black prince. Her gaze quickly went to his hand. The familiar ring on his middle finger confirmed her suspicion.

She had thought him large and imposing then. Now he seemed even more so. The short dark hair she remembered him having now fell in thick waves past his broad shoulders. His eyes were a clear blue; so striking against his dark skin and hair she couldn't help but stare. His hips were narrow, his legs muscular and well defined in navy breeches.

To Arlie's horror, her knees actually felt weak. She gripped the chair tighter.

"So...you are Arlie Whitman." His voice was low, appealing.

She focused solely on his face, not letting her gaze drift further to his powerful body. She'd seen many men in her time, but no other had looked like this man. White teeth flashed when he gave her an easy smile. Uncomfortable with her reaction to him, she stumbled over her words. "Y-yes, my lord."

"You may sit."

She immediately did as he asked, glad to be off her wobbly legs. He walked toward her, and she forced herself to sit tall instead of sinking back into the cushion. She let out the breath she'd been holding when he sat down in the chair just opposite her, stretching his long legs out in front of him, to where his boots nearly touched hers.

"Miss Whitman, I wish I could say I remember your father well, but to be perfectly honest, I don't. I only met him on a single occasion, yet it is obvious he thought it enough to appoint me as your guardian." His brows furrowed into a frown. "But I suppose that is beside the point. My lawyers have assured me that the will is legal and binding. Therefore, it appears you will be living at Rochford Manor as my ward."

Arlie saw the nerve in his jaw tic and as he lowered his eyes, she noticed his incredibly long lashes. How unfair that one person should have so much physical beauty. She shook her head clear of her wayward thoughts. *Good Lord, what was wrong with her?* The man was her guardian. A connoisseur of women. He used them, then tossed them aside when he tired of them — which he did with great regularity, or so she'd heard.

"Are you listening?"

"Yes, my lord." She nodded, trying hard to concentrate on what he was saying, rather than what had been said about him.

"I will not be around a great deal, but my butler, Joseph, is well informed as to what I expect as far as your education is concerned."

His blue eyes, so magnetic, kept her riveted. Pinching her wrist to stay alert, she replied, "Yes, my lord."

He ran his hands down his face, then attempted to look pleased, but failed. He was not happy about her presence there, that was obvious. For all that she'd told herself she would not throw herself on anyone's mercy, she realized that whether she liked it or not, this man held her fate in his hands. Penniless and homeless, she needed his help.

"My lord, I am aware that my position as your ward came as a shock. Trust me when I say it surprised me equally. I can assure you I will not be a burden. I've lived an independent life since the age of ten." She took a deep breath and continued, "I guess what I'm trying to say is, I will stay out of your way…that I promise."

He sat forward in his chair, his long fingers playing with the tassel of a pillow. The side of his mouth lifted slightly. "Miss Whitman, your time here is not a prison sentence. On the contrary, you will have tutors like every other young debutante in London. Soon you will be introduced to all the eligible bachelors of *the ton*. Who knows, within a few months' time we may be placing a wedding announcement in *The Times*."

She could feel the blood drain from her face. "Marriage?" A gasp followed the word. As she stared at him, she hoped he would tell her he only teased, but by his expression, she knew he meant every word. Tears stung the backs of her eyes, but she blinked them back. By God she would not let this…*this rakehell* marry her off! She'd endured too much in her short life to let some stranger tell her who she would marry.

Her stomach clenched into a tight knot. A husband would expect an obedient wife to throw galas and tea parties for his friends and their wives. And he would no doubt see she conceived right away and then leave her at some country estate to spend the rest of her days, while he kept a mistress in town and drank until all hours of the night. She had read far too many stories about such instances, and she was not about to let her life take that turn. She would rather find work somewhere, perhaps as a governess or maybe a housekeeper. After all, she'd taken care of her father for her entire life. How hard could it be to manage a large household, or to care for children? She sighed heavily. Why hadn't she just been born a male? At least then she could set off on her own and not worry about having to answer to anyone.

"Did you hear me, Miss Whitman?"

"Yes, you mentioned marriage," she replied, her voice barely audible.

He smiled, the gesture softening the harsh lines of his face. If possible that small gesture enhanced his good looks. "Arlie, I believe…it is all right to call you Arlie?"

She nodded, confused that her heart jumped at hearing her name on his lips.

"Arlie, I believe marriage to be the perfect solution for this predicament that we find ourselves in. After all, you're of age, and I can't imagine you'd want to live here for long. Believe me, it won't take any time at all to find a suitable beau. In fact, after careful preparation, we will be sure to arrange your coming out at one of the most influential balls of the Season."

Too stunned to reply, Arlie bit down on the inside of her cheek. She nodded obediently, knowing that arguing would get her nowhere. What had she expected from this man—for him to be overjoyed about being a guardian of a penniless stranger? He wasn't that old himself, and to be strapped with a ward was obviously the last thing he wanted, or needed. What better solution than to marry her off?

"I can see you are in need of a wardrobe," he said, his gaze moving down her body once again. She clasped her hands together in her lap and sat up straight.

He frowned, and a slow blush crept up her neck to her cheeks. She cleared her throat. "I am accustomed to wearing breeches rather than dresses."

His frown lines eased. "I realize that the life you led in Wales was...different than the one you are now living. You will dress appropriately, which means you will wear gowns, not men's breeches."

Forcing herself to meet his gaze, she replied, "Yes, my lord." Her fingernails dug into the skin of her palms. How subservient she sounded. What had happened to her bravado? It had all but disappeared the moment she met him. Oh, but he was so dark and sinful-looking. Women no doubt fell at his feet. And to think that at one time in her life she had looked upon him as her black prince, dreaming that one day he would come and sweep her off her feet.

He stood abruptly. Following his lead, she stood as well, trying earnestly not to stare directly into his baby-blue eyes, but it was impossible. His striking features demanded attention.

He nodded. "Miss Whitman, I'll see you this evening at dinner. Joseph will show you to your room. Please take the rest of the day to make yourself at home."

Like magic, the butler appeared at her elbow. Obediently Arlie followed the older man out of the room, glancing over her shoulder to see her guardian watching her.

* * * * *

Dominic waited patiently in the dining room, occasionally glancing at the clock. Only a few hours had passed since he'd met his ward, and he was still trying to come to terms with the fact he was a guardian. He shook his head. He could scarcely take care of himself, let alone a seventeen-year-old girl. It wouldn't have been so difficult had she been a young man instead. He would simply give the boy an allowance, point him to the best social events and encourage him to marry well. But a young woman was altogether different.

Nor had he imagined she would be a beauty. When he first saw Arlie standing in his study, her wisps of blonde hair falling out of the thick braid, Dominic figured he had to be the butt of a joke Langley had cooked up. He waited for his friend to step out and shout "surprise". Yet as the moments ticked away, Dominic realized with a sinking feeling that this was no joke.

The young woman watching him with green almond-shaped eyes was indeed his ward. Her very appearance startled him. Her baggy breeches hung off her slender frame, and the well-worn shirt actually had patches at the elbows. Yet she stood before him like a princess, despite her beggars clothing.

No doubt her maturity came from spending months alone in an isolated shack while her father captained a fishing vessel; one Dominic had helped buy Alexander Whitman out of gratitude for helping him one evening when he'd been caught in a rainstorm. An act of gratitude he now regretted. Celebrating his twenty-first birthday with friends, Dominic had been well into his cups, so much so he barely remembered the burly man who walked with a limp and had a fondness for poker. Not many would have invited him into their home and made him so at ease. In fact, when Dominic's carriage had broken a wheel, the man had stepped outside his small cottage and asked to be of assistance. Since the footman said he did not desire help, Alexander had offered Dominic a drink and some company.

Arlie had been just a young girl at the time. Dominic vaguely remembered a child with a head full of pale blonde curls, asleep on a cot in the corner of the cottage she shared with her father. Who would have thought that child would come to be his ward? And who would have imagined she would grow to be such a beauty?

What a shame Alexander had lost everything to drinking and gambling. Even the vessel Dominic had bought him had been taken as repayment for his many debts.

"She's quite a lovely lass, isn't she, my lord? A little rough around the edges perhaps, but lovely all the same."

Dominic glanced at Joseph, whose mouth held the slightest hint of a smile. "Indeed, she is lovely," Dominic agreed.

"The maids told me she is quite friendly, not to mention gracious. She is delighted with her quarters. With a bit of polish you should have no difficulty finding a husband for her, my lord."

Finding Arlie a husband was exactly what he intended to do, posthaste. Not only did he not have time for a ward, he didn't like the idea of spending too much time with a young, beautiful woman. Not that he didn't trust himself—well, on the other hand, he didn't. He shook his head. Good Lord, *what* had her father been thinking?

"I say, when she has her coming out, every dandy in town will be beating down the door," Joseph added, smiling widely.

If Dominic didn't know better, he would think his butler waited expectantly to see how he handled his new "parental" responsibilities.

Before he could respond, the door opened and the woman who had been burning in his thoughts walked into the dining room. Arlie wore her hair up, in a chignon that made her look years older. The borrowed dress, compliments of his latest mistress, was most becoming on her slender frame. Her tightly corseted body displayed an impossibly small waist, and full breasts that pushed up against the silk of her low bodice until they threatened to spill over. He would never have guessed a beautiful body existed beneath the horrible male attire she had arrived in.

Joseph pulled out her chair, and Dominic was grateful for the few seconds her attention was elsewhere. It gave him a chance to watch her when she was unaware of his scrutiny. A diamond in the rough. Her long lashes fanned against high cheekbones. Her cheeks, like her lips, were pink...and bloomed with color by the second.

He bit back a smile. How charming she was. And how very young, he reminded himself.

Nodding at Joseph to proceed with dinner, Dominic became intrigued by the lovely young woman who had been made his responsibility. He watched her through dinner, pleased to see her take dainty bites of food. She used the correct silverware, and kept her elbows off the table. A surprise, especially since her father had not appeared to be concerned with etiquette. "Your father — was he a good man?"

At the mention of her father, a transformation came over her. Her green eyes sparkled and her mouth split into a wide smile, showing small, white teeth, and deep dimples that creased her cheeks. He shifted in his chair, uncomfortable that his ward, this young lady who he should be thinking of as a daughter, he instead found attractive...very much so.

"He was a wonderful man, very loving and kind. When he went out to sea, I would miss him terribly. But when he returned, we would celebrate into the wee hours of the night. He enjoyed cards. Perhaps too much," she said, her voice losing its luster.

"I remember his laugh," he said, wanting to protect her. He could not bear to see sadness come over her gorgeous face. "And his smile, with those large dimples, which I see, you were blessed with."

Instantly the smile returned in force, and to his disbelief, his heart missed a beat. "Indeed," she said, "his laughter could bring a smile to anyone's lips. Though he did sometimes laugh at the most inopportune times. And his voice boomed so, I could hear him coming from a great distance. He was quite a character."

"You have no other family?"

She shook her head. "No, none. My mother died when I was very young."

"Tell me of your life."

"There is not much to tell." She shifted in her seat. "I grew up in Wales. I was alone a lot, except for our neighbor, Johanna Hopkins, a spinster who taught me to read and write. She had been a music teacher at a school in Cardiff. I remember hearing her play the piano at night, the soft notes floating over to our house." She closed her eyes and smiled, obviously reliving the memory.

Dominic sat entranced by her innocence. The memory of a simple moment in time had stirred Arlie, and he could see the passion on her face.

"I feel as though it were yesterday," she said.

"How old were you?"

She opened her eyes. "About ten. Johanna was a good friend to me and my father, who I missed terribly when he left." Her voice faltered as she stared down at her lap. "I often feared he would never return."

"But he always did."

She nodded and met his gaze. "Yes, he always did. When he lost the boat you'd bought him, he was so sad. I tried to get him to stop drinking and gambling, but he couldn't. They were as much a part of him as breathing, I'm afraid."

"I understand you like to read."

Her eyes lit up, and he made a mental note to thank Joseph for the information.

"Very much, my lord." She sat up straight, her face full of joy.

Dominic did not expect such a reaction from something as simple as books.

"I'm quite impressed by your library, my lord. You have so many titles, and I..."

As she continued talking, Dominic couldn't help but think that she would make someone a wonderful wife. His gaze fell past her chin to her swanlike neck, then down further to the soft swell of her breasts. The firm globes were perfect—not too large, just about a handful. The tight corset made her slender frame appear even smaller. His cook was renowned for her skill—it wouldn't take long to put some meat on Arlie's bones.

His innards warmed as he stared at the curl that had escaped her chignon and lay against her bosom. He wondered what she would look like with her soft hair flowing down her back in thick pale curls. An image came instantly to mind, one in which she stood before him wearing nothing. The blood stirred in his groin, rushing to his cock, making his breeches achingly tight. He took a deep breath, and tried to diffuse any notion that she would become his lover. Yet the image would not fade and to his distress, his penis throbbed painfully.

She stopped abruptly, her brows furrowing into a frown. "What's the matter?"

Taking a long, steadying breath, he sat up straighter. The trembling hand that had been adjusting his breeches a moment before now held firmly to his glass as he drained the brandy. *I should be struck by lightning*, he thought, disgusted by his attraction to this young woman who, no doubt, considered him to be an old man.

"Nothing," he said, managing to sound not at all disturbed by her presence, when in fact, he felt very out of control. He dreaded word getting out that he was the guardian of this gorgeous, desirable young woman.

The ton would have a heyday.

But he would prove, not only to them, but to himself, that he could be a guardian. In a few months she would be married off, and he would forget about this nightmare.

Why was he fantasizing about a virginal young woman anyway? He liked his women experienced, and preferably married, just like his current mistress...who would have a fit when she saw Arlie. "Do you like your room?" he asked, hoping to divert his attention.

"My quarters are lovely. I've never had anything so fine, and the bed…it's so soft. When I first lay down on the mattress, I found it impossible to get up."

If he had his way, she would never get out of *his* bed.

He cleared his throat. "I'm glad it pleases you. Feel free to request whatever it is you may need," he remarked, forcing his thoughts to the rugged conditions she had once lived in.

He'd had his lawyers search her background thoroughly. Aside from the knowledge that Arlie had in essence raised herself, her relationship with her father had been a strong one. He knew she would give anything to have her father back, and perhaps her way of life as well. In fact, maybe she would be better suited for his country home in Whitley, the estate he stayed away from since his grandmother was always in residence. The manor was a good five hours ride from London — far away from him.

He dispelled that notion a moment later when she said, "I can hardly wait to see the sights of London. One of the footmen said it is less than an hour away. Do you think that perhaps one day we could take a ride?"

"Perhaps," he said, and immediately he saw the disappointment in her eyes. He had never been known for stinginess. In fact, he treated his mistresses with the utmost respect and lavished them with baubles and flattery. Seeing his ward's disappointed expression made him want to give her anything she desired, even a trip into London. Though he couldn't form the words because he felt she was not quite ready for Society. The moment he introduced her to *the ton*, all hell would break loose. Like Joseph had said; men would be knocking on the door at all hours. He closed his eyes, already dreading the future.

And once again an image of Arlie, naked in his bed, rose to taunt him.

If only she knew his thoughts, she would run far and fast. He opened his eyes to find her watching him, frowning. She must be terrified, he thought, managing a smile for her benefit. "I apologize. It has been an awfully long day. In fact, if you don't mind, I think I'll retire." He stood, and nearly knocked the chair over in his haste to escape the room. And his wicked thoughts.

"Of course, please do."

He headed for the door, and stopped, realizing his manners had been deplorable. "Would you like me to escort you to your room?"

She shook her head and flashed a soft smile. "No, I think I'll stay here and enjoy my tea. Sweet dreams, my lord."

Sweet dreams? He'd be lucky if he slept at all tonight.

Exiting the dining room, he wondered why this had happened to him. Of all people to become a guardian to a young woman, he was the least capable candidate. And if he had to have a ward, then why could she not have been homely?

As he shut the door behind him, he wondered if this wasn't God's way of testing him to see if he did have a soul. If so, he was surely heading for the gates of hell.

Chapter Two

The next few weeks saw Arlie besieged with dressmakers and tutors. One dressmaker, Mrs. Candora, had praised her for her straight posture, but lectured her about her preference of men's clothing when Arlie had showed the woman her wardrobe.

Arlie endured hours of being poked by the woman's needle. She wondered if the hateful woman pricked her repeatedly on purpose. If she thought the woman spiteful during the measuring process, she turned absolutely heinous when she burned Arlie's favorite breeches and shirt before her very eyes. The fire roared in the fireplace, and Arlie watched with inner fury as the comfortable clothes turned into a charred mess.

Arlie had been able to save only one pair of breeches. That pair remained safely tucked under the mattress, where hopefully no one would be the wiser.

If she had thought Mrs. Candora had been stern, her long list of tutors had been exasperating. Deportment came first and foremost on the earl's list. Apparently he was under the impression she knew nothing of how to behave in Society. Under Miss Elridge's instruction she would, within six weeks' time, become the perfect lady.

No matter how much she did not want the lessons, Arlie gave every one of her tutors her undivided attention, hoping her guardian would be pleased and treat her with a trip to London. At times she found it difficult to concentrate on her studies when there was a whole other world out there just waiting to be explored.

But Rochford had been specific that her lessons take top priority, leaving her time to do little more than walk the gardens and yearn for the day when she could escape the manor's walls—walls that were slowly closing in on her.

Rochford usually left first thing in the morning, and never returned until after seven in the evening. Each night was like the one before. They would have a cordial dinner, talk briefly of their day, then he would excuse himself.

Later, while reading in her room, she could hear the murmur of his voice as he and his friends burned the midnight oil. Not once had he requested her presence, and she had yet to meet any of his acquaintances.

Her teeth sank into her bottom lip as she contemplated why Rochford had not seen fit to introduce her. Could it be he thought her so ill mannered as to embarrass him? Surely if he would just take the time to get to know her, he could see for himself she had been well educated and didn't need the tutors who came in a steady stream day in and day out to teach her things she already knew. If his embarrassment came from the way she dressed...well, she had not worn a pair of breeches since her arrival. Instead, she wore the new, constricting gowns that she found far too heavy and cumbersome.

She sighed heavily. With every day that passed, she became more bored and lonely. She'd tried to strike up conversations with the servants, but none seemed interested in talking with her. And her tutors had been paid to teach her, not talk, as they told her every time she tried to initiate any form of dialogue.

Leaning her head back, she squinted as the sun peaked through the clouds. It would be a perfect day for a ride. How she missed the feel of a horse beneath her, the wind whipping her hair, the adrenaline racing through her body.

She smiled to herself. *Did she dare?* Rochford had left and wouldn't return for hours. Even the shortest ride would get her mind off her loneliness and burn some of her energy. She raced to her room to don her riding habit.

The stable master was an older gentleman who took his job seriously. He made it quite clear that Arlie should not venture from Rochford land alone. After assuring him she would take a short ride and stay close to the manor, she mounted the horse effortlessly. The stable master had been right, the mare was an excellent ride, much like her own had been before she had sold her in order to put food on the table.

Going against the stable master's advice, Arlie rode south, straight for London. She had heard it took the earl a good hour to get there via his carriage, but if she hurried, she could be there in less time and back before he even knew she'd left the manor.

The horse seemed to sense her excitement and bolted. Arlie leaned over the horse's neck as they raced across the flat land. This is exactly what she needed — the wind whipping her face as she flew over the hard-packed ground.

She kept going, eating up the miles, losing track of time, not caring about anything other than the exhilaration of being on horseback and the prospect of seeing the city she had longed for. Having lived her entire life in a small village, she knew not what to expect of a city such as London.

At the thought of her childhood home, melancholy washed over her in waves. She remembered the life she had once led and envisioned the one laid out meticulously before her. She hated the structure, hated the way every minute of her day was planned to the seconds. Every day it was the same thing, absolute repetition. She did not deny being thankful for a roof over her head, clothes that actually fit, and going to bed with a full stomach every night.

If only her guardian could see how desperately she needed his friendship...

Though Rochford had taken her in and given her the best of everything, he hadn't taken the time to get to know her. Every day, she yearned to ask him when she could see the sights of London; attend parties, soirees, the theater...anything. But always he seemed preoccupied, and she ultimately lost her nerve.

At least she was out now. Away from stuffy servants and the same walls of Rochford Manor. She knew every inch of her guardian's home, having explored its depths whenever she had a free moment away from her tutors. Slowing the mare to a gallop, she smiled triumphantly as her stress slipped away. She needed to be patient with Rochford. Perhaps he was still experiencing the shock of having another person under foot, something he was not accustomed to.

When she came upon a passing carriage, Arlie slowed her pace. She lifted her chin, nodding at others who acknowledged her with a smile or curt nod. When they passed by and out of sight, she continued at a breakneck pace.

As she approached the city, it became increasingly difficult to keep her excitement at bay. There were people all about—and the noise sounded like a constant humming. Elegant carriages, simple wagons, gentlemen, ladies, and commoners filled the streets.

She noticed more than one person staring at her, and she knew she had been foolish to continue into London alone, but she could not help herself. For too long she had wanted this. Now she was here, she could not bear to leave.

Fancy gas lampposts stood on every corner. Charming brick townhouses with intricate iron rails lined one side of the street, while shops, clubs, and a hotel lined the other. She smiled to herself. London was everything she imagined it to be and more.

The women, dressed in expensive gowns, looked so refined. It served to remind Arlie that these ladies were what Rochford strived for in her deportment. He wanted her to be a true lady, so she could snag herself a man who would take her far away from Rochford Manor.

Her good mood darkened at the thought. She turned her attention to an enormous park filled with extravagantly dressed individuals. This must be Hyde Park of which she'd read. The books had not done the park justice. In her mind it had been but an acre of grass with trails where one could walk or ride on horseback. This enormous park sprawled out over many city blocks, a place to see and be seen.

With head held high, Arlie passed by a group of women, who lifted their brows at her. They said nothing, but she could see the disapproval in their eyes. Did they stare because she rode alone? Miss Elridge told her a young woman such as herself never, under any circumstance, went out without a chaperone. It could easily cause a scandal.

Arlie fought back the wave of guilt that assailed her. She had made a mistake by coming to London. She cringed, hearing the whispers of the women passing by in a curricle, their laughter burning in her ears.

She must leave at once.

"Hello there."

Arlie jerked toward the sound of the masculine voice. The man, sitting astride a large dark horse, watched her intently. About the same age as Rochford, the man had pleasant features: hazel eyes, hawkish nose, full lips, which complimented his golden hair. Arlie's gaze strayed to the fine cut of his dark green coat, then to the buff-colored pants and black high-polished boots. With a single glance, she knew without a doubt this man belonged to *the ton*.

"Allow me to introduce myself." With hand on heart, he bowed slightly. "My name is George Hawthorne. My friends call me Langley."

She released the breath she'd been holding. He had not mentioned a title. Perhaps he did not know Dominic. She smiled warmly. "And I am Arlie Whitman."

His brows furrowed. "Arlie Whitman? Whitman? Hmm...by any chance are you related to Terrance?"

"No," Arlie said a touch too quickly. "I fear I have no family in London."

His frown deepened.

"Actually, I am living with my guardian for the time being."

A smile replaced his frown. "And may I inquire as to your guardian's identity?"

Arlie swallowed hard and replied, "Dominic Santrell, Earl of Rochford. Do you know of him?"

Langley's mouth dropped open for a scant second before he caught himself and snapped it shut. Yet, as he continued to stare, the corner of his mouth curved into a smile.

Arlie could only imagine what he was thinking—and preferred not to.

"Rochford is one of my closest friends. I saw him just yesterday. Odd, but he didn't mention a word about you."

The words cut at Arlie's heart, confirming her worst fear...Rochford hated her.

"How long have you been staying with Dom?"

"A few weeks."

"I must say I'm surprised. Dom just isn't the type I figured as a guardian. Are the two of you related?"

Though she expected this line of questioning, she found herself at a loss for words. What did one say when the guardian her father had picked for her despised her? Before she could form a reply, she heard Langley laugh under his breath.

"Tell me, Miss Whitman, does Dom know you are in London?"

The way he looked at her made her uneasy—like an unruly child in need of discipline. She wanted to tell Langley—and Rochford as well—that she could take care of herself, that before coming to live with the earl, she had spent months alone without any supervision, save Johanna, coming and going as she pleased. Her life had been free of ridiculous schedules, and continuous studies.

She shifted in the saddle. "Well, I did not *exactly* tell him I would be visiting London."

"Do you realize how far you've come from Rochford Manor?"

"No," she said, hoping she sounded surprised. "Though it has been some time since I last rode. I suppose time just got away from me."

"And you found yourself in London," he said, his voice sounding unconvinced. Pulling his pocket watch out of his waistcoat, he winced. "It's almost half past five now. Soon it will be dark. I'm afraid if we don't hurry, your guardian will come looking for you himself. And I've a feeling he would not be happy to find you in London."

True, Rochford probably would not be happy, yet why should he care? He had not even told his good friend about her. Why should he care if she came up missing? In fact, he would probably be thrilled to learn that she'd left.

She should leave Rochford Manor. Being walled up in that mausoleum, learning things she already knew until he was good and ready for her launch into Society, was making her insane.

"Shall we go?" Langley asked, breaking into her thoughts.

She wanted to tell him she could make her own way back. She could ride fast and make it to the manor in no time. Perhaps before Rochford returned. However, the horse beneath her was exhausted, and the man at her side would probably not take kindly to her riding alone, especially since he and Rochford were friends.

They rode at a leisurely pace, Arlie in her own thoughts, saying little to the man at her side. Keeping her gaze focused ahead, she could only hope Rochford had not made it home early.

She winced. The tutors would have arrived by now, and those tutors cost good money. A wave of regret washed through her. Perhaps it hadn't been wise to leave the manor without telling someone exactly where she planned to go. And it certainly had not been smart to venture into London alone.

"How did you come by Dom as a guardian?" Langley asked while straightening the lace at his cuff.

"My father met Rochford many years ago, when the earl had need of assistance. In appreciation for the help he received, Rochford told my father to look him up if he should ever need anything."

"How very interesting," Langley remarked, the corner of his mouth lifting in a charming smile. "He must have made quite an impression in order for your father to entrust him with your life."

"We have no family, and my father had few friends that he trusted. I suppose he felt Rochford, of all people, could give me the best life."

Langley stared at her thoughtfully. Arlie knew he wondered if she was a blue-blood aristocrat like he and Rochford. She met his level gaze, keeping her chin up. Let him wonder. He didn't need to know the truth — that her father was a fisherman, her mother, an actress turned prostitute.

"Well, Dom is a wonderful man. He is certain to take good care of you."

"Yes, he is a good man," she replied, meaning it. Though Rochford had not given Arlie the welcome she would have preferred, he at least had not turned her out. Instead, he did the best he knew how — showing interest in her studies, asking her questions every evening over dinner, listening to her while she played the piano. He did those things for her. She had faith that in time he would come around. She had confidence that in time they could be friends.

When the manor came into sight, Arlie suffered from fear and trepidation. Turning to her companion, she forced a smile she did not feel. "Thank you, Langley. I'm certain I would have gotten lost had you not come along. I appreciate your assistance."

"Think nothing of it." He lifted her hand in his and kissed it lightly. " I've enjoyed this time with you, and though I would love to drop in on my dear friend, Rochford, I feel it would be most inappropriate at this time." He dropped her hand. "I'm certain we'll see each other soon." With a wink, he turned and headed back down the tree-lined drive.

Arlie knew something was amiss when she saw the stable master pacing near the front steps of the manor. There was no welcoming smile on the man's face. Instead, he waited for her with hands on hips, his jaw in a rigid line. "Ya said you'd be right back. Ya promised me. Do ya know how upset his lordship is?" he asked, all but ripping the reins from her hands.

Alarm raced through her. "His lordship is home?"

"Aye, and he's not very happy with ya, right now," he replied. "Nor was he happy with me for letting ya go."

"I'm sorry. I did not mean to get you in trouble."

He ignored her apology and walked past her with the mare in tow.

Brushing out her skirts, she ran her fingers through her hair, trying to look as presentable as possible. She walked briskly down the pathway to the house, praying Rochford was too busy with his work to give her any mind.

Slowly, she opened the front door, and then quietly shut it behind her. Holding her breath, she walked lightly on the tips of her toes toward the staircase.

"Miss Whitman!"

She jumped hearing her name being yelled from the hallway. Closing her eyes, she breathed in through her nose and out through her mouth, trying to calm herself. With head held high, she walked toward Rochford's study.

Her heart hammered so loud she could scarcely hear anything above it. Entering the dark-paneled room, she saw Rochford sitting on the edge of his desk, his long legs crossed at the ankle. His arms braced either side of him, the sleeves of his shirt were rolled up exposing strong forearms. His hair looked disheveled and as he ran his fingers through the raven tresses, she noticed his hands shook. He was either nervous—or very mad. She feared the latter, and his next words confirmed it.

"Where the hell have you been?" he asked, his voice dangerously low.

"I'm sorry," she blurted. "I—"

He lifted his hand, immediately silencing her. The expression on his face frightened her. He was furious.

"Do you realize I've been worried sick wondering where in the world you've been for the past hour? When I arrived home early, I found your tutor pacing the drawing room floor, waiting for you, and not one of the servants could account for your whereabouts. I've been envisioning all kinds of horrible things that could have happened."

"I didn't mean to alarm you."

He pinned her to the spot, his blue eyes unrelenting. "You have yet to answer me. Where were you?"

Knowing he would not be happy with anything she said, Arlie considered lying. But having met Langley, she knew it would only be a matter of time before he learned the truth. She decided to stretch it a little. "I took a wrong turn and ended up in London."

"London?!" he exploded, the veins in his forehead prominent. He closed his eyes and shook his head. "God help me."

"I met your friend Langley," she blurted, hoping the words would ease his anger.

He opened his eyes. "Langley? As in George Hawthorne, Viscount Langley?"

"I believe so," she murmured, not recalling the man's title.

Muttering something under his breath, he ran his hands down his face. "This is just wonderful."

"I sincerely didn't mean any harm. I only wanted to get away for a little while. I've been closeted up for weeks now, with nothing but studies and deportment. I have been so bored...and I wanted desperately to see London."

His expression softened as he watched her, yet his eyes were still intense. Slowly his gaze moved from her eyes, down to her mouth. Her pulse skittered as his gaze moved lower...down her neck...over the swell of her breasts.

Her throat grew tight as he continued to stare—and her body responded to that stare. Her nipples grew tight under the velvet bodice of the riding habit, sending a pulsing need to the very core of her. She pressed her hands against her stomach, afraid of her body's reaction to his hot stare. "I meant no harm."

"So you decided to leave here without telling another soul where you planned to go?" He slowly lifted his eyes to where they were once again level with hers.

She could not think. Her mind raced, wondering if she had only imagined the way he had looked at her mouth and breasts just seconds before. No, she had not imagined it. Her body had reacted to that stare, and still it betrayed her, her nipples chaffing against the soft material of her bodice. She felt the need to run from him, and away from her wicked thoughts.

"Need I remind you, Miss Whitman, that you have only just arrived. There are ruffians about, particularly in London, who would just love to get their hands on you. This is not a fishing village." He stood, his height overpowering her, making her feel small and exceedingly feminine. He took a step toward her, not taking his eyes off her. "I am certain that word is already spreading throughout the city that I have no control over my ward."

"Is that why you worry?"

He took another step toward her, and stopped. He crossed his arms over his impressive chest. "Pardon me?"

"Were you worried about *me*...or about what people would say about *you*?"

The surprise showed on his face, and for a moment he merely stared at her. Then there it was, the smallest hint of a smile tugging at his full lips.

"Both, actually. Just promise me you will never venture into London again. Is that understood?"

She nodded. "Yes, my lord."

He took a deep breath and released it. "Had I known you had a liking for horseflesh, I would have included riding lessons in your schedule."

She shifted on her feet, relieved that his anger had fled. "I would very much enjoy lessons, my lord."

He nodded. "Please, call me Rochford. "

Arlie smiled genuinely. "Very well. Yes, I would enjoy lessons, *Rochford*." The name sounded awkward to her ears, but he smiled.

"If you wish to leave the premises again, I suggest you tell me first. I will see you have a proper chaperone. " He lifted his chin a notch. "I hope I've made myself clear."

"Quite, my lord. Er, Rochford."

He grinned, the gesture making him seem boyish. Gone was the intense man of a few minutes ago. Now he seemed...approachable. He looked past her shoulder to the door. "Well, I suppose you should get some rest before dinner."

Arlie wanted to spend more time with him. She felt they had made immense progress today, and the last thing she wanted to do was sit in her room until dinner and wait for the maid to come and get her. No, she wanted to learn all about her guardian. She wanted to know about his past, what he did all day when he left the manor, who his parents were, and why he was still not married...

Their eyes held for a long moment before she turned and walked out of the room.

* * * * *

Dominic was not at all surprised when Langley made an appearance the following morning, conveniently right when breakfast was being served.

Putting the newspaper down, Dominic sat back in his seat and watched as Arlie and Langley conversed about the weather, gardening and horseflesh. He listened intently, surprised how much his ward knew about horses. Her knowledge and experience were obvious, as well as unexpected.

Not that he had presumed her to be anything but bright, yet from what he knew of her background, he knew she had no formal schooling. He was fast realizing that he shouldn't be shocked about anything she did. Not many women her age would venture into London alone, particularly when they had never been to the bustling city.

Her intelligence delighted him. Every one of her tutors praised her work, bragging that she needed little guidance and took to her studies with a zest they had seldom seen. With her beauty and brightness, he knew he would have no trouble finding her a husband. Langley's enthusiasm gave evidence of that. Langley had reprimanded him for not telling him about Arlie, making Dominic wonder why he *had* been keeping her a secret. Could it be that since she'd come into his life, he'd arrived home every night looking forward to sharing dinner with her, hearing about her day, listening to the sound of her laughter as she told him about something she had done or seen? It seemed so insane that he, a man who spent precious little time in the company of any one woman, should choose to seek out the very one who had turned his life upside down.

"Oh, Langley…!"

Dominic's brow lifted as Arlie playfully hit Langley's arm. Her smile was devastating—big dimples and small white teeth. Worse still, Langley, who never backed down from a woman's advances, pounced. He took Arlie's hand in his own and brought it to his lips, looking very much like the rakehell he was known to be.

Dominic's eyes narrowed in suspicion. Could it be that his ward already fancied the charming viscount? The very thought was disquieting to say the least. Before he could stop himself, he cleared his throat.

Langley dropped Arlie's hand and turned to Dominic with a sheepish smile.

"Did you say you had an early meeting this morning, Langley?" Dominic prompted. "If you don't leave soon, I fear you'll be late."

Langley kept his features carefully schooled as he stood. "Indeed, I shall, Dom. Thank you kindly for reminding me," he said, blandly.

"My pleasure," Dominic replied, watching as Langley took one last moment to charm Arlie, his lips mere inches from her ear. Arlie's blonde hair stirred from his breath. Dominic clenched his fists, surprised how very irritated he had become with the man he thought of as a brother.

A confirmed bachelor until the last year, Langley had recently become engaged. A woman he had known for only two months, and who brought to the marriage enough money to subsidize his way of life—which went well beyond extravagant at times.

"Please tell your lovely fiancée hello for me." Dominic could not help adding the last as Langley headed for the door.

Langley tripped and Dominic winked as his friend, looking a tad irritated, shut the door behind him.

"My lord, I would like to say something," Arlie said, bringing him out of his unpleasant thoughts.

Intrigued, Dominic sat forward in his chair, trying to keep his thoughts pure and his gaze focused on his ward's face...a difficult feat when the dress she wore emphasized a great deal of her feminine charms.

"I apologize for yesterday. I did not think of the consequences. I know I caused you distress, not to mention embarrassment for going into London without a chaperone." She reached across the table and put a hand over one of his. Much to his surprise, his heart gave a jolt. Her small hand, so tiny compared to his own, pressed down on his, her fingers moving in a circular motion. "I scarcely slept last night knowing all I put you through. I want you to know I would never knowingly hurt you. I just—"

"It's all right," he replied, surprised as the hair on his arms stood on end. How could he be so aroused by such a simple touch? The touch of his ward—a loyal, devoted woman who he wanted in his bed. He shook his head at the wicked thought. He could not look at her in such a depraved way.

She appeared skeptical of his sincerity. "Are you certain you are not angry with me?"

To his amazement, her fingers moved along his in an up and down motion, as though she sought to comfort him. The woman could not possibly know what she did to his senses. His cock throbbed with need, and he resisted the urge to pull away from her touch, knowing it would appear ridiculous.

For a moment he forgot what she said. Yet her hopeful expression prompted him to respond. "I know you will never leave this house again, without first telling me where you are going."

"Indeed, I will not. Thank you, my lord, for your understanding." She stood, her hand leaving his for a moment, only to be replaced by her lips.

The breath caught in his throat. The sight of her lips against his hand sent waves of desire down his spine, straight to his rigid cock. He stared at the pale curls on her head, then into the cleavage that nearly spilled out onto the table. Grateful for the table that hid his obvious erection, Dominic forced a smile and breathed a sigh of relief when Arlie sat down.

"Langley is a nice fellow."

The abrupt change in conversation caught him off-guard. "Yes, he is. My friend is a good man, but remember—he is a flatterer. He is quite charming, but he is also to be married soon."

She stared at him, one brow lifted in silent question as she bit into her lower lip. Had he hit a nerve, he wondered? Had her show of affection been merely a way to learn more about Langley?

She sighed. "His fiancée must be beautiful."

His fears had been confirmed—she cared for Langley already, which could be very dangerous indeed. He knew Langley's fiancée, Rose, was no beauty, but instead of giving his ward false hope he said, "Yes, his fiancée is quite charming. Langley and Rose are well suited and will be very happy together." He lied. Langley had no intention of giving up his mistresses.

That was one of the many reasons Dominic chose to remain a bachelor. Marriage was far too cumbersome a lifestyle. Plus, he'd been engaged once before, and he'd learned first-hand how cruel love could be. Never again would he fall victim to a woman's charms.

He would play by his own rules, and never, ever, surrender his heart.

"We will be going to the Banfield ball as well? I've heard it's quite an event…five days filled with games, dancing…even hunting."

He stared at her, pondering her question, surprised she even knew about the ball. Knowing Langley, he had probably planted the seed in her mind. Already he could see the hot stares the men would send Arlie's way. He burned with jealousy.

And now what choice did he have but to take her? She told him just yesterday that she had been bored.

She leaned across the table and grabbed his hand again. She squeezed it within her own, then proceeded to slide her fingers through his. He looked from their joined hands to her wishful expression. He had no choice but to agree. Whether or not he liked it, he would be introducing her to society. "Yes, we will go."

She squealed joyously and rounded the table. A moment later she stood behind him, her arms around his neck, her face beside his, her lips at his ear. "Thank you, my lord. Thank you for your kindness." The words stirred his hair, and sent a ripple of awareness through him. *Sweet Jesus he wanted her!*

Dominic closed his eyes, inhaling her soft scent. Her full breasts pressed against his back, making him think of things he had no right to. One of her hands drifted from his chest, down toward his stomach, splaying there as she hugged him tight.

Her fingers were mere inches from his cock. If they ventured even an inch further, they would come in contact. He put his hand over the one on his stomach and pressed it tight to him, not wanting it to drift lower. He would be horrified if she discovered the battle that raged within his body. He was astonished she did not see the enormous bulge in his breeches.

He patted her hand. "You're very welcome, Arlie. Now you had best get to your studies."

"I will not disappoint you," she whispered, her lips grazing his ear.

His heart skipped a beat.

She pressed a kiss against his neck. "I shall see you later, my lord."

Chapter Three

Lights shone brightly in the night sky as the sleek black carriage with the Rochford family crest emblazoned on its doors approached the home of the Duke and Duchess of Banfield. Awash with multicolored lights, the large mansion appeared even more enormous and imposing.

Arlie glanced nervously at her guardian. Rochford looked gorgeous in a black suit that fit him like a second skin. The dark material spread across his broad shoulders and his breeches fit perfectly, molding to narrow hips and strong, muscular thighs. Of all the men she knew, he was by far the most attractive and desirable.

She mentally shook herself. She could not, under any circumstances, fall in love with her guardian. Particularly a guardian who wanted her married off immediately.

"Would you like a drink?" he asked, holding out the silver flask he'd been taking sips from since they'd left Rochford Manor.

She shook her head. "No, thank you."

Arlie tried to convince herself that her feelings for Rochford were simply misplaced adulation for a man who had taken her in when she had no one. A man who had given her the finer things she'd never had. But was that really it? Was she simply grateful? Would she feel this way with any other man?

He had a mistress. There was no way she could compete with a woman like that.

Memories of a few nights before burned in her mind. Arlie had been in her room reading, when she'd glanced out the window. There stood Dominic, his arms braced on the iron railing, staring out at the night sky, like a hero out of one her many books. Arlie had touched the cold window, wishing she could touch his body. How magnificent he was—all hard muscle beneath dark, olive skin. Broad shoulders, well defined chest, rippled stomach. A movement behind him caught Arlie's eye, and a moment later a redhead walked out on the balcony. Her smile was sultry and seductive as her arms encircled Rochford's waist.

"*No.*" Arlie said the words to the empty room, watching helplessly as Rochford turned in the woman's arms. Bending his head, he kissed her long and passionately, and Arlie imagined he kissed her instead of the other woman.

With a gentle shove the redhead walked away from him, and Arlie saw her teeth flash as she grinned, teasing him, urging him with her sultry stare, back into the room. Rochford pushed away from the rail and followed, leaving the balcony door open just wide enough for Arlie to see clothes hitting the floor.

"Are you ready for this evening?" Dominic asked, his voice breaking into her thoughts.

She smiled, but her lips trembled and she quickly pressed them together.

The corner of his mouth lifted into a smile and she wondered if he was mocking her. Dear Lord, what if he had guessed her wicked thoughts, or worse, seen her watching him and his lover from her bedroom window? Heat raced up her neck to her cheeks.

"Perhaps I'll have a drink after all," she replied, noticing the uplifted brow as he handed her the flask.

Avoiding contact with his fingers, she focused all her attention on not dripping any of the liquor on her new cloak— another generous gift from Dominic. No doubt it cost more than her father had made in his lifetime.

Taking a long swallow of the liquor, she smiled as the brandy warmed its way down to her knotted stomach. She handed the flask back to him. He took it, his fingers grazing hers—long fingers that could bring pleasure to a woman. She had touched him before, but that had been different. She had wanted to prove her loyalty to him. Yet that touch had ignited a longing in her, a desire to be more to him than just a ward. She wanted to experience what his mistress experienced. She longed to know what his fingers would feel like on her...and *in* her. She yearned for his long, hard body to cover her own—his sex pressed against her—to enter her and show her what it was to be a woman.

The carriage stopped, breaking into her unwanted thoughts.

The door opened and the footman helped her out. Arlie glanced up at the enormous manor that looked as though it could house all of London. She took Rochford's arm and tried to keep from trembling. How would she make it through the night? Already her nipples pebbled against her gown from just touching him.

Entering the enormous foyer, Dominic turned to her and helped her out of her cloak. She kept her eyes averted, but she could feel him staring at her. The dress was a daring style—so much so, Arlie could hardly believe when Mrs. Candora had suggested it. The dressmaker finally persuaded Arlie to go with the ball gown of lavender French gauze over a cream silk slip. The squared bodice sat lower than anything Arlie had ever worn before. She felt positively naked without her cloak. She held her breath and turned toward Dominic.

All her fears were put to rest in that moment. Rochford's gaze moved quickly from the low bodice of the gown to the ankle-length scalloped hem. "Beautiful," he said, his voice barely above a whisper.

"Thank you," she replied, enjoying the rare compliment and the stare of appreciation. She knew he usually thought of her as a child, instead of a desirable young woman.

With Rochford's hand at her back, Arlie stood in the receiving line looking past the others to the open doors of the ballroom where hundreds of people socialized and danced. Three enormous chandeliers hung from the gold-trimmed ceiling on which pictures of cherubs smiled down on the rich and powerful of London.

Never in her life would she have imagined herself in such a setting, rubbing elbows with *the ton*. Taking in the swell of people, Arlie breathed deeply to calm herself. Rochford had brought her here to find someone suitable for marriage. She straightened her back and lifted her chin. Maybe finding a beau wasn't such a bad idea. Maybe then she would get over this silly obsession with her guardian.

As they approached the host and hostess, she glanced up, and her breath lodged in her throat. Ahead of them in line was the redhead who had been on the balcony with Rochford the other night.

His mistress.

The woman was even more beautiful up close.

The redhead acknowledged Arlie with a sweeping gaze, her green eyes narrowed slightly as she stared at the low neckline of Arlie's gown. She turned her attention to Dominic. Jealousy flashed in the woman's eyes before she could mask it with lowered lashes and a false smile. Her expression alternated between friendliness and lust. Anyone watching her could surely tell the two were lovers.

The older man at the woman's side introduced himself as the Duke. The husband of Dominic's mistress! Arlie's stomach knotted. Not only was she beautiful, she was a duchess as well.

And an adulteress.

The Duke of Banfield was a kindly man with a quick smile. Arlie could only stand back and watch with fascination as Rochford shook hands heartily with the older man, who beamed at him like a favorite son. Arlie frowned. The man couldn't possibly know the betrayal taking place right under his nose. If he did, how could he tolerate the deception?

When the Duke took Arlie's hand, she smiled easily, her heart aching for him. What a fool he would feel if he knew. But Rochford would be careful, discreet.

A sense of relief filled Arlie when they moved toward the ballroom. As Rochford ushered her into the crowd, she refrained from taking his arm, mad at him for cuckolding such a nice man. It didn't matter that she knew nothing of the Duke, she simply hated infidelity in any way, shape or form, remembering too well her father's pain at having an unfaithful wife.

A married woman—why did it surprise her so that Rochford would stoop to such a level? The man was notorious; she'd even heard of his reputation in her village, which had always seemed a world away from London.

Knowing she had to spend five days in Rochford's mistress's house didn't help Arlie's disposition. Had she known then what she did now, she would have told Dominic she wasn't ready to "come out," yet here she was in a mess of her own making. She'd wanted to come even knowing that he'd agreed only to find a suitor to take her off his hands.

If he wanted rid of her, then she *would* look for a man, one who would make her happy...a man who would never stray. A man unlike the deplorable Rochford, who would never be content to spend the rest of his life with one woman.

Schooling her features, she smiled sweetly at the crowd who turned to stare as she and Rochford passed. Her stomach tightened nervously. Never had she seen so many people in one place. It was terrifying and exhilarating but she willed herself to relax, knowing tonight she would make a whole new beginning.

* * * * *

Dominic kept trying to make small talk with Arlie, but she seemed preoccupied. He assumed she would talk to him when she was ready.

For all that he hated to admit it, he was proud to be her guardian. She carried herself with the grace of a princess. Her beauty always stunned him, yet tonight she was breathtaking. The pale hair piled high atop her head had pearls woven throughout and spilled tiny tendrils that framed the delicate features of her face. Her breasts were pushed up so high her nipples were in danger of spilling over the lush lavender bodice. Though she looked incredible in the gown, he wished he would have seen her before they'd left. He would have suggested she wear something a bit more demure.

Now every man within fifty feet stared at her like she was the main course, and it unsettled him, to say the least. Many of the married men gawked at her with lustful eyes, no doubt fantasizing about her becoming their newest mistress. But there were also younger men — good candidates for marriage. He pushed aside the resentment that thought caused, a difficult feat when a group of men in their early twenties beared down on her. He felt Arlie tense at their approach and it was all Dominic could do not to whisk her up in his arms and carry her away...back to the manor, behind closed doors, to where she would be safe from these scoundrels.

Scoundrels like him. What he wouldn't give to take her into a nearby drawing room, lift her skirts, and fill her with his cock.

With a shake of his head Dominic cleared the image from his mind, and took a step back as Daniel Bryant, a handsome American from a wealthy family, approached Arlie. He took her hand in his and lifted it to his lips. Dominic's eyes narrowed as the man, who still held her hand, introduced himself. Even more discomfiting was Arlie's expression. She appeared completely besotted with the man. When Daniel took Arlie's hand and headed for the dance floor where he held her tight, Dominic felt the impulse to follow behind and rip her out of the man's arms and take her to the drawing room, or better yet back home where he would make love to her the entire night. His body tightened imagining her beneath him, her long legs wrapped around his hips as he pounded into her.

The minutes ticked by endlessly, and all the while Arlie's laughter vibrated in Dominic's ears. He clenched his teeth together as Daniel twirled her around the dance floor. Other guests watched with a mixture of approval and knowing smiles on their faces. A few acquaintances lifted their glasses in a toast to him, apparently their way of congratulating him for having taken on such a fine, respectable young woman. If they only knew her true background, they would have nothing to do with her. But he could lie with the best of them, and he was prepared to protect her at any cost.

"Dom, your secret is finally out I see."

Dominic smiled at his friend. "Hello, Langley," he replied, not taking his gaze off his ward and the too-handsome American. "Yes, I suppose I can thank you for telling her about the ball."

"You're very welcome," Langley replied with a wicked smile.

"Well, what do you think of her?" Dominic asked, nodding toward Arlie. "Or need I ask, since you made a spectacle of yourself by showing up on my doorstep like a lovesick fool."

Langley had the grace to chuckle. "I think you are either the luckiest bastard in all of England...or the most unfortunate."

Dominic couldn't help but smile at his friend's analysis. "Indeed, I'm beginning to think it's the latter."

"You haven't had her yet?" Langley asked, his voice filled with surprise, his gaze following Arlie around the floor.

Dominic shook his head. "No, and I won't."

"You won't what?"

He knew the familiar voice, not to mention the overpowering perfume of his mistress, the hostess of the ball. He and Veronica had become lovers nearly a year ago, at a party held in honor of her thirtieth birthday. Her aging husband had no idea of his wife's infidelity, and Dominic had no intention of the older man finding out.

"Tell me what you won't do. I'm intrigued," Veronica whispered, throwing Langley a sultry smile.

Langley lifted his brows and said under his breath, "I bid you good luck, dear friend, for I fear you will need it." A second later he had made his way to the dance floor, conveniently right as the music ended, where he took Arlie off Daniel's hands.

"Veronica, you look lovely," Dominic said to his mistress, finding it hard to keep from looking past her shoulder to his ward, who by all appearances seemed to be having the time of her life. Light on her feet, she smiled widely as she went through the steps of the quadrille.

"She is far more beautiful than you said, Dominic. Should I be concerned?"

He grinned and turned to face Veronica. "She is my ward. Plus, I already have a lover...a very hot-blooded woman who keeps me satisfied." His gaze dropped to her full breasts, the tops of her nipples clearly visible at his height.

"Let's go outside, Dom. I need you desperately," she whispered against his ear. "Remember last year in the labyrinth?"

"How could I forget," he replied, tempted to give her what she wanted, until he saw Langley walking Arlie toward the open doors of the veranda. The bastard! "Perhaps later, darling," he said, and without a backward glance, headed toward the double doors with every intention of cutting them off.

Dominic made eye contact with no one, not wanting to give his friend a single minute with his ward. He knew Langley far too well. They had spent many a day together, in brothels and beyond, and he knew the man's voracious appetite for women— especially young, beautiful women. It made no difference that he was engaged or that Arlie was Dominic's ward. In fact, Langley probably found it even more enticing to see if he could outwit him.

By the time Dominic stepped out on the veranda, he caught sight of lavender skirts disappearing into the labyrinth. He shook his head in disbelief. He'd *kill* Langley. Knowing the maze well, he cut the pair off in mid-stride.

Langley's grin quickly faded under Dominic's scowl. Arlie looked up at him innocently.

"Langley, I'll speak with you later," he managed to say without doing his friend physical harm.

Langley let out a heavy sigh. Bowing over Arlie's hand, he lifted it to his lips. Dominic took a long breath, trying to refrain from pushing Langley out of the way. But the man kept him from doing anything rash when he finally dropped Arlie's hand and walked off.

Dominic waited a few silent moments in an effort to control his anger. He wasn't sure who to be mad at; Arlie, Langley...or himself. Taking another deep breath, he said, "Under no circumstance are you to leave the ballroom without a chaperone, or any other room for that matter. I believe we've had a similar discussion about chaperones before. You cannot risk having your reputation ruined."

Her eyes widened in surprise. "I'm sorry," she whispered. "He's your friend. I didn't think..." Her hands moved up and down her arms as her gaze slipped to the ground at his feet, obviously waiting for a lecture.

Dominic could remember his father's wrath, his lectures, the sting of the belt on his backside for the slightest misdeed. His anger slowly ebbed.

"You're cold?" he asked, surprised since the night was fairly warm. But then again, he'd been drinking and his temper had flared.

"A little chilled," she replied, dropping her arms back to her sides. "I guess we should go back. We don't want to start any gossip."

Even though the words dripped with sarcasm, Dominic didn't smile. Didn't Arlie know it was too late for that? The gossip had started the second they entered the ballroom, and would only gain in momentum with every day that passed. The Earl of Rochford, the guardian of a young beautiful woman unrelated to him? Speculation was already at a fever pitch.

She turned, and he grabbed her wrist, stopping her. His gaze fell to her parted lips, and before he could stop himself, he pulled her into his arms. He pressed a gentle kiss to her forehead, the sweet smell of her instantly enveloping his senses. She stiffened for a moment, but as his hand caressed her back, she relaxed. She fit so perfectly against him, as though she were made just for him. He told himself he touched her to warm her and for no other reason, yet his body told him he was a liar. Heat filled his veins, racing to his cock. He could take her here and now and no one would be the wiser.

She moaned low in her throat and pressed closer.

He would give anything to make her writhe with passion. "Men like Langley can be dangerous," he said, the words sounding absurd even to his own ears, especially since his cock strained his breeches.

"He seems innocent enough," she replied, her voice just above a whisper. "I like him."

He held her tight for a moment longer before he put her at arm's length, looking down into her trusting, upturned face. "Langley may appear innocent, but he is anything but."

The moments ticked by as she stared up at him, her eyes searching his. A man could get lost in those green depths. His gaze shifted to her mouth. He bent his head, she lifted hers— their lips just inches away, so close.

A peal of soft laughter coming their way made him abruptly aware of what he was about to do. His arms dropped to his sides. "We'd better go," he said, his voice a mixture of anger and regret.

She stared at him, her gaze fastened on his lips before she blinked rapidly. "Yes, we should go." Without another word, she turned on her heel and started up the walk.

He followed behind her, willing his blood to cool and his cock to soften. He took a deep breath and released it slowly. One day someone would hurt her.

He resolved it wouldn't be him.

Chapter Four

As Dominic entered the ballroom with Arlie on his arm, he could literally feel the excitement of the guests that milled about. "Have a wonderful time," he told her, releasing her hand. Instantly, men of all ages pounced. The American was at the forefront, but another young man argued that the dance belonged to him. And off Arlie went on the arm of another beau.

Dominic motioned a waiter over and plucked a drink off the man's tray. He drained it, then grabbed another, his gaze never leaving his ward. The seconds ticked away endlessly, and from the corner of his eye, Dominic could feel someone watching him. He turned, and his gaze locked with his grandmother's.

It was too late to ignore her and apparently she wouldn't give him the chance. She walked toward him, her steps slow and somehow regal, despite the fact she leaned heavily on her gold-tipped cane. Dressed in a royal blue gown she'd owned for decades, rings on every finger and heavy diamonds that weighed down her ears, the Dowager Countess of Rochford lifted her chin a good two inches when she stopped before him.

"Dom, I wondered when you would finally arrive." Her eyes raked him from head to toe. "I knew you would not forego the chance to bed your current paramour under her own roof."

Ignoring the jibe, Dominic managed a smile. "Grandmother, you are looking quite fetching this evening. How have you been?"

She let out a sigh. "I've been faring well, though I've pondered when my only grandson would come calling."

Dominic knew his grandmother thought him made of the same cloth as her only child, Dominic's father, a man who had been renowned for his rakehell ways. Throughout the years, Dominic had tried in vain to win the woman's affection, but to no avail. She was cold-hearted, and it seemed that no matter what he did to please her, it was never quite enough. So he simply had stopped trying.

"I've been busy," he replied, instantly noting the disapproval on her face.

"So I hear."

He refused to take the bait, and instead glanced over her shoulder to where Arlie danced with an older gentleman, who was staring down at her bosom.

"She is quite a lovely young lady, Dom. When did you plan to introduce me to your new ward?"

It did not completely surprise him that she already knew about Arlie, since it seemed word had spread like wildfire through *the ton*. He was amazed word had reached as far as Whitley though. "She has been busy with lessons and the like."

"Indeed. Well, I should think she might like a stay in the country. Bring her to Whitley, boy. I would dearly love to get to know this young lady who has the *enviable pleasure* of having you as a guardian." Her sweet smile belied the words laced with sarcasm.

"Perhaps I will be sending her sooner than we both know."

His grandmother's gaze riveted on Arlie. "She is a fair beauty. It's hard to imagine she is but a commoner." She lowered her voice so that it was barely audible. "You'd best come up with a good story, boy, or we will all be made a laughingstock."

"For both our sakes we must keep the truth quiet."

Her gaze flicked over him. "It was nice to see you, Dom. By the way, your hair is getting far too long. You look like a gypsy."

Without another word, she left him with a swish of her skirts. He shook his head, wondering if there would ever come a day when she would not voice her opinion.

"My lord."

Hearing Arlie's voice, Dominic turned abruptly. "I'm sorry to bother you, but I am not feeling very well. I hoped you might escort me to my room."

Her face was a bit pale, and just beyond her shoulder he saw the throng of young men coming toward her. "Of course," he replied, extending his arm, taking great pleasure in turning his back on the crowd of young bucks who no doubt cursed him as he took Arlie out the double doors and up the stairs to the second floor to her room.

But he didn't care. He had Arlie away from them.

Neither of them spoke a word as he opened the door to her room and entered. She sat down on a nearby settee, and he lingered at the door, feeling awkward. "I'll summon a maid."

"No," she said quickly, shaking her head. "Please, just stay with me for a moment."

Concerned, he joined her on the settee. "What's wrong?"

"I have a terrible headache," she said, pressing her fingers to her temples. "I am not accustomed to so many people in one place, and I must say that the smells are almost overbearing. The last gentleman I danced with wore too much cologne."

He relaxed when she smiled softly at him. She was simply overwhelmed, and it was no wonder when she had every dandy in town chasing after her. "Is there anything I can do to help?"

Her eyes closed for an instant, long lashes fanning her cheeks. His stomach tightened as desire filled every ounce of his being. He imagined her just as she was now, but naked, waiting for him, ready to surrender.

She opened her eyes, her gaze settling on his mouth before meeting his once again. "Would you read to me? My father used to read to me when I did not feel well. It always helped me fall asleep."

A strange request, yet a pleasant one—he was more than happy to do her bidding. "What would you have me read?" he asked, but before the words left his mouth, she was walking toward the bed. She reached beneath a pillow and pulled out a well-worn book, which she handed to him. He lifted a brow at the simple title, *Enraptured*. She lay down on her bed and turned toward him, her eyes wide, watching him intently, obviously waiting for him to start reading.

He cleared his throat as he opened the book, then frowned as he skimmed over the first passage printed on the marble-colored paper. "This is highly unsuitable for a young lady such as yourself."

"It's my favorite book. My father bought it for me on my twelfth birthday. I always talked of a prince dressed in black, and the hero in this story is a prince."

"You obviously have a great imagination."

"Not really. I was just a girl with a lot of time to daydream."

"And you dreamed of this prince dressed in black often?" he asked, trying hard to keep a straight face.

"For a while. But one day I just stopped thinking of him."

He wanted to ask her why her dreams had faded but didn't. "I shall read then," he said, and he began. As he read, he could feel Arlie's eyes on him, watching him intently as he told the story that she no doubt knew by heart. From time to time he glanced up, and always she would smile softly. He found it strange that he would rather sit with his ward in her room reading her a story, than be downstairs drinking with friends.

Arlie's eyes drifted closed and Dominic set the book aside and stood. "I will call your maid," he whispered, fighting the urge to kiss her tenderly.

She smiled sleepily. "Thank you for reading to me. I feel much better now."

He touched her soft cheek with the back of his hand. "I'm glad I could help."

Dominic left Arlie's room and summoned a maid. Heading for the stairs to return to the party, he stopped. He had no desire to return. Instead, he preferred some much-needed time alone.

Sitting in the confines of his dark room, Dominic realized being alone was a mistake. His mind kept wandering to what was happening in the room next door. He envisioned Arlie preparing for bed—stepping out of the gown, her nipples hardening at the cool air while she waited for the maid to help her into a nightgown. He moaned, wishing for a hole in the wall that he might see for himself what he imagined. He ran his hands down his face. What was wrong with him?

All night he'd had to fight to keep his jealousy at bay whenever a man even looked in Arlie's direction. Daniel Butler, the young American, had stuck to her side as though to proclaim to all others she belonged to him. Not that it deterred anyone. Men would never leave Arlie alone, at least not until she was married—and that wouldn't stop many of them, himself included. Dominic shook his head, glad that she had asked to leave the party early. He didn't think he could stand another moment of her being ogled. Already he was mentally exhausted. He cringed knowing he had four more days of festivities to contend with.

He knew Arlie wanted to experience everything. He couldn't very well tell her they were leaving in the morning, even though he wanted that most of all. *Why had he brought her to begin with?* He asked himself the question, even though he knew why. She had wanted it, needed it, deserved it. She'd proven to him and everyone else what a well-mannered young lady she was. She had surprised even him.

A knock at the door brought him quickly to his feet. Arlie? He crossed the room with long strides. Perhaps her headache had returned? When he flung open the door, his mistress's sultry smile instantly put *that* fear to rest.

Veronica brushed past him and he closed the door behind her. "I want you," she whispered against his neck.

Her body flush against his, Veronica licked the lobe of his ear, her hands ripping the shirt off him. Before he could pull away, she pushed him onto the settee and straddled him.

"What if Alfred comes looking for you?" he asked. This moment had been inevitable. He'd merely hoped it would come much later...long after his ward had gone to sleep, and long after he had consumed another bottle of brandy.

"Forget about Alfred," she whispered against his ear. Even as Veronica kissed his neck, he couldn't get Arlie off his mind. He closed his eyes and saw her face, felt the softness of *her* skin beneath his fingertips, the feel of *her* lips against his throat.

Veronica nipped at his ear and it reminded him of when Arlie's lips had grazed his ear that night not so long ago. "I don't care about Alfred. I just know I want you, and I can't wait another minute." Pulling her skirts up, she smiled as she unbuttoned his breeches and yanked them down around his hips.

Dominic heard a pounding in his ears. His groin filled with blood as her fingers closed around his erect shaft. Though his heart was not into the seduction, his body could not help but respond. Veronica moaned as she kissed him.

"My lord?!"

His eyes widened. Arlie. She was standing outside his door calling out to him, needing him. He abruptly lifted Veronica off him, and buttoned his breeches.

"She'll go away," Veronica whispered, disappointment evident in her voice. "Please, Dominic—"

He was already at the door, whipping it open. His heart lurched at the sight that met him.

Arlie stood in a thin wrapper, her feet bare, her long blonde hair a riot of long silky curls that fell to her slim hips. Never had a woman looked so desirable to him. He wanted to pull her in the room—and into his bed. He'd make love to her until she couldn't stand.

"What's wrong?" he asked, pushing aside the wicked thoughts. "Are you ill? Does your head still ache?"

She tilted her head slightly and shifted on her feet. "I...couldn't sleep, and I thought I heard something. I wanted to make sure you were all right."

She watched him with such wide-eyed innocence he knew that she told the truth. "You thought to protect me?" he asked, trying hard not to laugh at how preposterous that sounded. Yet he was oddly touched by her concern. This young woman who had burst into his life *cared* for him.

She gave him a blinding grin and his heart skipped a beat. She felt something for him. True, it might not be the same desire he felt for her, but she cared. Her gaze shifted to something beyond his shoulder and the smile disappeared.

Veronica.

Arlie's mouth opened then she quickly snapped it shut, her cheeks flushing crimson. "I'm so sorry...I didn't know. Forgive the interruption."

Veronica's hand rested on his shoulder, and he felt it like a heavy weight as Arlie's eyes lost their sparkle. He wondered what she was thinking. Was she upset that he was with another woman, or that the other woman just happened to be married? Veronica's breasts pressed into his back, her hand encircled his waist, coming to rest on the band of his breeches, right above his now deflated cock.

Arlie's gaze fixed on Veronica's hand, and she opened her mouth...but no words came. The silence was deafening. With a deep breath, she turned on her heel, and left him staring after her. A heartbeat later her door closed behind her, and then locked.

"Now, where were we?" Veronica purred, pulling him back into the room.

"I think we need to return to the party," he said, pulling out of her arms, suddenly ashamed of the relationship he had with Veronica.

Veronica pouted. "I can't stand another hour watching you with other women. They're all falling over themselves to be near you. To sit and listen to their endless fantasies...I simply cannot stand it a moment longer!" Her voice was almost demanding, and he lifted a brow in silent warning. She hardly had the right to be angry.

"Dom, it's been so long since last we spent time alone," she said with a sweet smile, her voice more controlled.

"Nonsense. It's only been a few days."

"But it seems like an eternity."

An eternity. That's what the next four days would be. It was insane to have come to the ball, especially with his ward in tow. He had set himself up for disaster, and now he found himself in a most undesirable situation. Arlie had caught him red-handed with a married woman. How could he justify his actions to a young woman who knew nothing of life? Would she think this behavior was common—that this is what she should expect of her marriage? He groaned inwardly at the odd twist his life had taken, that suddenly he should care so much about what Arlie thought.

"Later," he promised Veronica, ushering her out the door. "We don't need anyone talking, especially this first night."

Knowing he had many days to pass in her company made him uneasy, yet his words must have pacified her since she smiled seductively. "You're right, darling, we have all sorts of time."

"I'll return to the party shortly."

He watched the sway of her hips as she walked away from him, her head held high. She was a very desirable woman. A woman who liked to have sex in every position known to man. She had tried everything at least once, and took great pleasure in all forms of sexual play, particularly being bound. Despite the pleasure she'd given him, he found his desire for her diminished. As she descended the stairs at the end of the hallway, she glanced back, blowing him a kiss, letting her hand trail down the banister as she returned to her duty as hostess, a job she relished.

He sighed heavily and shut the door behind him. He felt compelled to either go to Arlie and explain or lose himself in the bottle of brandy that sat on a nearby table.

The brandy won.

* * * * *

Arlie woke early the following morning, joining the others who had got an early start despite the late night. She had taken special care in her appearance this morning, wanting to capture the interest of one man in particular. Who knew? Perhaps she would be wise to walk away from this party with a bona fide fiancé. At least then she wouldn't have to contend with a guardian like Rochford.

Last night she had truly felt close to him for the first time, especially when he had comforted her in the labyrinth, and then later in her room when he had read to her. He genuinely had been concerned about her. But then she'd made the mistake of going to his room to find him with the duchess, Veronica. Despite her exhaustion, Arlie had stayed awake for hours last night, tossing and turning. Memories of the woman's face as she stared at Arlie over Dominic's shoulder came back to haunt her time and again throughout the long night. It was as though Veronica somehow knew what was going through her mind, and in a sense had been saying, *Ha, I have him and you never will!*

Arlie lifted her chin. No wonder Dominic didn't want her underfoot. He believed such a life to be customary for his kind. Well, if Dominic Santrell wanted her out of his life, then so be it. She would find a man worthy of her love and affection, a man who suited her, and her guardian would have no more say in her future, whatsoever. If he wanted to bed married women for the rest of his life, she would not stand in his way.

Convinced she was about to change her destiny, Arlie headed off and immediately ran into Daniel. Looking well rested, and quite handsome in a dove gray suit with knee high boots, he took her hand in his and kissed it gently. "Miss Whitman, how are you feeling this morning? I was quite concerned when you retired early last evening. I heard you had taken ill."

She smiled, touched by his concern. "I had a slight headache," she replied, noticing he didn't drop her hand, but rather kept it firmly within his own. "But I feel fine this morning. I'm sure it was just the excitement."

"I can't tell you how happy I am that you are well." He stared at her, his gaze slipping to her mouth.

Uncomfortable, she shifted on her feet, and Daniel immediately released her hand. "We are all going for a stroll. Would you care to join us?"

He motioned over to where a large group already crested a hill. The day, though a little brisk, showed promise, and rather than stay and brood over her guardian's lack of morals, and her silly infatuation with him, she decided it would do her good to take a walk with the American. She nodded. "I would love that."

He rewarded her with a boyish grin. Taking the arm he offered, she followed, enjoying the company and the leisurely pace.

It seemed the further they went from the manor, the more comfortable she became with the young man at her side. Daniel was easy to talk to, quite clever, and had a good sense of humor—all desirable qualities for a husband.

"You were quite the talk of the ball last night," he said, bringing her out of her thoughts.

"I hope that is a good thing."

He chuckled. "Of course, it is a good thing. Dear Miss Whitman, you are much too naive when it comes to your beauty and fairness. Yet I must say your innocence is refreshing and others feel likewise. I fear I have some rivalry for your attention."

His words were like a double-edged sword. She wanted the young man to like her, perhaps even pursue her. Yet, at the same time she was reluctant. It would be difficult to fall in love with anyone when her feelings for Rochford kept her awake at night.

She could not understand what she felt for her guardian. She did know that when she touched him a charge raced through her, straight to her breasts, and caused an ache between her thighs. No one had ever made her feel that way...and she feared no one else would.

"You've been called London's best kept secret," he added.

"Really...why?"

After Daniel steered her around a large stone, the hand he had rested on her back to guide her remained. "Because Rochford never said a thing to anyone about you. Langley leaked word, but none believed it, of course. Not that Langley is a liar, but he has been known to start a few stories. And I'll be honest, the idea of Rochford being a guardian is...well, surprising."

"His lordship only kept quiet because he wanted to make sure I would be ready. He wanted me to have time."

"Time for...?"

"To mourn the death of my father and to become accustomed to my life here. Where I come from things are different. The pace is slow, and you could go days without seeing another human being." For all she had told herself she would be closed-mouthed around these people, she found Daniel so easy to talk to words just seemed to slip out. Yet Dominic's advice to be aloof about personal details came back to her and she clamped her lips together, deciding some things were better left unsaid.

"And to think many call him a rakehell."

Though Arlie hated to admit Dominic was a rakehell of the worse sort, she knew it was true. But despite that knowledge, she still felt unwanted desire whenever he was around. All he had to do was look at her and the hair on her arms stood on end. He made her thoughts turn wicked — to things no virgin should ever think of, yet she couldn't help it. She wanted to see his body, to learn every line, every muscle. She longed to touch his dark skin, to feel the length of his manhood. She wanted him to take her virginity, to take her to the stars and make her feel like the heroines in those naughty stories she read. "Why do they call him a rakehell?" she asked, although she already knew the answer. She had witnessed it firsthand.

"My dear Miss Whitman, it's not right for me to go into any of that, especially since you are in the man's care. Let me just say that many find it hard to believe he is a good choice to serve as your guardian. He has a reputation with women that is not, how do I put this, flattering."

She bristled at the words, hating how protective she felt of Dominic. She released Daniel's elbow. "Rochford is a wonderful guardian. He's given me the best of everything."

Daniel walked over to the shade of an old oak tree, just far enough from the others to have a little privacy, yet close enough for propriety's sake. She followed him.

He took one of her hands within his own. "I've upset you."

He appeared distraught, so she smiled. "Rochford's my guardian, and he doesn't deserve what is being said about him."

He nodded, and they spoke no more of Rochford, much to Arlie's relief. Time passed quickly and Arlie enjoyed Daniel's companionship. He took the liberty of introducing her to many of the guests, most of whom she had met the previous night but had forgotten in the excitement. All were very kind, as well as curious about her life before coming to live with Dominic. One man in particular asked a lot of questions, mostly about her background. Arlie carefully answered, hoping she sounded convincing when she lied and told them her father had been a baron.

When the group turned back to the manor, Arlie sensed Daniel's disappointment at returning so soon. With a sigh he extended his arm and they headed back, lingering behind the others.

Arlie took the arm he offered and enjoyed the peacefulness of the late morning. She breathed deeply of the morning air and smiled as a flock of sparrows flew overhead. Content, she listened to Daniel talk about his family in America.

"Will you be staying in London long?" Arlie asked as the manor came into sight.

Daniel's eyes gleamed as he stared down at her and then stopped altogether. Arlie guessed he thought her question meant she hoped he would be staying on for a while. He turned to her, taking both her hands within his own. "It depends..."

Rather than ask what it depended on, she smiled, letting him come to his own conclusion.

"I would like very much to spend more time with you, Miss Whitman. I know we have only just met, but I feel I have known you for —" His gaze had shifted to something beyond her shoulder. "Your guardian does not appear happy, Miss Whitman." Daniel dropped her hands, and Arlie turned.

On the manor's steps, hands planted firmly on his narrow hips, stood Dominic. Though Arlie could not see his expression from where she and Daniel stood, she could guess by Rochford's body language alone that Daniel was right. He was not happy.

She frowned. What in the world could he be so upset about? Certainly it couldn't be that she and Daniel had gone for a walk. Good gracious, it was ridiculous that he should be angry with her, especially when it was mid-morning. Plus they'd been surrounded by a crowd of at least twenty or more people, and Daniel had been a perfect gentleman...a quality Dominic would know nothing about.

And why did she care what he thought anyway? Why wasn't he off with his married mistress?

"It's fine," she said softly, reassuringly. She took his hand in her own, finding a perverse pleasure in doing so, knowing that Dominic watched her every move. As though reading her thoughts, Rochford walked down the steps and onto the gravel. He looked menacing. Thankfully the others who had returned before them had gone into the house, and no one else was about, save for a gardener who paid them no heed.

Arlie glanced over at Daniel and noticed the sheen of sweat on his brow. "He is harmless, really."

"I hope you're right, Miss Whitman."

"Miss Whitman." Dominic's voice was lethal.

Arlie noticed the change in his appearance from the night before. Rochford had dark circles beneath his eyes, and he was sallow beneath his usual olive tone. Dark stubble along his jaw line made him look even more dangerous. Apparently, he'd had a little too much to drink—or his mistress had kept him up all night.

"Yes, my lord," she said, trying hard to sound civil.

"I thought you still abed yet I hear it on good authority you decided to take a stroll with Mr. Butler here," he said without even glancing in Daniel's direction.

"There were others with us, my lord. We were not *without a chaperone*."

"Oh?" he queried, one dark brow lifted high. "About a quarter of an hour ago a small group returned from a walk. When I asked if you were with them, they told me that you were with Mr. Butler. So, I waited patiently...and then I waited some more. Everyone came back to the house together, save the two of you, which would leave you *without a chaperone*."

She wanted to tell him that she and Daniel had only been alone for a brief period and that nothing could happen in that space of time. Then she remembered who she spoke to. The Earl of Rochford could accomplish a lot in a matter of minutes. Arlie sighed heavily. "I am here now." A small group had walked out onto the steps, and Arlie could feel their stares. Her cheeks grew hot. "Please, you are making a scene," she said under her breath.

Daniel stepped forward. "I apologize, Lord Rochford, for my impropriety. I take complete responsibility. The time simply got away from us. It shall not happen again."

Dominic's gaze shifted abruptly to Daniel, his blue eyes blazing with a fury Arlie had never witnessed. She could sense the tension in Daniel as he met her guardian's brutal glare. "You're damn right it won't happen again."

Daniel flinched as though he'd been struck, but to his credit he remained silent.

"I suggest you use more sense in the future, Mr. Butler. That is, if you value that handsome face of yours. Now I will have a word with my ward *in private.*"

Daniel's throat convulsed as he swallowed hard, and turned to face Arlie. "Miss Whitman, I apologize for having caused you trouble. I hope to see you again." With a curt nod, he walked away.

Dominic stared at her. She could see the nerve tic in his jaw and again wondered why he was so angry. It wasn't as though she and Daniel were married to other people and cuckolding their partners right beneath everyone's noses. The man had not even attempted to kiss her.

When he continued to say nothing, she moved past him, but his hand swept out and grabbed her wrist. "We need to talk. Will you walk with me?"

Though it was a question, Arlie knew she had little choice but to go with him. He dropped her wrist, and she released the breath she'd been holding. Her heart pounded—from anger or reaction to his touch, she knew not which.

She walked the immaculate and private garden in silence, watching him under her eyelashes as he kept a good distance between them. Arlie turned her attention to the carefully tended rows of flowerbeds, gravel pathways and enormous fountain in the center. Knowing the beautiful gardens belonged to Veronica took the pleasure from her.

A good five minutes passed in silence before Dominic said, "Arlie, I'm not used to being responsible for another person. After last night I was concerned—"

She turned abruptly, surprised to hear him apologize. "We didn't do anything wrong. I swear it."

"I know. You just worried me."

"I can take of myself. I'm a grown woman."

He ran a hand through his hair and looked to the distance. "I'm reminded of that every time I look at you."

At one time she might have taken that as a compliment, but now she didn't know how to take such a comment. She didn't understand him. One minute he wanted her to find a husband, and the next he was angry with her for doing exactly what he wanted her to do.

His gaze shifted back to her. "I know how men can be, and even Mr. Butler is no exception."

Undeniably, he was right, but she couldn't resist saying, "You should remember your words to me when we met. You said you planned on finding a husband for me. How can I do that without spending time with a man?"

He actually looked stricken at her words. "It is only your first outing. You don't have to court the first man you meet."

"True, but you said yourself that within a few months' time you expected to place an announcement in *The Times*. By my estimation, I have less than two months to go. And to be perfectly honest, I don't want to waste any more precious time. There are a few nice men here, and Daniel is..." she groped for the right words. She glanced at Rochford. His eyes narrowed, but she continued, "He is a nice man, handsome and very kind."

All expression slid from Rochford's face, and Arlie smiled, glad to see her words hit a nerve. "He is witty, charming and I *adore* his accent."

"Well, I wish you and Mr. Butler all the best," he said through clenched teeth.

"Your approval of Mr. Butler means so very much," she said in her sweetest voice. He opened his mouth, but before he could reply, she kissed him on the cheek. "You see my lord, being a guardian is not so difficult."

Chapter Five

It was the longest day of his life.

Dominic sat back in his chair, watching the group of young men surround Arlie. She had just played a minuet, and as always, she enraptured one and all. Dominic was amazed by her talent, and even more so by her elegance, wondering again where she came by it.

Glancing at the clock, he moaned inwardly seeing it was only eight o'clock. He was exhausted. He wanted nothing more than to find his bed and sleep off his hangover, but he couldn't when he had to play chaperone to his ward and her following of eager young men.

He caught his grandmother's bemused expression from across the room and quickly looked away. She was enjoying his discomfort far too much.

Dominic declined the glass of wine a servant held out to him. He had no intention of having a repeat performance of the previous night. Last night after drinking a carafe of brandy, he'd gone back to the party and continued to drink, thinking alcohol could wipe away thoughts of his beautiful young ward, and it had for a little while. Yet when he woke this morning, his head ached so much it felt like it would split in two. Then memories of the night before marched through his mind, reminding him how disastrous the combination of too much alcohol and a willing woman could be.

Veronica had come to him and they had had sex. He had hoped he could slake his desire, but it didn't work. When Veronica had caressed his cock and wantonly taken it in her mouth, it had been Arlie's elegant fingers and sweet mouth he'd wished for. And when he'd cried out his release, finally, he had very nearly moaned Arlie's name. What the hell was wrong with him? Arlie was a complete innocent. He had to stop thinking about her.

When Veronica had left she'd mentioned visiting him again tonight. *Dear Lord, he hoped not.* He had no intention of carrying the affair on a day longer. For too long he had pretended to have no conscience concerning Veronica, but now he had someone else to think of.

Arlie's laughter brought him out of his musings. What a fair beauty—like a flower waiting to be plucked. Daniel was obviously enthralled with her. He'd been her constant companion all day.

It annoyed Dominic that Arlie and Daniel's names had already been linked as a couple. Before he knew it, rumors of marriage would start flying...and they still had three days of the party left. Now more than ever he dreaded them.

To make matters worse, Arlie's anger had not abated, even though he had apologized for his behavior earlier. Obviously she was angry with him for being with Veronica. Would she think differently if she knew he'd been thinking of her while fucking the other woman?

He closed his eyes. He was beyond redemption.

"Do I sense trouble between you and your pretty little ward?"

Dominic turned to Langley who took the seat beside him. His friend, as always, had a drink in hand and wore the smirk he liked to call a smile.

"Tell me, old boy, when will you tell yourself that you feel something for the girl?"

"Langley, I'm tired and you're talking in riddles."

His laughter vibrated in Dominic's ears. "I think you drank far too much last night, my friend. That is the only reason it sounds like a riddle. Tell me you don't desire her."

Dominic shook his head, realizing Langley's tongue loosened whenever he drank. He did not need more rumors flying.

"I only want the best for her."

"Do you now?"

When Dominic glanced at his friend, he noticed Langley wasn't smiling. "Yes, I do." And to his dismay, his voice even sounded unconvincing.

"Sometimes what we want is right under our noses. You've never been the jealous type, my friend, yet one can see by the expression on your face that it doesn't make you happy to see her with other men, myself included."

Knowing Langley wouldn't shut up, he patted him on the shoulder. "And this from a man who has bedded every woman in this room, save only a few."

Langley looked around the room, his smile returning in force. "Indeed, I would have to say that for once you are right. Except of course for your grandmother, who can't take her eyes off you by the way—oh, and I haven't had the chance to get close enough to that little filly over there," he replied, nodding in Arlie's direction.

Dominic frowned. "And you won't get anywhere near her in the future."

"Well—"

"Langley..."

He sighed dramatically. "True, I am to be married, but Arlie would make a nice mistress. Indeed I wonder what she would think of my rented flat near Hanover Square."

A young woman sat down beside Langley, cutting their conversation short. Dominic turned to find Arlie involved in a game of charades. A light breeze blew through the room, beckoning him outside for fresh air.

Stepping out onto the lit veranda, he stared up at the full moon, wishing himself a long way from here...from all these *snobs*. Strange, but he wished himself at his country estate, Whitley—a place he usually avoided, except for emergencies, since his grandmother had laid claim to the home. His mother had always teased him, telling him there would come a day when he would yearn for his country home and be tempted to sell the others.

God, was that what was happening to him now? Was he actually getting tired of all the people, the parties, the gossip? Perhaps it was his age. He was almost three and thirty and not getting any younger. Many of his friends had already settled down, some had children and spent most of their time at their country homes, except for a short season in London.

"My lord?"

He turned at the sound of Arlie's voice.

"Are you ill?" she asked, her voice mirroring the concern on her face.

Aside from his mother, who had long been dead, he could not recall a time anyone worried about him the way she did. "I'm fine," he replied, instantly warmed by her presence.

Pulling the shawl tight around her shoulders, she looked up at the moon. "I love it when the moon is full. As a child I used to imagine it was a big ball of cheese and that if I reached high enough, I could pick off a piece."

He smiled at the image of a young Arlie reaching out to the sky, trying to capture the moon in her hands. "Are you enjoying yourself?"

She nodded. "Yes, I have had great fun. I look forward to the hunt tomorrow."

Despite his effort not to, he frowned. "You will be participating?"

"I would like to," she said with obvious hesitance. "With your permission."

Surprised that she had actually asked his approval, he was ready to say yes when she added, "Daniel has asked me to ride with him."

"I prefer you come with me…"

She nodded. "All right."

Her quick answer delighted him. All day she had avoided him like the plague, yet now she sought him out, making him believe that she wasn't as angry with him as he'd originally thought. Or perhaps her anger had simply ebbed with time. He knew he had acted rashly this morning—like Langley said, rather like a jealous suitor. Thankfully, no one else, save Daniel, had taken much notice. He had to wonder if he could contain his emotions for a few more days. It seemed he had no choice…he was committed for the duration.

"I'll see you in the morning then," she said, already heading back inside.

"Are you going to bed?"

She stopped and turned to face him, her eyes bright. "It's been a long day and I didn't sleep last night."

He watched her, wondering why she hadn't slept well. A horrible thought crossed his mind. What if she'd heard he and Veronica together? Something in the way she stared at him made him think that might just be the case.

* * * * *

Arlie headed toward the staircase and stopped mid-stride upon hearing her name being called from the parlor. Frowning, she walked into the ostentatiously decorated room to find an older woman sitting in a Queen Anne chair. The woman had sharp features, and on her head she wore a turban that matched the pale green of her gown.

Though the woman's feet barely touched the floor, there was a regal quality about her.

"Did you call me?" Arlie asked.

"Yes, my dear, I did. Please, sit down."

Doing as the woman asked, Arlie took a seat beside her.

The woman's gaze swept over her. "You favor your mother, dear child."

Arlie's stomach clenched into a tight knot. "You knew my mother?" she asked, sitting up straight, trying to act composed — a difficult task when her cheeks burned under the woman's scrutiny.

"Yes…an actress was she not?"

Arlie glanced over her shoulder at the empty room, and then to the door that stood ajar.

The woman's lips curved into a smile. "You need not fear your past will be discovered by others. I am the Dowager Countess of Rochford, Dominic's grandmother, and therefore your secret is safe with me."

Arlie released the breath she'd unconsciously been holding. *Dominic's grandmother?* It took Arlie a moment to digest the information. "I apologize. I did not know Rochford had any family."

The dowager rolled her eyes dramatically. "Of course you didn't. Dominic barely acknowledges me as it is. Why would he bother to introduce his ward to me?"

"I am pleased to meet you, madam."

The woman gave her a sharp, calculating look. Arlie had the impression she wanted something from her.

"How are you enjoying yourself so far, Miss Whitman?"

"I am having a wonderful time."

"I'm certain you are," she replied. "What a different life this is compared to the one you left behind. Tell me, what do you think of my grandson?"

Arlie could feel her heart begin to accelerate and her cheeks flush again. "He is very kind, and more than generous."

"Is that all?"

Since her arrival at the manor, Rochford had not bothered to tell Arlie about his grandmother. In fact, by the older woman's grim expression, Arlie had to believe the relationship between the two was less than amicable. She elected to speak carefully. "He is a wonderful guardian. He's seen that I have the best of everything."

The countess tapped her bejeweled fingers on the chair's arm. "We must not be speaking of the same man, for my grandson is not setting a very good example, now is he?"

"Sorry?"

"Hrmph," the dowager said beneath her breath. "You know who, or rather *what*, the Duchess is to Dominic."

Arlie merely nodded.

"A fine example he's setting, particularly when he is searching for a suitable husband for you. What you must think of the institution of marriage..."

"I am not so young that I don't understand these things."

The dowager smiled then, and she appeared years younger. "Dear girl, though we have only just met, I could be of great assistance to you in your quest to find a suitor...that is, if you wish for my help."

How could Arlie possibly tell the woman no, especially when she looked entirely too pleased at the prospect of helping. Plus the dowager knew everything about Arlie. "That would be wonderful."

"Good, good," she replied, patting Arlie's hand, the bracelets on her wrist rattling. "There are a number of suitable and wealthy men here, but I must insist that you not stake claim to anyone just yet. You must let them all know you are a woman who deserves to be treated with respect and dignity. You must be courted as though you are a princess, and you must not, even for an instant, believe you deserve less."

Arlie nodded.

"Well, I suppose you have had enough for one day. Tomorrow we will take up where we have left off. Now remember, my grandson may not take my interference well, so I would ask that you not tell him we have met."

"Certainly," Arlie replied, standing and helping the woman from her chair. As expected, the dowager barely reached to Arlie's shoulder.

"We will talk soon," the dowager said, and without another glance, walked out the door.

* * * * *

The horse sensed Arlie's excitement.

Though she could not ride astride like the men, Arlie did not let that small factor keep her from enjoying the hunt. She reveled in the fact that Dominic had been true to his word and kept by her side all morning.

Last night she had been so exhausted she'd fallen asleep the moment her head hit the pillow. Once she thought she heard footsteps outside her door, but her dreams lulled her back to sleep, and when she did wake, she felt well rested and more than ready to join in the hunt.

Dressed in a royal blue riding habit with a matching hat, she shifted in the sidesaddle, getting as comfortable as possible. It was so ridiculous to make a woman ride this way. It was unnatural, making one feel off-balance. But she made do, knowing that complaining would get her nowhere. Very few ladies participated in the hunt at all. Unfortunately, Veronica was one of those that did.

The Duchess wore a maroon riding habit. Exquisite, down to the black velvet derby she wore on her head at a jaunty angle. Arlie felt a jab of jealousy. The woman's beauty and sense of style rivaled all at the party.

Arlie noticed the Duchess kept glancing in Dominic's direction, but he seemed not to notice. In fact, he kept his attention on Arlie the entire time—perhaps to detract attention away from his relationship with the Duchess.

Arlie watched Dominic from the corner of her eye. His tall frame astride the black horse made a powerful impression. Dressed casually in a white shirt and navy breeches tucked into black knee-high boots, he appeared completely at ease, as though born to the saddle. His unruly dark hair only added to his rugged good looks. Arlie's heart swelled with affection and desire for him. Not one woman at the party could keep their eyes off Dominic, herself included. No matter where he went, hot gazes followed.

As though sensing her perusal Dominic turned, his smile devastating. "Let me guess, you yearn to rip that sidesaddle off your horse and ride astride?"

Her heart did a little flip as she returned his smile. She wanted to do far more than rip the sidesaddle from her horse. She wanted time alone with him. Time to show him what she felt for him, to prove to him once and for all she was a woman and not a child. "You know me too well."

And just when she thought nothing could ruin her present good mood, Veronica brought her mount up alongside Dominic. She smiled wide, her eyes sparkling like gems. "It's a wonderful day for a hunt, don't you agree?"

"Yes, it is," Dominic replied, while Arlie tried in vain to smile.

Arlie watched Dominic closely, waiting for the smoldering fire in his eyes as he talked with his mistress. Yet as the minutes ticked by he offered Veronica no lust-filled stares—just cordiality. Over the years he probably had learned how to mask his emotions, especially if he was accustomed to bedding married women.

Veronica turned to Arlie. "Miss Whitman, you are quite an accomplished rider. Perhaps I can interest you in a race later today?"

"I would love—"

"I think that would be inappropriate," Dominic cut in.

"Oh, *Dom*, really. It would be such fun, and I am so weary of always having to ride against men. Two women competing should add a little excitement to the party. So, what do you think?" Veronica stared at Arlie, waiting for a response.

"I would love to," Arlie replied, realizing she meant it. Having raced against many a man in Wales, Arlie knew she could give the woman a run for her money and then some. "But only if I am able to ride astride."

Veronica's brows lifted. "A woman after my own heart. We shall see you soon then." With a wave of her hand, the duchess cantered off.

Arlie glanced at Dominic who frowned. "I think you just made a grave mistake. Veronica prides herself on her horsemanship."

Arlie smiled innocently. "Come now, it will be fun."

"What if you were to fall, or perhaps—"

"What if? What if?" She smiled and a thrill ran through her seeing the side of his mouth lift. "Truly, I'll be fine. I promise."

Five hours later, Arlie sat astride her mount, blood pumping in her veins as she waited for the sound of the gun. At her side, Veronica was dressed similarly in a split skirt, her face a mask of concentration. The duchess was obviously bent on winning. A shame...because Arlie had no intention of letting her.

The gun blasted, and they were off. The blood pulsed through Arlie's veins as the horse beneath her ran like the wind. The flag they rode for sat just over a hill, down in the valley.

Arlie heard Veronica behind her, gaining on her. Leaning lower over the horse's neck, Arlie urged the mount faster. Up ahead two men held flags. The women took the turn at the same time. The crowd appeared tiny from the distance, yet Arlie heard their excitement, yells of encouragement urging her on. Perhaps some would be tempted to throw the race, particularly when the lady of the manor rode in said race.

Arlie had to win, that's all there was to it. Somewhere in the sea of faces was Dominic—she would make him proud. And she would prove a point, if not to Veronica, then herself.

"Come on!" She urged her horse on, leaning lower, leaving Veronica behind her in a cloud of dust.

The finish line was a blur, and when she passed it the crowd went wild, sending up cheers. Turning in the saddle, Arlie looked back to see Veronica at least fifteen feet from the finish line. She'd dismounted and was having a groomsman check the shoes of her horse. The woman couldn't even lose graciously.

Turning back to the awaiting crowd, Arlie caught sight of Dominic's grandmother. She stood, leaning heavily on a cane, her expression unreadable, yet Arlie could swear she saw amusement, and perhaps even surprise there. Arlie nodded in her direction, and the Dowager discreetly nodded in return, then turned and headed toward the manor.

* * * * *

Dominic stood back from the crowd and watched in stunned silence as Arlie crossed the finish line. Langley clapped him on the back, and he nearly choked on the breath he'd unconsciously been holding.

"Incredible!" Langley said, a broad grin speaking his delight.

Arlie turned in the saddle and looked back at Veronica who played the poor sport. Her husband ran over to console her, and Dominic's gaze returned to Arlie.

She gave an animated grin and Dominic's heart tripped like a schoolboy's. What a treasure this young woman was. A woman whom fate had decided to drop into his lap.

How he yearned to fight his way through the crowd and lift her up into his arms...and back to his bed. His body burned with the need to take her beneath him, to drive into her ripe body until she trembled and cried out his name in ecstasy.

Arlie dismounted then turned to someone in the crowd. She smiled timidly, biting her lower lip, a nervous habit of hers—one he'd noted long ago. The glance only lasted but a few seconds, then she nodded, almost in understanding. Dominic willed himself not to scour the crowd to find who she had connected with, but he had to.

He was not surprised to find that the American, Daniel Butler, who stood next to Dominic's grandmother, had been on the receiving end of that smile.

Daniel boisterously congratulated Arlie and stepped forward with a single red rose. Arlie took the flower, brought it her nose, and then wrapped her fingers around his extended arm. Unable to watch, Dominic told Langley he would see him that evening, and headed back to the manor.

He could not understand his emotions where Arlie was concerned. One minute he cursed her presence in his life, the next minute he wondered what he would do when she was no longer a part of it. He wanted to give Arlie the best life he knew how. Yet he could not bear the thought of handing her over to another—a man who would take her to his bed and fuck her as soundly as Dominic wanted to.

What would he do if Arlie professed her love for the young American?

Dominic entered the manor, and climbed the stairs to the second floor, cursing himself for having brought her to this place at all.

"Could you please draw a bath?" he asked a passing maid, who appeared happy to oblige him. "I'm the second door on the right."

"Right away, my lord," she said, her cheeks turning pink while her gaze raked over him hungrily. Another time he might have been interested, but now Arlie filled his mind completely.

He opened the door to his room and shut it behind him. Stripping off his shirt, he glanced out the window and saw that the crowd had thinned, yet others still celebrated. Leaning forward, he searched for Arlie. Not seeing her, he kicked off his boots and began unbuttoning his pants when a knock sounded at the door.

Thinking it was the maid come to draw his bath, he opened it to find Arlie.

"Rochford, I..." Her eyes went wide at his state of undress. "Is this a bad time?"

He re-buttoned his pants and motioned her in. "Not at all, please come in."

She stepped into the room and he closed the door behind her. She turned to him, her gaze wandering down his body, stopping just shy of his cock. He wondered how often, if at all, she had seen a man's body. *How he yearned to show her more.*

As though realizing where it was she stared, she ripped her gaze back to his.

"Congratulations on your win," he said, grabbing the shirt off the back of the chair, and hastily put it on.

"Thank you, my lord. I enjoyed it, though I think I may have angered many people by not letting the duchess win."

He shrugged. "It doesn't matter what anyone else thinks."

Her brows furrowed into a frown. "But it does, really. For all that we'd like to think other peoples opinions don't matter, it does. It matters a lot."

Something in the tone of her voice gave him pause. She looked so wild and vulnerable...and desirable, standing there, her beautiful hair in disarray, her cheeks glowing with excitement, her green eyes gleaming with the triumph of her victory.

Unable to resist, his fingers moved along the edge of her jaw as he lifted her chin. "You cannot worry what the world thinks, Arlie. What matters most is what's in your heart. Only you can be the judge of your emotions. Let them guide you."

Her eyes instantly softened, the expression on her face blissful as she stared at him — with what? His heart missed a beat. He knew well what that look meant. He'd seen it a thousand times. Could it be that she desired him as much as he desired her? He dropped his hand, unsure of what to make of it.

Her gaze fell to her feet, obviously uncomfortable. When she glanced up a moment later, the fire in her eyes had vanished, making him wonder if he had only imagined it.

"You're right, I alone can make my happiness."

Her full lips parted slightly as she stared up at him. Unwelcome emotion raged within him.

"You should prepare for tonight's festivities."

He walked over to the door and opened it. She said nothing as she passed by him. He wanted to reach out and stop her, pull her up against his body, kiss her pouty pink lips until they were swollen, and teach her everything about sex.

He shut the door behind her, and let out the breath he'd been holding. Dear Lord, what was he to do now?

Perhaps he had imagined the desire in her eyes. Perhaps the atmosphere, or the excitement of winning the race had made her appeared interested in him. He ran a hand through his hair. At the end of the week, he would take Arlie and they would leave this place and return to Rochford Manor, where she would resume her studies.

He would have his work, and she would have her studies.

Liar!

Arlie had got under his skin, and the only way he could put her from his mind was to see her married off, and soon.

Which made him think of the young American. Up to this point, Dominic had tried to deter the man from continuing his pursuit of Arlie, but Daniel was by far the best choice for her. And if Daniel did marry her, they would eventually live in America—far away where he could forget about her. Then another dark thought followed that one. Could he actually handle a lifetime without seeing her again? Definitely not.

He was still contemplating all sorts of things a few hours later as he stood in the ballroom watching Langley and Arlie waltz among the other masqueraders. Where others went to the extreme to mask their faces, Arlie did not and he was glad. Her beauty was breathtaking. Dressed in a sleek white gown that hugged every curve of her body, Arlie was a sight like no other. He would have loved the gown on anyone else, but not the woman whose virtue he was supposed to protect. She had worn her pale hair high on her head, long curls cascading down her shoulders and midway down her back.

A Greek goddess, and a very fair one at that, he thought, frowning when he noticed she had once again foregone a corset—and if he wasn't mistaken, undergarments as well. His gaze ripped back to her face, but it was too late, his body had already come to life. Blood rushed to his groin, causing a deep ache in his already rigid cock.

A moment later, Langley, as though sensing his discomfiture, brought Arlie to his side after the dance. "Rochford, the lady tells me you are her next partner."

Arlie smiled up at him and he wasn't about to tell her no, even though he didn't really care to dance, especially in his current state of arousal. He would much prefer to go for a walk in the cold air, but instead he took her arm in his and led her out on the floor. His hand rested on her hip, the small amount of fabric between his flesh and hers proving he'd been right about her wearing nothing beneath. As she stared up at him, he knew he had never seen anyone as beautiful or desirable.

"My lord, who are you supposed to be tonight?" she asked with an arched brow and a playful smile.

He returned the smile, feeling more lighthearted than he had in days. "Once I dressed up like everyone else, but I find it much too tiring. Instead, I choose to come as myself."

She laughed. "Sometimes you sound so old."

The words struck a barb within him, and his smile faltered. He didn't think of himself as old, yet since Arlie was a mere seventeen, she probably thought him ancient. "I'm only sixteen years older than you," he reminded her. "Sure, old enough to be a brother, but—"

"Or an uncle," she added, her smile saying she enjoyed the game far too much.

He grinned. "Touché."

"Actually, sixteen years is not that much," she surprised him by saying.

"Is it not? I was under the impression you thought different."

She shrugged. "No, but as you've said before, you've probably tired of the things that I find exciting, only because you have experienced so much more."

He stared at her, wondering if she was teasing him, but her gaze never faltered. "What would you have had me dress as?" he asked, curious of her thoughts.

"You would be a black prince," she said, her lips curving into a devastating smile that showed her adorable dimples.

"The black prince in your dreams?" His voice sounded low and husky to his own ears.

Her gaze dropped to his mouth. "The very one. When I first saw you, I thought that's who you were. *My* prince, dressed all in black, come to take me away. So elegant with your long black coat, coming out of the storm. Your black hair slicked back from your chiseled face, and that lion on your finger, its ruby eyes staring at me from across the room, hypnotizing me." Whether she did it self-consciously or not, Arlie's fingers grazed the ring he still wore on the middle finger of his left hand—a gift from his grandmother on his eighteenth birthday.

Her words were fanciful, yet he felt them all the way to his bones. *He was her black prince?* He could not deny the delight her words brought him.

"I thought you asleep that night." He pulled her tighter to him, needing to feel her soft curves against him. He glanced down and could see her stiff nipples against the soft thin fabric of her gown. He ached to fill his palm with a firm breast, to lave the nipple with his tongue until she groaned low in her throat, begging him for release.

"I watched you under lowered lids. You looked at me once, but I closed my eyes. I tried to stay awake, but I fell asleep to the sound of your voice, and after that day, I dreamed of you nearly every night."

"You said that the dreams stopped in time."

Her gaze shifted to his chest. "I stopped believing in dreams long ago."

"And now?"

She looked at him once again, and the desire in her eyes took his breath away. "I believe that dreams are images we create to escape from real life."

Those were not the words he wanted to hear. He wanted her to say she believed in love, that she believed her black prince would sweep her off her feet and make her infinitely happy. But she did not, and there was no more time to speak of such things. The music had stopped, and her anxious suitor waited eagerly to claim her.

Dominic turned to the young American, and with smile firmly in place, nodded. Daniel took Arlie's hand, and off they went.

Watching the two, Dominic noticed with annoyance how perfectly suited they seemed. Taking a glass of wine from a side table, he drained it in a single motion, and resisted the urge to crush the crystal in his fist when Daniel pulled Arlie even closer.

Throughout the night, Daniel stayed at Arlie's side, playing the ardent suitor to perfection. With trepidation Dominic realized his ward was slowly slipping through his fingers, and he could do nothing but stand by and watch.

As Daniel walked Arlie out onto the veranda, Dominic instinctively headed in that direction. Nearly to the doors, he stopped in mid-stride. He could not watch her every move. He had to allow what was going to happen, to happen.

They would all be better off for it. She would marry, and he would go on as usual.

For some reason the future seemed so incredibly bleak.

As the minutes ticked away, Dominic drained three glasses of port, and was working on his fourth when Arlie stepped back inside with Daniel. The American walked off, and before Dominic could have a word with Arlie, another man asked her to dance. Daniel came back to where Arlie had been, a glass of punch in hand, looking disgruntled when he found Arlie on the dance floor with another man.

Someone tapped on his shoulder and Dominic turned. His grandmother smiled up at him. "Your ward has made quite a name for herself, has she not?"

"Indeed, she has," he agreed, steadying himself for a lecture.

"Arlie and Mr. Butler make a pleasing couple, don't you think?"

He nodded.

"Already word is circulating that the two will become engaged before the end of the Season." She tilted her head in contemplation. "I wonder, will they be right?"

"It is much too soon for her to consider any beau. She has only just entered Society."

"Could it be that you have a soft spot in your heart for the young woman yourself, Dom? I've been watching you, and I've noticed that you seem...uncomfortable when she is with Mr. Butler."

"I am only concerned about her welfare. She is young and knows little about the world. And in case you've forgotten, I am her guardian."

His grandmother's knowing smile set his teeth on edge.

"I believe she knows much more than she lets out. I had the opportunity to meet her the other day, and she is quite charming. She will make Mr. Butler a fine wife. I can just envision what attractive children they will have."

Dominic bit back a curse as an image of Arlie beneath Daniel Butler came to mind.

"Well, I've had a most tiring day, and I must get my rest. I will see you on the morrow."

"I bid you goodnight, Grandmother," he said to her back as she walked away.

As the night progressed, his grandmother's words came back to haunt him time and again. Obviously everyone thought Arlie and Daniel would end up together. Even a few of the men who had been in the running early on in the party now bowed out, having come to the conclusion that Arlie had chosen Daniel.

Was Daniel Arlie's choice? Did she desire the American? The thought twisted in his gut like a knife. Now as he watched her dance with Daniel, he saw what everyone else saw; a young couple who fit perfectly together. Arlie looked happy, her smile radiant. Dominic realized in that instant that she was well on her way to getting the young man she clearly coveted.

He forced his gaze away from his ward, and looked across the way at his mistress who stood beside her husband. As though sensing his perusal, she glanced up and met his smile. She lifted her brows, and he immediately caught her meaning.

And he thought, *What the hell?* What better way of forgetting the desire he felt for his ward than with a night of mindless fornication with his more than willing mistress?

Chapter Six

Even though Arlie was dancing with Daniel, she didn't miss the silent communication going on between Dominic and Veronica. The two were across the room from each other one minute, the next they both exited from opposite doors.

Jealousy ate at Arlie's insides, and though she knew she had no right to feel such an emotion, she did — with a vengeance. She knew where they would go, what they would do. An image of the two making love burned in her mind, torturing her, reminding her that she would never experience the pleasure of being in Dominic's arms.

Obviously Dominic felt he had done his duty by her. He usually watched her like a hawk, but now he had left her alone, *without a chaperone.*

When the dance ended Daniel excused himself and Arlie took the opportunity to slip away. Running up the stairs, she tiptoed past Dominic's room, then entered hers, telling herself she was there only to freshen up. Instead of refreshing herself, she pressed her ear against the wall. The minutes ticked by and she heard nothing. It was *too* quiet.

She left her room and walked down the hall, brow furrowed into a frown. Why was she acting like a lovesick fool? She should go back to the party, enjoy herself, and forget about Dominic. He was a grown man with a voracious appetite for women. She could do nothing to change that fact. To pursue the infatuation was asking for her own destruction.

Arlie rejoined the party, but she could not enjoy herself. Her traitorous thoughts returned to Dominic and what he was doing with Veronica.

By midnight Arlie was emotionally exhausted and she allowed Daniel to escort her to her room.

She opened the door a fraction, and looked up to find Daniel smiling down at her. "I bid you goodnight, Miss Whitman. I look forward to your company tomorrow."

"Thank you for a wonderful evening," she replied, ready to shut the door behind her when his hand braced it open.

"Could I have a goodnight kiss?"

Surprised by his request, she quickly nodded and closed her eyes. A second later his dry lips touched hers. Disappointment washed over her in waves, and she opened her eyes to find Daniel looking down at her, a look of pure wanting on his face. "Well, good night then."

Daniel grinned. "I can scarcely wait until tomorrow."

"Good night," she said again, glancing at his arm that still braced against the doorframe. He dropped the arm to his side and took a step back. Arlie shut the door and rested her forehead against the hard surface. She locked the door and breathed a sigh of relief having heard Daniel's departure. "Thank God," she said, kicking off her slippers. She turned, lifted her skirts, and bent over to remove her stockings.

"You're retiring early."

She jerked upright, her gaze moving to the dark corner where Dominic was sitting in a chair.

"Rochford!" Her hand went to her pounding heart. "I couldn't find you."

He said nothing. He just stared at her for a few unsettling moments. When he did speak, his voice was low. "I took a walk. Then I came back to my room, but when I couldn't sleep I thought I'd wait for you. I hope you don't mind."

She shook her head. "No, not at all."

"Did you have a good time?"

"Well…yes."

"You don't sound so sure."

She shrugged. "Actually I had been enjoying myself, but when you left, I went looking for you. I thought you had gone with Veronica, but then she came back."

"Was that Daniel who asked for a kiss?"

"Of course!"

Again, he said nothing, and as the seconds ticked into minutes she began to feel uncomfortable. Had it been a mistake to tell him she'd been looking for him? What must he think? Oh, how she wished he'd say *something*.

Sitting down on the bed, directly across from where he sat, she took the pins from her hair. "Do you love her?" she asked, unable to help herself.

His eyes followed her movements. When she finished, he smiled. "Do I love who?"

"The Duchess...your mistress."

He laughed without humor. "No, I don't love her. For a long time I lusted after her, but I find lately that I've grown tired of her."

"Yet you were with her tonight?"

A dark brow lifted, and the smile on his face turned wicked. "No, I was not. At least not in the way you're implying."

She let out the breath she had been unconsciously holding. "But you left together."

He came quickly to his feet, making her heart leap. As he walked into the light, she noticed how tired he looked. She wanted desperately to comfort him.

"Do you want to know why I wasn't with her?" he asked, running a hand through his hair. "I wasn't with her because I want someone else. I yearn for the touch of her, yet I know it isn't right."

The pulse in Arlie's neck quickened as he took another step toward her. She had to bend her neck to look up at him. "Does she know this?" Her voice was barely a whisper.

The side of his mouth lifted at the same time his hand reached out to lift a lock of hair from her shoulder. He wound it around his finger, then placed it against the swell of her breast. His finger lingered for a moment, barely touching her sensitive skin, but she felt that touch all the way to her soul. "I'm telling her now."

He wanted her?

Arlie swallowed hard as she watched him watching her, obviously waiting for her reaction. His nearness kindled a desire that warmed her blood. Standing, she went on the tips of her toes and kissed him lightly. He didn't move, and she felt a blush race up her neck to her cheeks. Her embarrassment was forgotten a second later when he pulled her against his hard body and his mouth covered hers.

The kiss was slow, thoughtful one moment, the next almost savage in its intensity. His hands explored the soft lines of her back—her waist, her hips. She moaned softly when his lips left hers and traced a line down her throat to the swell of her breasts. Her nipples tightened. Liquid fire raced through her veins, down low into her belly, making her ache for what only he could give her.

"It's wrong these feelings I have for you," he whispered against her overly sensitive flesh. "I want you desperately, yet I know it's not right."

"Why is it so wrong?" she asked breathlessly, feeling disconnected from herself. All these new sensations—her body felt like it had a will of its own.

"You're my ward. I should be protecting you against men like me. You deserve a husband."

The words were like a dash of cold water to her face. The fire she had felt but a moment ago began to ebb as his meaning became clear. He wanted a single night of passion. It would cost him some of his conscience, but it would cost her virginity...and the chance of gaining a man who would actually marry her.

She abruptly stepped away from him. The back of her legs hit the bed, nearly knocking her off-balance. "I cannot give up my virginity for only one night," she said in a resigned voice.

His dark, seductive stare pinned her to the spot. "I want you."

"I want you, too," she said hesitantly, noticing the side of his mouth lift. "Yet I cannot surrender everything and gain nothing."

As he stared at her, she saw many emotions play over his face, most of all regret. He nodded and took a step away from her. She felt it like a hard blow to her stomach.

"I shouldn't have come," he said, closing his eyes for a moment. He opened them a second later. "Good night, sweet Arlie."

Then he was gone, just like that.

* * * * *

The day dawned gray and cold, matching Arlie's mood perfectly. For hours now she had lain awake staring at the ceiling, waiting for the sound of others, but it seemed only she could not sleep

The entire night she had tossed and turned, all the while wondering where Dominic was—or more importantly, with whom he had spent the night.

Several times she'd been tempted to go to his room to talk about what had happened between them. Always, she talked herself out of it, knowing it would only cause them both pain in the end.

But with the dawning of a new day, Arlie was desperate to speak with him. After all, they would be returning to Rochford Manor and things could not stay as they were between them.

She dressed and went to his room, determined to set things right. How she would accomplish that task, she wasn't certain, but it had to be done—she felt too wretched to leave things as they were.

Her knuckle almost grazed the hard door when she looked down and saw a key in the lock. Should she dare open it without knocking first, she wondered, glancing down the long hallway. Seeing it clear, she grabbed the handle and turned it. A sliver of light shone through the sheer curtains, falling on the figure of her guardian, sprawled on silk sheets. At his side, the Duchess. Her long auburn hair fell across their naked bodies like a voluminous cloud. The sheets wrapped around their hips, the Duchess' ample bosom cradled against Dominic's strong chest.

Arlie swallowed a scream. How dare he come to her last night professing desire, and the next make love to the very woman he professed not to love—a married woman whose husband slept in another wing, who no doubt expected his wife to be asleep in her quarters.

How tempted she was to slam the door and wake them. Unable to stand the sight any longer, Arlie closed the door behind her and went downstairs.

She passed servants on her way out the front door. She walked down the long drive, her strides determined, her jaw set, while swiping at the tears that burned a path down her cheek. Why was she so upset? Last night he had told her he wanted her, and she had been the one to send him away by saying she expected marriage. What man wouldn't run?

Daniel. Daniel was the kind of man who would respect her. Daniel was the kind of man who would actually marry her.

Daniel was not anything like Dominic.

And at this moment you could be in Dominic's bed, her traitorous mind taunted. Right this moment she could be in Dominic's arms. If she had said nothing she would have experienced true bliss, but no, she said she wanted marriage, and that single statement had ruined everything. The knowledge was so sobering she stopped in mid-stride. What did she think she was going to do? Walk all the way back to Rochford manor?

What would everyone say once she came up missing, her clothes in her room, no note. She sighed heavily. She *would not* wallow in self-pity like the child Dominic thought she was. She lifted her chin. She was a woman, and she'd better start proving it to all of them.

She would have to grin and bear it. Lifting her chin, Arlie returned to the house, resolved to move forward with her life.

She made the mistake of looking up at the window where Dominic slept, and she wavered on her feet. She had no mind to sit in her room and listen to the sounds of Dominic and Veronica stirring. Instead she walked to the private garden, opened the iron gate, and took a seat on a stone bench, staring at nothing.

"Child, why do you look so down this morning?"

Arlie glanced up to find the dowager looking at her.

"May I?" the older lady said, pointing to the bench.

"Please, "Arlie replied, patting the place beside her.

The dowager sat down, and turned to Arlie with a smile. "You look tired, my child."

"I did not sleep very well." She found it difficult to remain indifferent in front of the older woman. The dowager had become a dear friend these past few days, and aside from Daniel and Langley, she felt she hadn't another friend in the world. But she could not tell the dowager of her feelings toward Dominic. She would probably give her a good set-down and remind her that Dominic would marry someone of the gentry, someone of his own station, and that she would be better suited for someone like Daniel, an American man with money who could offer a good life.

"I have not seen my grandson this morning. Have you, Miss Whitman?"

Arlie swallowed the lump in her throat. "No, I haven't," she replied, keeping her voice level. "I suspect he is probably still in bed."

The dowager nodded. "He is no doubt with that brainless twit of a mistress of his."

"Do you mean the Duchess?" Arlie blurted before she could stop herself.

The dowager nodded and released a heavy sigh. "Indeed. I often wonder if he will ever settle down. He is too much like my own son, who I had no control over. It seems it is in their blood. I hope for the day Dom realizes he needs an heir. I would hate for the title and lands to be passed on to those silly great-nephews of mine."

"Perhaps one day he will find a woman," Arlie said, hoping she sounded convincing, when the thought of Dominic marrying made her ill.

"When hell freezes over." The woman laughed. "I don't know why I agonize so. He does not care much for me."

"Why is that?"

The dowager shrugged. "I suppose I was not easy on him when he was a child. I tried hard to be a good mother to my son, but he was so headstrong, and he always did the opposite of what I wished. I realized early on that Dominic was much like Randolph, my son and a complete rake. Dominic's mother was a mouse, she was frightened of her own shadow and was no help in such matters. She allowed my son to walk all over her. It is such a shame."

The dowager had been looking straight ahead, but she turned her gaze directly on Arlie. "Don't ever let a man treat you thus, Arlie. After all, women are stronger than men. You must show them that you will not stand for such treatment. Promise me here and now that you will stand firm and never allow yourself to be treated unjustly."

The forcefulness of the dowager's words surprised Arlie. Obviously she was sincere and meant every word. "I promise," Arlie agreed, smiling in the hopes to put the woman's fears at ease.

The dowager nodded. "Good, with that said, I want to know all about Mr. Butler. How are things progressing in that area?"

The last thing Arlie wanted to do was make the woman think she really desired Daniel, but the dowager would not be put off easily. "Well, I don't know, really. Daniel is quite nice, but I don't really feel...how do I put it? — tingly all over."

The dowager's laughter filled the morning air and made Arlie laugh for the first time in days. "You are quite the little tart, aren't you? Well, perhaps in time he will make you feel...*tingly*. You will give him a chance, yes?"

"I shall, but only for you," Arlie injected and sat up straight, noticing that Daniel was making his way toward them. Dressed in a somber gray suit, he smiled, and Arlie was reminded of the dry kiss they had shared last night.

How different that chaste kiss had been compared to the one she'd shared with Dominic. His kiss had stirred the blood in her veins, making her feel alive . . .and yearning for more.

"Madam," Daniel said, bowing toward the dowager, before turning his full attention to Arlie. "Miss Whitman, I had hoped I would see you this morning. Langley has asked several of us to go for a ride, and being that he is a good friend of your guardian, he is prepared to act as our chaperone. Would you come with us?"

"Yes," Arlie said quickly, wanting to get away from the mansion and more importantly, Dominic. "Give me but a moment to change."

"Perhaps you can meet us at the stables?"

"That would be fine," she replied. "I'm sorry to leave you like this," Arlie said to the dowager.

"Think nothing of it, child." The dowager winked at Arlie. "You forget, I'm an old woman. Already I'm in need of a nap."

Arlie kissed the dowager's cheek, then ran for the manor and up the stairs to her room. Not wasting any time, she slipped into her riding habit, tidied her hair, and walked quickly toward the stables, looking forward to the day ahead.

Rounding the building, she nearly missed her step seeing Dominic at Veronica's side. To Arlie's immense displeasure, the woman looked the picture of contentment.

"Well, here she is," Langley said, a playful smile on his face. "Dearest Arlie, I have procured the very steed who saw to your victory yesterday."

Veronica turned to face Arlie, her gaze raking over the royal blue riding habit. It was one of Arlie's favorites and she was glad she'd brought it along.

Langley walked toward her. "Oh, and Mr. Butler said he would be right back."

Arlie smiled at Langley and saw from the corner of her eye that Dominic watched her. Just being in his presence brought every sense to life. How could she be so aware of him? She glanced at him and he stared back, his face showing no emotion. He wore dark breeches, black knee high boots and a white shirt open at the throat. He had tied his hair back, making his high cheekbones more prominent. Never in her life had she seen such masculine beauty. How she wished he was not her guardian but a suitor instead. How she wished she had told him yes last night instead of no.

She felt a hand at her back and jumped, startled. "I'm sorry," Daniel said, his hand lingering at her hip. "Apparently I just missed you. I didn't want to leave without you so I raced to your room, only to find you'd left."

"How very sweet," she said, smiling her most charming smile, determined to have the time of her life no matter how grueling the day might be.

Daniel glanced past her and immediately his smile lost its luster. His hand slowly slipped from her hip. "It appears that your guardian is the only one allowed to act as chaperone," he said under his breath, his voice laced with venom.

"Don't mind him," Arlie whispered.

"I fear that's impossible. Even now he is staring daggers at me."

Arlie didn't look at Dominic but instead put a hand on Daniel's arm. Instantly his dark eyes lit up. "He is harmless. Plus, he'll soon be occupied with *other* things."

Daniel immediately took her meaning and grinned.

For the next few hours Arlie made a valiant effort to have fun, a difficult feat since her guardian and his mistress watched her every move. Arlie didn't want to use anyone, but she found herself paying special attention to Daniel. She smiled, listened attentively, and laughed at everything he said, funny or not. But all along she remained conscious of the blue eyes that watched from a distance.

By the time they stopped to rest their horses, Arlie had wearied of hearing Veronica's soft, throaty laughter. Even though Arlie had a handsome man at her side, the man she craved was with another.

Dominic was an aristocrat, and the woman with him, though married, was his equal in every way. Though Arlie now rubbed elbows with members of *the ton*, she herself was not one of them, and never would be, no matter how hard she tried. The thought sobered her, and it must have shown in her expression because Daniel lifted her chin in his hand.

"What has put a frown on that beautiful face?" he asked, his expression full of concern.

How thoughtful…a true gentleman. Why could she not feel for him what she felt for Dominic?

As his hand drifted back to his side, she smiled reassuringly, though she knew well it was forced. "I am just a little light-headed. I didn't eat this morning, and I fear I am paying for it now."

He brightened instantly. "I just so happened to bring along a few things that may come in handy," he replied, producing a basket. He unloaded apples, grapes, a variety of cheeses and two biscuits.

They ate in silence, content to take in the setting and Arlie was grateful. She had grown weary of conversation.

Veronica's laughter reached out to her once again and Arlie turned. Immediately she wished she hadn't. Lying on a blanket, looking as relaxed as ever, Dominic ate a berry right from Veronica's fingers. The woman stirred another in her glass of champagne, then again proceeded to feed her lover. It was an erotic display, especially when the duchess licked her fingers, the same fingers that moments before had been in Dominic's mouth.

To her chagrin, Arlie's thoughts returned to the night before. She remembered the way Dominic's lips had felt against hers, the heat of his hands on her body, touching her like no one else had.

"Would you care for a grape?" Daniel asked at her side, reminding her she was staring.

"I would love one," she said with renewed enthusiasm. She refused to sit and pout, especially when her guardian obviously had been well into his cups last night. So much so that he'd propositioned her. He had probably been so drunk, he didn't even remember what had transpired between them.

Daniel handed her a small cluster of grapes and their hands touched briefly. She noticed the fire in his eyes immediately, the darkening of the already chocolate brown orbs. Though she had limited experience with men, she recognized the look in a man's eye when he desired a woman. Something about his face changed, the way his eyes slightly lowered and wandered down her body, scrutinizing her as though she stood before him naked, as though he could picture it so.

Like the way Dominic had looked at her last night.

"You are so very beautiful, Miss Whitman. Your hair is like spun silk. Your light eyes exotic."

She had never heard words so flattering, except of course in novels, but this was the first time someone had said anything like them to her face. "Daniel, you are too kind," she replied, lifting her hand and running the backs of her fingers along the length of his jaw. His mouth opened slightly and realizing his shock, she dropped her hand, then her gaze, and proceeded to eat despite the fact she wasn't hungry.

What was she doing? Good Lord, she might well be two different people: one good, who wanted desperately to win this young man over; and the other bad, who acted scorned by her guardian and his lover.

* * * * *

Dominic glanced in Arlie's direction. His ward still busily made conversation with the young American. How could they find so much to talk about? He stared at her profile, mesmerized by her soft beauty, her innocence, her excitement at all things he took for granted.

He had told himself when she had come into his life that he would waste no time finding her a suitable man to marry. By all appearances it was happening before his eyes, and now he wanted nothing more than to stop it.

By the besotted expression on Daniel's face, it appeared Arlie's fate had been determined. Daniel would ask for her hand, and she would soon leave Dominic's home and join Daniel in America. Things couldn't have worked out more perfectly if he'd planned it himself. Which in essence, he had.

He regretted the plan now, almost as much as he regretted coming to the party. If Arlie were home at Rochford Manor now, no one would even know of her, save Langley. The two of them could still have their time together where no one besides the servants could intrude. But that time in his life was gone, and there could be no going back.

He hated the thought of what would happen when they returned home. The peaceful life he had once known would be nothing but a savored memory.

Veronica's fingers skimmed along his spine, bringing him out of his musings. "Darling, you must give her the space she needs. You are becoming paranoid. You haven't been able to take your eyes off her since we left the house."

"She is my responsibility. I'm all she has."

"For now."

His gaze moved to his mistress. He saw the victorious gleam in her eyes having said aloud what he himself feared these last few days. It had been obvious from the beginning that Veronica was jealous of Arlie, as were a majority of the women at the party. He'd witnessed firsthand the envious glances as Arlie danced with man after man, especially the highly coveted Mr. Butler.

"Come now, darling, you mustn't look so grim. Mr. Butler is a gentleman through and through. He would never take advantage of someone as innocent as Arlie." She glanced past his shoulder to the two she spoke of, and her smile widened. "How very sweet, he is feeding her grapes. See, she is learning the ways of seduction already. Before you know it, you will be walking her down the aisle."

Dominic looked over to find Daniel grinning while he fed Arlie a grape, his fingers lingering longer than necessary on her full, pink lips. Dominic's blood boiled in his veins. Arlie's color was high, her eyes sparkling with merriment as she smiled at the younger man. Her laughter reached out to Dominic, mocking him.

He should have known better than to have given into his feelings last night. Good Lord, what could he have been thinking? Lust had overpowered him, and he'd made a spectacle of himself. Even worse, he remembered only bits and pieces of their conversation. However he recalled vividly that she had refused him.

All day he noticed how she avoided his stare. No doubt she was terrified by his open display of affection toward Veronica. More than once he'd been tempted to walk over and request a moment of her time. He would tell her it had been a mistake to go to her room and wait for her, and deplorable to have told her he desired her. But the opportunity never arose, and in the space of hours they had become strangers.

"Look, Dom, they're coming over."

He glanced up to find Arlie and Daniel, hand-in-hand, looking down at them. They looked so happy, so perfectly suited that he wondered if he hadn't ought to give the young man a chance and help him in his pursuit of his ward. The thought fled a moment later when he met Arlie's gaze.

"Would you care to join us?" Veronica asked, motioning to the small space of blanket remaining.

Daniel cleared his throat and looked at Arlie with a charming smile. "Actually, Miss Whitman and I wanted to ask if you would permit us to take a stroll down by the lake. It is not far."

Dominic lifted a brow. "You are wanting to take Arlie there without a chaperone?" His gaze shifted back to Arlie, who stared back at him, a fair brow lifted.

Daniel smiled tightly, proving he preferred to go alone. "Of course not...I wondered if perhaps you and the duchess would like to join us."

Veronica jumped to her feet and exclaimed, "What a wonderful idea."

Outnumbered, Dominic had little choice but to join them.

At the lake, Daniel took off his shoes and stockings then proceeded to wade into the water. "Come, Miss Whitman, the water is not too cold. Actually it is rather refreshing."

Arlie glanced in Dominic's direction as though waiting for approval. Their gazes locked for a moment. He saw the hurt and vulnerability there. What a letch he was. He had thought there had been a mutual attraction. Instead, she probably felt nothing more than adulation for taking her from a depressed surrounding into one that offered limitless opportunities. What a depraved fool.

Veronica kicked off her shoes and pulled off her stockings. With a wicked grin, she lifted her skirts to mid-thigh and walked into the water after Daniel.

As the pair in the water became more daring and walked out further, Dominic noticed Arlie had slipped out of her boots and was now peeling off her stockings.

"I'm sorry about last night," he said, his gaze slipping to her firm calves that were exposed to him.

"We both said things we didn't mean," she said with a forced smile.

She didn't give him a chance to try and explain himself. She stood, bunching up her skirts as she waded into the water.

He swallowed hard, his gaze taking in the long, silken legs, and slim, creamy thighs. Blood rushed to his already engorged cock. She was so ripe for the taking...

"Dom, aren't you coming in?" Veronica asked, bringing his attention back to where it should be.

He needed to cool off. He felt on fire, his desire for Arlie mocking him as a fool. Even now as she took the young American's hand, he wondered if he hadn't ought to leave and let nature take its course. That, or perhaps he should send her to stay with his grandmother at Whitley. Some time away from each other could only do them both good. Perhaps if she wasn't constantly underfoot, he could forget about her.

And perhaps he could quit breathing, too.

Chapter Seven

Dinner that evening was torturous. Arlie sat beside an elderly couple with Dominic directly across from her, conveniently right beside Veronica. Arlie couldn't help but think how daring the duchess was placing herself next to her lover while in full view of her husband. But the duke seemed blissfully unaware of his wife's cheating. That, or he turned a blind eye to it.

Time and again visions of the two as she'd seen them that morning raced through her mind. The image haunted her, to the point where she couldn't concentrate on the conversation going on around her. When the dowager's quick-witted humor couldn't bring her out of her bad mood, Arlie excused herself and went straight to her room.

At first, she attempted to read, but the story of the prince had suddenly lost its appeal. When there was a knock at her door, her heart raced. *Could it be Dominic?* But it was only Daniel, stopping by to see how she felt. She told him she'd been exhausted by the long day, and he left, but only after she gave him a chaste kiss on the cheek.

In a misery of her own making, Arlie sat on the edge of her bed. Sleep was out of the question. She glanced around the elaborate room and yearned for her quarters at Rochford Manor. She wanted to be home. Only one day left...she could stand it.

Preparing for bed, she sat at the vanity brushing out her hair when she heard the door to Dominic's room open then close. A moment later she heard giggles, then a masculine voice, *his* voice, silencing the laughter. Her heart sank like a stone and she pressed her hands to her ears.

Tears burned the backs of her eyes as she lay back on the bed staring up at the ceiling. She swiped at the tears, cringing when she heard the soft moans on the other side of the wall. How tempted she was to knock on the wall to silence them. How desperately she wanted to go over there, throw open the door and slap her guardian's wickedly handsome face. How she hated him!

Another peal of laughter invaded the room, and Arlie sat up. With a curse she pulled a valise from under the bed and began throwing her things into it. She couldn't stay in this place a single day longer. Throwing on her gown, she marched out of her room, past her guardian's door, and out the front door, thankfully unnoticed by anyone.

The stable master would not give her a mount, but instead had the footman procure a carriage for her immediate return to Rochford Manor. He cautioned her about the roads at night, warning her of highwaymen and other riffraff who haunted the country roads. But she was adamant, uncaring of her safety, and finally the footman gave in, but only after she assured him it was an emergency.

She slept the majority of the way home, her dreams filled with visions of she and Dominic in bed. Naked, he lay over her, his lips teasing a nipple. Her hands moved to his head, anchoring him there. Her hips arched, aching for his throbbing shaft. Then he lifted his head, his brilliant blue eyes hot. "I need you," he said, and with a thrust, he entered her.

Arlie woke with a start. Recognizing the tree-lined drive of Rochford Manor, she released a shaky sigh. The dream had been so real this time. Her body throbbed with desire.

Joseph met her at the front door, his face the very picture of fatherly concern.

She hugged the aging butler, who seemed surprised by her affection, but he hugged her back. When she finally released him, Joseph smiled and told her that a maid would be up to her room shortly.

Once snuggled safely in her bed, Arlie fell fast asleep and didn't wake until late the following day feeling renewed. So renewed, a long horseback ride was in order.

At any other time she might have opted to wear her riding habit, but today she felt rebellious and instead pulled out the breeches she had hidden under her mattress. Donning a crisp linen blouse, she tied it at the waist and headed for the dining room.

The servants who passed her in the hall smiled warmly, showing no surprise at her attire. The moment she had walked into the manor, she had felt a calm overtake her. This was her home now. She was safe from prying eyes, vicious gossip and rakehell guardians. A moment later she pushed open the door to find Dominic sitting at one end of the polished table.

Her pulse skittered.

Silence met her as she walked across the room. Taking her time at the sideboard, Arlie filled her plate, knowing she wouldn't eat half of the food.

But it gave her time to get up the nerve to face him. Choosing the seat farthest away from him at the opposite end of the ridiculously long table, she finally looked up to find Dominic's piercing blue gaze on her. Strangely, he looked upset. Almost furious.

"Good morning," he said, sitting back in his chair and crossing his arms.

Arlie pretended indifference—difficult when he looked so handsome despite the frown that marred his perfect face. He could bend any woman to his will, herself included, but she must remain impartial at all times.

"Good morning," she replied, flashing a deliberately too-sweet smile before she dug into her ham. The meat may as well have been dirt for all she tasted, but she forced herself to eat every bite. As she swallowed, she could feel Dominic's gaze on her still, burning into her.

"Why did you leave without telling me?"

She looked up at him, her brow arched. "I didn't want to disturb you."

His eyes narrowed. "You might have left a note."

Arlie shrugged and continued eating.

"What are your plans for the day?" Dominic asked, clearly agitated that she had defied him.

"I'm going for a ride."

"Where?"

"I have no idea."

She could tell he was furious by the tic in his jaw. He appeared ready to question her again when the door opened and Joseph entered, holding a silver tray piled with calling cards. Without a word he set the tray before Dominic, who picked up the first card, scanned it, and tossed it aside. On it went—one by one, he threw each card aside.

"Well," he said, his voice edged with steel. "It appears you were quite a sensation. In fact, several callers are awaiting your presence as we speak."

Rather than be flattered by the attention, Arlie felt strangely disappointed. She wanted solitude, peace and quiet. She needed time to sort out her thoughts where Dominic was concerned. She needed to put an end, once and for all, to this infatuation that had taken over her entire being. She felt a prisoner in her own body, yearning for a man that would never be hers—suffering through erotic dreams that haunted her nights. She needed an end to the madness.

* * * * *

Dominic knew the surprise on Arlie's face was genuine. She had clearly not expected her suitors to chase her down, and found it shocking they now sat in the parlor awaiting her presence. He could only imagine the men's reaction to Arlie's clothing.

Did she have any idea how stunning she was—or how sexy? The breeches she wore clung to her skin, displaying her long legs and shapely buttocks to perfection. The outfit left nothing to the imagination. And the white linen shirt she wore with no undergarment beneath enticed a man to stare, to see her nipples beneath the thin fabric—should she walk out in the sunlight...

He cleared his throat. "You have suitors, Arlie. They are awaiting you."

She sighed. "I am so weary of company. I don't feel up to visitors. Would you tell them another time would be better?"

Would he tell them? He would be only too happy to throw the randy group out on their asses. Refraining from smiling wholeheartedly, he stood. "Of course," he replied like the caring guardian he should be.

As he marched toward the parlor, he tried to calm himself. He had become entirely too possessive of Arlie, and it was inappropriate. She lured him, like a moth to the flame. Her innocence drew him. She was a virgin, and he would give anything to be the first to take her, to feel her soft body against his hard one. To feel her arms encircle his neck, her sweet breasts press against him, her thighs spread wide for him and him alone.

He shook his head at his thoughts. Granted, he'd never cared anything about principle when it came to women. Older, younger, rich, poor, married or widowed—he'd never cared before. Sex was sex. He couldn't help but wonder if that was what all these men who came calling thought too.

He schooled his features as he entered the parlor where four young men sat, all bearing flowers, candies, and other trinkets, all for his ward. Jealousy ate him alive, and it didn't help that all of them, save one, were at least five to ten years younger than himself, and far more suitable husband material than he would ever be.

They all stood as he entered, their gazes straying past his shoulder to the hallway, obviously hoping Arlie would follow.

Dominic abruptly cleared his throat, drawing their attention back to him. "I regret to inform you all that my ward is not feeling well this morning. The recent party exhausted her and she needs time to recoup."

Masculine moans filled the air and Dominic managed an apologetic smile. "Thank you for coming, but I will ask that in the future you send word of your visit ahead of time, so I may see there is a chaperone available."

He motioned for them to follow him. He held the front door open as each man filed past him, each stating their disappointment at not being able to offer her their best in person.

Daniel Butler, the young American he'd actually liked before the Banfield ball, stopped at his side and pressed a bouquet of roses into his hands. "Lord Rochford, could you please give these to Miss Whitman along with a message? Tell her the last few days were the best of my life. When she left early, I was devastated and immediately returned to London. Her beauty has stunned me so that I can scarcely think."

Dominic clenched his fist. The man would have a tough time doing much of anything when Dominic finished pummeling him. Luckily, Daniel stopped his rehearsed speech and walked out the door before Dominic lost his composure. It took every ounce of will he possessed to refrain from slamming the door behind them.

Taking a deep, controlled breath, Dominic walked toward the dining room, his mind racing. He tossed the roses at a passing maid. "Throw them out," he said, his head pounding with every step that brought him closer to the dining room...and to Arlie.

Is this what life would be like from now on—diverting a bunch of randy men who clamored for time with his ward?

Would he be subjected to constant suitors on a daily basis? If so, how could he stand it?

Perhaps it was time he move Arlie to his country estate in Whitley. Lord knew his grandmother would be delighted to have her company. But Whitley was not far enough away…there was no place on earth far enough away. Wherever she went, men would surely follow. No, she must stay where he could watch her.

Watch…and turn every ardent suitor away. He wanted Arlie to himself. In the past week he had dealt with more suitors than he cared to. If people wanted to speculate, then so be it. He only wanted to be left alone with Arlie. The rest of the world could go hang.

Joseph hurried toward him. "I'm sorry to disturb you, my lord, but I wish to inform you Miss Whitman has taken the gray mare from the stables. Yancy tried to convince her not to, but she insisted. I know she's an accomplished rider…"

"Say no more," Dominic replied, striding toward the stables. If Arlie hadn't broken her neck already, perhaps he would do it for her.

* * * * *

Arlie rode at a furious pace, not caring that the horse was by far the fastest, not to mention largest, mount she'd ever ridden. She knew she should have been more cautious and picked a more suitable horse, but she desperately needed to escape the man who not only held her fate in her hands, but her heart.

She tried to tell herself that what she felt for Rochford was simple adoration. Yet how could it be simple adoration when her heart nearly pounded out of her chest whenever he came near, and the urge to touch him became overwhelming? She no longer lied to herself. She wanted him in her bed. She wanted to be his lover.

He was attracted to her as well, that much was obvious, but he had already said he would not marry her. She would simply be a diversion, a roll in the hay, and how long would that last? Look at Veronica. He'd said he had tired of her, yet within hours of the declaration he'd taken her to bed again.

For all Arlie desired Dominic, she had to admit the truth. Rochford would chase anything in a skirt. If she gave in to her desires and made love with him, then where would she be? In the end she would be hurt, and he would move on. She couldn't let that happen.

Letting her frustrations go, Arlie galloped on, eating up miles of land. Not until the horse became lathered did she slow, and then stop, allowing the mare a much-needed rest. As Arlie's heartbeat slowed, she looked at the countryside and realized she was lost. Knowing it would be foolish to continue, she dismounted and led her horse into a small alcove of trees set against the green hillside.

She would rest for a bit, then return the way she had come...hopefully.

She sat with her back against an old tree, and closed her eyes, taking in the silence around her. How peaceful it was. The only sound came from the stirring of the leaves overhead as a light breeze blew.

A moment later the sound of hooves interrupted the tranquility. Someone was coming her way. She considered hiding, but stayed put, figuring she could ask the person how to get back to Rochford Manor.

But it seemed that she was not going anywhere.

"Dominic," she whispered, her heart pounding in her ears as he raced toward her on his black steed. Dressed in black from his shirt to his boots, his very presence was so powerful, she wondered if any woman alive could resist him. He stopped just short of her. His eyes were as cold as ice.

What right did he have to be mad at her? She had merely gone for a ride by herself. She had not ridden into London, but in the countryside, so surely a chaperone had not been needed. She lifted her chin and met his stare without flinching.

"You know better than to take the gray. She's a feisty mount." His gaze shifted to her chest, lingering there a few seconds before slipping past her waist to her breeches.

Arlie's heart slammed against her ribs as his gaze found hers once again. "I thought all your breeches had been burned."

She stood and planted her hands on her hips. "As you can plainly see, I saved a pair from the fire."

"Young women should not ride astride, nor do they wear breeches," he said, his voice disapproving. "It's unseemly."

She bristled under his hard stare. How dare he tell her what was unseemly. Having sex with a married woman—that was *unseemly*. Telling his ward that he wanted to bed her, then saying he would never marry her—now that was *very* unseemly.

"What are you thinking?" He watched her intently, as though he could see into her very soul.

How did he read her so easily? It seemed he knew everything about her, while she knew nothing of him. "I never meant to upset you," she lied, knowing that's exactly why she had taken off alone...and on the gray.

He dismounted, and Arlie took a step back.

At Dominic's approach, Arlie could see a muscle twitch in his jaw. Her heart pounded in time to his steps, and a moment later she gasped when he pulled her up against him. He held his mouth inches away from hers. "I hate what you do to me. I hardly recognize myself anymore." His hot breath fanned her face.

She trembled, afraid of her desire for him. Her fear that he would abandon her once he got what he wanted.

A second later he released her and took a step away from her. He ran a hand through his hair, and it was then Arlie noticed he was trembling too. "I wanted to kill all of those men that came calling. Each one of them bringing you gifts, wanting to woo you with the hope of having you. I've endured day after endless day of men staring at you, touching you, only to come home to them beating down my door to see you."

"I didn't ask them to." He seemed so tortured, she had the sudden urge to comfort him.

"I know you didn't ask them to. You have no idea of the power you have over men. Look at you." His gaze moved down her body like a slow, deliberate caress. "You're a seductress and you don't even know it. You stand there in breeches that hug your skin, every curve nestled against soft wool. Slender hips, tiny waist, flat stomach, and those long legs—legs that were made to wrap around a man's waist. Your shirt is just thin enough to show the slightest hint of your rose-colored nipples. Your firm breasts strain against the material, taunting a man to feel their fullness in his hands, to taste their sweetness with his tongue until you're begging for him to take you."

Arlie's pulse skittered alarmingly. She could not believe what she was hearing, and yet she was strangely excited by his seductive words.

He took the steps that separated them and stared down at her, his eyes dark. "When a man sees you, all he can think about is fucking you."

Arlie swallowed past the lump in her throat. He looked past her shoulder, then turned and looked the other direction. He checked to see that they were alone. Arlie's stomach tightened, knowing what it meant.

He would take her here, and she would not stop him.

He confirmed her thoughts when a second later he brought his hand to the back of her neck, pulling her toward him and his lips crashed against hers.

Her heart pounded as he pressed his hard sex against her. Excitement raced along her spine as he coaxed her mouth open with his tongue. "Arlie, open for me," he said against her lips.

And she did.

* * * * *

Dominic was beyond redemption. He wanted Arlie with a desperation that terrified him.

When she didn't resist him, he couldn't stop himself. Breaking away from her kiss, he unbuttoned her shirt with trembling hands. He had not felt this way since he was a young man. Finally when he had completed his task, he took her perfect breasts into his hands. Hearing her moan, he smiled, and lifted her, wrapping her long legs around his waist, while he took a nipple into his mouth. She moaned again, and it was all he could do not to take her then and there.

She watched him as he suckled her, first one pebble-hard nipple then the other. "Oh, Dominic," she whispered, her fingers weaving through his hair, pulling it as she pressed her hips against him.

He would not be able to last.

With a groan, he fell to his knees, and lay her down on the soft grass. He went on his elbow, wanting to see her sweet body, and her beautiful face while he made sweet, passionate love to her.

His heart gave a jolt seeing her eyes half-closed, dark with desire. He felt a strange thrill knowing he made her feel thus. He leaned over and rained kisses along her face, down her slender neck, over her bared breasts, and down her taut stomach. Unbuttoning her breeches, his hand wove through her soft curls and lower, along the moist cleft that he'd yearned to feel for weeks now.

* * * * *

Warning bells went off in Arlie's head, but she could do nothing to stop them. It was too late for that. She wanted Dominic more than she'd ever wanted anything. As his fingers worked their magic, stroking her until she writhed against him, crazy with need, she wondered if she would regret what was surely to come.

His lips met hers once again, then slowly moved down her body, kissing her neck, her collarbone, the valley between her breasts, one nipple, then the other. His eyes met hers, then a second later his tongue flicked out, licking a diamond-hard nipple once again. She held him there, keeping him positioned over her breast. As he suckled, her nipples turned hard and a tingle began deep inside her stomach, and spread down between her legs. She moaned, not wanting the pleasure to end.

He was merciless in his torture as he suckled her breasts, all the while, his fingers worked their way downward, over the mound of her womanhood, and then inside her. Arlie's heart raced, and heat filled her veins as he moved his long finger in and out of her. He slipped another inside her and her breath caught.

"It's all right, Arlie. Let yourself feel," he said, his fingers pulling in and out, in and out. Something within her built, to the point she felt like screaming out loud for all the world to hear. Then it happened; her insides contracted, like a dam giving way—an unbelievable sensation that wracked her entire body, leaving her spent and her body humming.

Minutes passed, and she lay with her arms spread wide, staring up at the bright blue sky. She glanced over to her right, to find Dominic watching her, a soft smile on his face, and a warmth in his eyes she had never witnessed before.

She grinned like a fool, and he laughed softly under his breath.

She felt his hand on her stomach, and ever so slowly his fingers moved over her belly then beneath the sensitive flesh of her breasts. Her hard nipples tightened as his mouth descended. Immediately, the wicked sensations began all over again. His fingers played with the other nipple then slowly worked their way down to the dampness of her cleft, where all her nerve endings seemed to stem from. "I feel like I'm on fire," she whispered.

"Let yourself go, Arlie." He kissed her, first soft, tenderly, then harder with a desperation that excited her.

She met his kiss feverishly and opened her legs wider, giving in to the pleasure.

* * * * *

Dominic could not take much more. His cock felt near to bursting. If she touched it, he would spend himself before he entered her.

He fought an inner battle. Every part of him demanded he take her here and now. Yet he pulled out a thread of sanity — long enough to take in their surroundings. They were out in the open, and anyone could come upon them.

And he would be ruined. A disgrace — just like his father.

His fingers moved in and out of Arlie's tight sheath, and in response her hips lifted. He applied pressure to her clitoris with his thumb, and a moment later she let out a low moan as she climaxed.

Chapter Eight

Dear Lord, what had he done?

Dominic woke the following morning, wondering what in the world had possessed him to take advantage of the woman he had sworn to protect. Last night he had dinner with Arlie, then they had played a game of chess. He had walked her to her room, and left her there with a light kiss on the lips—and he had seen the disappointment in her eyes.

With the dawning of a new day came a large dose of reality. He had seduced his ward. He had touched her, kissed her, and had come very close to making love to her out in the open. Though he still had those same urges, he realized that he could not take the relationship any further. Arlie deserved more—a husband. A man who would marry her, spoil her, and get her pregnant with child.

The very thought of Arlie sharing another man's bed made his blood boil.

"My lord?"

Dominic turned to find Joseph standing at the study door. "Lord Malfrey is here—"

"Lord Malfrey?" Dominic repeated.

"Yes, and though he has asked to visit with you, I've a notion that he is interested in Miss Whitman."

"What gives you that idea?" Dominic asked, certain that his butler would tell all, especially when he looked full to bursting.

"Well, first off, he is dressed quite elegantly for this time of day. And he is carrying a rather large bouquet of roses, which I assume are *not* for you."

Dominic walked to the window. There on the gravel drive sat the most ostentatious carriage Dominic had ever seen.

Instantly he recalled Lord Malfrey. The man had acquired the title of viscount from a distant uncle whose only heir had died under mysterious circumstances. Malfrey, if memory served, was newly married. His bride, a most unattractive woman, spent the majority of the year in the highlands of Scotland — at her parent's country estate.

"Send him in," Dominic said, taking a seat behind his desk. Malfrey entered, wearing a heinous suit of dark purple velvet, and in his hand he held an enormous bouquet of red roses. Joseph had not lied — Malfrey had dressed as though to attend a wedding, particularly his own.

"Rochford," the Viscount said with a curt nod.

"Malfrey," Dominic replied, hoping to keep the venom out of his voice. He knew why the man was here. Like an animal in heat, he'd come calling for Arlie. "To what do I owe the pleasure, or need I ask, since I assume those roses are not for me?"

The man laughed easily. "You are correct, my lord. Actually, they are for your lovely ward. I have just discovered I made a huge error by not attending the Banfield Ball. And since others are speaking so highly of her, I wished to come and make her acquaintance, so I would know of whom they speak."

"Malfrey, I mean no disrespect, but you are a married man."

Malfrey appeared stricken by his direct statement. "Indeed, I am newly married. You misinterpret my intentions. My visit is a friendly one. I have no immoral intentions toward Miss Whitman."

He lied. Malfrey wanted Arlie, as did most every single, married, or widowed man who had ever set eyes on her. Dominic could not stand it. He could not endure another day under the same roof as Arlie — wanting her, turning men away, knowing that one day she would belong to another.

"Today is not a good day," Dominic said, the pleasure of doing so surprising even himself. "Miss Whitman is busy with her studies, not to mention exhausted from the week's festivities."

Malfrey's disappointment was so obvious, it was all Dominic could do to keep a straight face.

To Dominic's great dismay, he heard Arlie's voice and soft footsteps in the foyer.

He pushed aside his disappointment and stood. "It appears that you have a stroke of luck, Malfrey, for I hear Arlie now."

"Miss Whitman," Dominic called, and a moment later Arlie walked into his study, dressed in a flattering peach-colored dress. Malfrey's mouth opened for a scant second before he snapped it shut. He moved so quickly, Dominic could do nothing but watch in silence as the Viscount extended his leg and nearly bowed to the floor before her.

"Miss Whitman, it is a pleasure to make your acquaintance. I apologize that I did not have the opportunity to meet you at the Banfield estate. I fear business kept me away. I am Reginald Leopold Franklin Stanford, Viscount of Malfrey," he said, his voice full of self-imposed pride.

Arlie curtsied. "It is a pleasure to meet you as well," she said, her cheeks turning a flattering shade of pink.

"Lord Malfrey is a newlywed, Arlie. And if I'm not mistaken, Malfrey, your wife is expecting your first heir," Dominic quickly injected.

The man's shoulders stiffened and he gave a curt nod. "Indeed, I am to be a father soon. How very astute you are, Rochford."

"I would love to meet your wife one day. Does she live in London?" Arlie asked, her smile genuine.

"No, she is in Scotland."

Arlie's smile quickly turned into a frown. "How difficult it must be for her to have you so far away. I hope my husband and

I will be inseparable, for I could not bear to be alone during such a difficult time."

Two bright spots of color appeared on Malfrey's cheeks. "Yes, well, my beloved enjoys the country, and the pregnancy has been without difficulty," he said, as though righting a wrong.

"Perhaps one day I shall meet her. When next she is in town, would you be kind enough to bring her by for tea?"

Completely flustered, the man could do little but nod.

"Excellent," Arlie replied, then turned her full attention to Dominic.

"My lord," she said, a soft smile coming to her lips. "I wondered if I could request a special menu for supper tonight."

Feeling the viscount's ardent gaze on him, Dominic frowned. "Is the menu not to your liking?"

Arlie shook her head. "No, my lord...I simply wanted tonight to be special."

Dear lord, he knew what that meant. She expected their relationship to continue on the course it had been heading. Damn, why did she have to look so desirable? Why did he want to touch her soft skin and pull her into his arms every time she walked into a room? She was ripe, ready and willing for the taking.

"Joseph," he called louder than intended, making the other two occupants of the room jump. He glanced at Arlie. "I am afraid tonight you will eat alone. I have business to attend to in London."

"My lord," Joseph replied, appearing at the door.

"Will you please see Lord Malfrey out and then return to my study."

"Yes, my lord."

Dominic barely heard Malfrey's goodbye. Instead he saw the devastated expression on Arlie's face. She clutched her hands before her. "When will you be returning?" she asked, her disappointment obvious.

"I'm not certain," he replied, standing. "I have taken enough time away from business and there are matters that need my immediate attention. I'll return as soon as possible."

Avoiding her gaze, he opened the desk drawer and pulled out a ledger. "I will tell Joseph he is to serve as chaperone when suitors come calling — as I know they will be storming the gates." He forced a smile. "I shall see you upon my return."

* * * * *

A week later Arlie sat down to dinner, her gaze straying to the head of the table where Dominic usually sat. He was still in London. The past days had been excruciatingly long. Not even her lessons had helped pass the time.

With every hour Arlie yearned for the sight of Dominic. *When would he return?* She tried to tell herself he really had business to handle, yet part of her wondered if he intentionally stayed away. After that afternoon in the meadow, when he had brought her to her first climax, he had become sullen, speaking only about trivial things such as her lessons, pretending the intimate moment had never occurred.

But he *had* touched her, and she relived that afternoon almost every waking hour.

Her body had betrayed her that day, but her mind had not. She knew she still possessed her virginity, but what she had experienced in his arms had made her feel like a wanton, out of control. Worse still, she had taken the greatest pleasure from it. Never in her wildest dreams could she have imagined a man's touch could be so wonderful.

She realized with a pang that she wanted it to happen again. She wanted Dominic as a lover with a desperation that terrified her.

But she had no idea what he thought of her. Did he find her lacking as a lover? Did he regret what had happened between them?

She picked at her food, glanced at the clock, and with a sigh, pushed the plate away. It was nearly seven o'clock, and she wondered if her evening would be interrupted by yet another man. The suitors who visited were kind and courteous, but try as she might, Arlie could not picture herself married to any one of them. Men—they spouted poetry and gave her trinkets, yet there wasn't one among them that made her feel the way Dominic did.

Arlie jumped as the door to the dining room flew open and Dominic strode in. He faltered when he saw her, then grinned boyishly. Arlie stood, and could not help but return the smile. She could tell he had been drinking by the way his glazed eyes brushed over her, his expression sinfully seductive.

She drank in everything about him. So handsome—it hurt just to look at him. She pushed back the chair and took a step toward him when a gorgeous brunette walked into the room, her red lips curving into a provocative smile as her heels clicked on the marble floor.

Dominic pulled out a chair and fell into it. The brunette followed, landing on his lap, her arms encircling Dominic's broad shoulders. The blood roared in Arlie's ears and she stood frozen to the spot.

The woman licked Dominic's ear, as though Arlie did not stand ten feet away, watching them.

Just when she thought things couldn't get worse, Langley and another harlot came in, their laughter filling the room. "Could I borrow a room, old man?" he asked crudely, releasing a growl while kissing the woman's neck. The redhead all but purred as her arms encircled Langley's waist, her hands drifting down, grabbing his buttocks and squeezing. Langley's gaze locked with Arlie's and the shock she saw there would have been funny under different circumstances. But now it wasn't funny in the least.

"Miss Whitman!" Langley said, releasing his hold on the woman.

Arlie's gaze shifted from Langley to Dominic, so busy with the brunette, he didn't notice her distress. All week Arlie had envisioned him working hard on his ledgers, putting his business in order. All along he'd been off cavorting with another woman.

Everything became clear in that moment. She meant nothing to him. The moment they'd shared had happened, and now it was over. He probably never gave it any thought. In fact, he must surely be disappointed in the whole experience if he could fondle this woman right in front of her. Did the man have no shame?

Arlie closed her eyes, took a deep breath, then opened them again. Without saying a word, she left the room. The moment she was on the other side of the door, she covered her face with her hands. The sound of laughter filled her ears. Were the women mocking her? Were they making fun of her, she wondered. They couldn't possibly be ladies. Their clothing was cut far too provocatively and they wore too much makeup to be members of *the ton*.

Arlie raced up the stairs to her room and sat down at the vanity. She stared at her reflection for a long time to see what everyone saw when they looked at her. Her pale blonde hair was as shiny as silk but a bit too wavy. Her lips were too full, her nose small and tipped up slightly at the end. Her eyes were probably her best feature. Almond-shaped, they were green in color and framed by long, dark lashes. She stood and her gaze moved down her body, taking in the unflattering dress.

Since Dominic hadn't been around, Arlie hadn't given much thought to her appearance.

That was going to change.

With a little polish, she could be just as enticing as those women downstairs. After all, didn't the blood of a true whore run through her veins? From her reaction to Dominic's passion play, she would certainly enjoy making love to a man. Well, she would prove to him, and to herself, that she was the kind of woman any man would desire as his own.

* * * * *

Having survived a sleepless night, Arlie spent the entire morning and afternoon preparing for the night to come. Dressed in a new gown of the finest rose-colored silk, Arlie took a deep breath and glanced down at the dress's incredibly low bodice. Her breasts were pushed up so high she was in danger of falling out.

The sides of her hair were pinned up by pearl encrusted combs, leaving the length to fall down her back in thick waves. With Mary's help she had lightly powdered her face and added rouge to her cheeks and lips. The diamond earrings and necklace had been an afterthought. Dominic had bought them for her weeks ago, when she had scored perfectly on her French test, and this was the first time she had worn the jewels.

Joseph met her at the bottom of the stairs, his brows lifting in silent appreciation. "Let me do the honor," he said, opening the door to the dining room with great aplomb.

For a moment Arlie felt the incredible urge to run back to her room and change. Steeling her nerves, she took a deep breath, lifted her chin a fraction, and entered the room.

Dominic had already arrived and sat at the head of the table, wine glass in hand. He set the glass down and stood. "Expecting company tonight?" he asked, a dark brow raised in question.

She forced a smile. "Yes. In fact, I'm surprised he's not here yet."

"*He?*" The word had scarcely left his lips when Langley entered the room via the servant's entrance, a bottle of champagne in hand. He stopped in mid-stride, his gaze raking over her. He whistled between his teeth. "My dear Miss Whitman, your beauty astounds me."

"Langley?" Dominic said in disbelief, glancing from his friend to Arlie.

Arlie avoided her guardian's stare and instead went to meet her dinner guest. Taking the champagne from him, she handed it to Joseph who stood at the ready.

Langley took both her hands in his and brought them to his lips. His eyes sparkled with devilish intent. "How thoughtful of you to stop by today and extend me the invitation to dine with you. I must say, I was sorry to have missed your call."

She shrugged. "No matter, I looked a mess."

"Mmmm, I doubt it."

Dominic cleared his throat. Arlie ignored him and kept her attention focused on Langley, who pulled out a chair for her. Taking the seat beside her, Langley sat down. Dominic cleared his throat again.

"Do you need me to pound on your back, old boy?"

Dominic sat down. "Would you prefer that I leave?"

Langley shrugged. "No, that's all right. The more the merrier, I always say."

"Which reminds me. I thought Rose was in town?"

"No, not until tomorrow," Langley replied, turning his attention back to Arlie.

Dominic frowned. "Is Mr. Butler coming as well?"

"Not unless you invited him," Arlie replied, her tone innocent.

He looked ready to choke her.

Arlie turned her attention to Langley, yet she was ever aware of the dark presence watching her every move.

One course followed another and Arlie enjoyed herself, finding Langley to be an excellent dinner companion. He gave her his undivided attention, commented on every course, and even managed to get in a few jibes directed at Dominic. Dominic, on the other hand, remained silent and left his food untouched.

When they had finished dinner, Langley stood and extended his arm to her. "Old boy, I'm taking Miss Whitman for a walk around the gardens. I would invite you along, but the truth of the matter is—I don't want you to come."

"You're my friend, Langley. I have nothing to fear, especially since your very rich, titled wife-to-be will be arriving tomorrow morning. That said, I can only assume your intentions toward my ward are honorable."

"Of course," Langley replied flippantly, his arm encircling Arlie's waist in familiar fashion.

Without another word, Arlie left the dining room on Langley's arm.

In the garden, away from Dominic, Arlie relaxed. She had succeeded in making Dominic angry, but oddly enough she didn't feel victorious, but rather devious.

"I believe your little game worked," Langley said, reminding her of the deceit.

"What do you mean?" Arlie asked, biting her lip nervously while glancing up at her companion.

Langley wrapped his arm around her shoulders. "I saw the look on your face last night when we came home with those women. You hurt far more than you would ever admit. I know the ways of women, Arlie. I've adored them for the last thirty years of my life. In that time I've learned their games and even some of their tricks. More often than not they work, but sometimes they don't."

"Meaning?"

"I know you feel something for Dominic, or you wouldn't have gone to the trouble of inviting me over. If it's any consolation, know that Dom also feels something for you. But like yourself, he's been fighting the attraction from the start. Perhaps out of honor, perhaps because he's afraid that if he gets too close, you'll flee." He smiled softly. "You see, Dom hasn't always been a notorious rakehell. In fact, once my good friend had a love, a woman whose beauty rivaled any in her time. Dom loved her desperately, perhaps too desperately."

Arlie stopped abruptly and looked up at her friend. "Who was she? Is she someone I've met?"

Langley shook his head. "She was several years older than him, and she played the game of love well. She wasn't titled, but he didn't care—Dom would have given up everything for her. When she told him she was pregnant, he was ecstatic, thrilled knowing she would have no excuse not to marry him. Unfortunately that bliss was short-lived. Just one week before the wedding, Dominic found his love in bed with another man. Suffice it to say, the baby was not Dominic's."

Arlie put her hand to her heart. "How horrible."

"Indeed, particularly since the man who betrayed him was his own father."

Arlie gasped in disbelief. "His father...how could he be so cruel?"

"It matters not. But that is the past, and I told you only because I love Dom, and I hate to see him lose something he wants so desperately." Langley lifted Arlie's chin with a finger and smiled warmly. "I am flattered that you think me a good enough friend to confide in and a good enough actor to pull off this little charade."

"I did not mean to—"

His finger moved to her lips, silencing her. "You need not explain. Though Dom may think otherwise, I would never hurt him. I care for him too much, and we have seen too many times together, both good and bad. We have never fought for the same woman, and I think what bothers him the most is that he would have, at one time, thought me quite suitable for you. But I knew the moment he hadn't told me about you that he was keeping you for himself. My thoughts are confirmed every time I see him look at you."

"He could never love me enough to marry me."

"Dominic is scared of marriage—as well you understand now. But rest assured, as titled men, it is our lot in life to marry and have heirs. It matters not if we love the woman we're bound to."

"How can you stand it?"

He shrugged. "We stand it by taking young, gorgeous mistresses to bed."

"Perhaps your wife will be different."

"Perhaps..." he said, even though he sounded unconvinced.

He glanced past her shoulder, a bright smile coming to his face. "Guess who's joined us," he whispered. "He is so jealous, he could kill me."

Without warning, Langley pulled her into his arms and kissed her full on the lips. A moment later he released her, a wolfish smile on his face. "Goodnight, dearest Arlie. Thank you for a most wonderful evening. Perhaps I will bring Rose over to meet you later this week." He turned to Dominic. "See you, old boy."

Silence fell over the gardens as Arlie watched Langley stride toward the stables. The hair on her arms stood on end, knowing that Dominic was right behind her.

When Langley was out of sight, Arlie turned to face him.

He had loosened his cravat, his waistcoat was opened as though he'd started to undress, then reconsidered. He stared at her saying nothing. She felt wretched. Wretched for pretending to be someone she was not, for using Langley, and for trying desperately to make Dominic angry. How disappointed he must be in her.

She longed for the protectiveness of his arms, for the passion and longing she remembered so vividly. She'd be happy just to have his friendship again.

His gaze burned into her. "I was under the impression that you wanted Mr. Butler. Am I mistaken?"

She shrugged. "I don't know what I want."

"That, my dear, is obvious."

"I suppose the same could be said of you," she replied, unable to keep the sarcasm from her voice.

His dark expression silenced her.

He took the step that separated them, making her lift her chin to look up at him. "I will live the life that I choose, Arlie. I am a grown man who is used to this way of life, but you are a young woman who has no idea how harsh the world can be. You have an opportunity now to marry a young man who can give you a good life. And as your guardian, it is my intention to see that happens."

"But what if it doesn't?"

His eyes narrowed, and he crossed his arms over his chest. "What do you mean?"

"I don't want to marry someone and then regret it. I suppose that I can take lovers, but—"

His shoulders stiffened. "A wife should be faithful to her husband."

"That sounds a tad hypocritical coming from a man who has just spent an entire week sleeping with another man's wife." To her surprise, her voice remained level, and she managed to keep a semblance of calm, when she felt anything but.

"The way I spend my nights should make no difference to you."

But it did matter—more than he would ever know. How could he stand going from woman to woman, making love, but giving nothing of himself? What a hollow existence it must be.

"You're right, it shouldn't matter." Having said as much, she turned and left him, knowing that if he called her back she would go to him. "But it does," she said softly. "It matters a great deal."

* * * * *

Dominic paced the length of his quarters. From time to time he glanced toward the bed where just last night he had brought a whore. He shook his head in disgust. *A whore?* It didn't matter that he had sent the woman home before he could bed her. In fact, he had not even kissed her. What did matter was that he'd brought her here in the first place, and he had seen the pain on Arlie's face. A pain he had caused.

Without Langley's knowledge, Dominic had hired the courtesans with the intention of driving Arlie away. After loving her in the meadow, he had wanted her with a desperation that frightened him. And she would have even given herself to him, but he'd pulled out a thread of sanity and had stopped his seduction before it was too late.

Instead, he'd run away, straight to London hoping to drink and whore away his confusion.

His grandmother was right—he *had* become his father.

Dominic closed his eyes and ran his hands down his face. Oh, but he was tempted to drown his sorrows in a bottle. Shaking off the urge, he went to the balcony wanting to cool his desire.

The night was clear, stars twinkling down at him, the moon shone down on the immaculate gardens below. He took a deep breath, his gaze straying to the bedroom window across the way. His heart jolted at the sight that met him.

Through the sheer curtains Arlie sat brushing her long hair. The silhouette of her naked form taunted him from across the garden, making him squint to see better. Already she was a natural vixen, sleeping naked while most women her age wore nightgowns that covered from neck to ankle. His body stirred to life, his cock throbbing as he continued to watch. She stood, and walked away—toward the bed. He held his breath and released it when he caught sight of her several windows down through the still-open curtains. For a scant second she stood there, staring out, and he saw all of her. The full breasts with rosy nipples, her tiny waist, the soft swell of hips, and the down of tight curls that covered her sex. His cock twitched and reared as he remembered the feel of her tight sheath against his fingers.

As though sensing his thoughts, Arlie drew the curtains, and a second later the room went black.

It would be so simple to end his misery. He could go to her, take her to bed, and be done with it. Maybe then she would be out of his blood.

* * * * *

The three months were over.

Arlie sat in her room and wondered if today would be the day that Dominic walked back into her life and announced that he had posted an announcement in *The Times*.

She hadn't seen him for weeks now. When she asked the servants where he was, they skirted her question, saying he'd gone off on business, but she knew otherwise. Daniel, along with other young beaus had commented about seeing Dominic here or there, yet he never came home, and she had to assume it was because of her that he didn't. Why else would he stay away, especially if he hadn't left London?

None of the young men who visited her would come right out and say it. It had been Langley who had told her Dominic had a townhouse near Hyde Park, a place Dominic stayed when he had business. But Arlie wasn't fooled. She didn't have to guess why he stayed there now. He obviously didn't want to see her, and in London he could entertain his never-ending parade of women without having to worry about her. Why should he change his ways, when all he had to do was take up residence somewhere else and continue on as always? Well, he could just live his life and she would go on living hers.

Tonight she had agreed to attend a soiree with Mr. Butler. When Daniel picked her up, she would be charming and happy, forgetting all about Dominic. It was time to move on.

* * * * *

Though the ball was not on as grand a scale as the Banfield's, still, the huge affair brimmed over with London's elite. There were a few familiar faces and as Arlie spoke with acquaintances, she was aware of the firm pressure of Daniel's arm around her waist. He had made it a point to touch her throughout the night, keeping an arm around her waist since they arrived. His possessiveness, though supposedly flattering, mostly irritated her.

But his behavior was only natural, especially since she had seen Daniel at least twice a week since meeting him. Apparently it had been just days ago when Daniel asked Dominic for his permission to escort Arlie to the ball. Dominic had readily agreed.

Daniel went in search of punch, and Arlie was grateful for the few moments she had alone. She stood near the veranda, closing her eyes, enjoying the cool wind that entered through the open window.

The room became quiet, though the music continued, a murmur raced through the crowd. Arlie opened her eyes. Dominic walked down the steps. Tall, dark and gorgeous, his gaze scanned the crowd.

Her heart slammed against her ribs as their gazes locked.

Then a virtual swarm of women ascended upon him, and the moment was forever gone.

"Miss Whitman, what a delight," Langley said, taking her hand in his. "Where is that devil, Butler? I dare say he is a fool to leave you alone. But that is his problem." He pulled her out on the dance floor.

"I'm so very sorry, Langley."

He lifted a brow. "Hopefully you're not referring to Rose, who by the way, is watching our every move."

Arlie smiled. "You know that's not what I meant."

"Then what are you sorry about?"

"I should never have used you the way I did. I want you to know that I genuinely care for you. I would never knowingly hurt you, and I'm ashamed that I used you to get to Dominic."

He grinned. "I appreciate your sincerity, but it is unnecessary. As I said before, I was, and remain, a willing participant."

"How has he been?"

"I can only assume you refer to Dominic?"

"Yes," she said wearily, feeling the heat race up her neck to her cheeks under his knowing grin.

"He is doing fine. Perhaps a little edgy of late, but he has a lot of business affairs to attend to. Apparently he just bought a good deal of stock in your intended's company, or perhaps it was Mr. Butler's rival's company."

"Daniel is not my intended."

"Really? One would think so by the way he is staring daggers into me. The young dandy must try harder to contain his emotions. Someone should tell him that it's not good to be so possessive early on. He hasn't even asked for your hand."

Langley kept her out on the floor for another dance, more out of spite than anything, she was sure. When the dance ended, Langley blocked Daniel. "Your guardian has asked for the next dance."

"Indeed, I have," the familiar voice said behind her.

Arlie turned to find Dominic standing with his hand extended, waiting for her to take it. Her eyes shifted from his strong, long-fingered hand up to his brutally handsome face. The sides of his mouth lifted and she was rewarded with a devastating grin. Why did he have to be so damn appealing? His blue eyes appeared darker as he stared, and she wanted desperately to know what he was thinking.

She took Dominic's hand and practically floated to the dance floor where he pulled her into his arms. Feeling strangely shy, she couldn't keep eye contact and instead averted her gaze.

"How have you been?" he asked, his tone formal.

"Fine."

"Joseph has told me you refuse to meet with your tutors."

"I feel I know enough." She met his gaze once more. "I always did, I only obliged before to make you happy."

"And now?"

She lifted her chin a notch. "I'm making myself happy."

He nodded. "So it would seem."

What did he mean by that comment? Anger and resentment of his treatment of her made her brash. "I've been thinking about returning to Wales," she lied, having no intention of returning to the village. She wanted to see his reaction.

Instantly the smile slipped from Dominic's face, and he almost stopped in mid-stride before he danced them off the floor. Before she could object, he pulled her out onto the veranda. "You will not leave Rochford Manor." It was a command, not a question.

Arlie took a step away from him. How dare he tell her what she could and could not do!

"Are you so unhappy?"

She nodded. "I am."

He actually looked startled. "I don't understand. I've seen to your every need—"

"Must it always be about money with you? Yes, you have been most generous, but that's not what I'm talking about." She took a deep breath, pondering her choices. She could tell him the truth or she could lie. "I shouldn't be in your home, especially since you refuse to stay there because of me. It isn't fair to either one of us."

His eyes searched hers as though he could see straight into her soul. She jerked as his fingers lightly brushed her cheek before moving lower to her neck, his thumb grazing her pulse that beat wildly. Slowly his lips claimed hers and she melted against him, opening to him, loving the feel of his velvet-smooth tongue against her own.

He pulled away slowly, staring down at her, his eyes dark with desire. "Dear Arlie, I'm not staying away because of you."

Even his voice lacked the conviction she needed to hear.

Another couple walked out and he stepped away from her, but only for a moment before the couple passed. He pulled her around the side of the house. "I've been distracted from my work, and there are certain things that need my immediate attention. I felt it was easiest to stay at the townhouse until I had finished my business."

"Dominic, don't lie to me. Rochford Manor is not so far from London that you could not stay there. Before you always managed to attend business and then come home. You are merely staying in town because you wish to be away from me."

He ran his hand through his hair, and then paced before her, leaving her to stand and watch him. Leaning against the stone banister, he looked out into the darkness of night. She almost wanted to leave him there, alone in his thoughts, but she couldn't bring herself to do it. For too long she had missed him. Now, being in his company, she didn't want the moment to end. Not like this.

When he turned to her, she saw uncertainty in his eyes. "Do you want me to come home?"

She nodded, afraid to say something for fear she'd cry.

He took the few steps that separated them, and she resisted the urge to throw herself into his arms. He lifted his hand and his fingers lightly touched her lips. "I'll be home tomorrow."

Chapter Nine

With the dawning of a new day, Arlie's spirits soared. Throwing open the curtains, she smiled out at the sunny day that greeted her. *Dominic would return today!*

The very thought made her want to dance around the room. No more lonely days and nights wondering where he was and what he was doing. Instead she would see his handsome face every single day.

Yet as the afternoon turned into evening, her mood soured and she wondered if he had once again lied to her. Here she'd worked so hard to prepare for his homecoming, taking extra care in her appearance, making sure the cook made his favorite dishes—and he hadn't even bothered to send word that he wouldn't be coming.

By ten o'clock that evening Arlie gave up hope that he would return. She went to the library, picked a book off the shelf, slipped off her shoes and plopped down onto a settee. The wind howled outside and she lay down on her side, resting an arm beneath her head, while she curled up and began the first chapter.

A door slammed in the distance, but she paid no mind. The door to the library whipped open and the book fell out of her hand.

Dominic strode toward her in long strides. Arlie stood abruptly.

He lifted her in his arms. His lips came down on hers, and she clung to him, releasing a moan while his tongue caressed hers.

Desire warmed her blood, swooping low into her belly.

"I've thought of nothing but holding you," he whispered against her lips.

"And I, you."

The words brought a smile to his face, making the creases at his eyes deepen. "Was I in your dreams as well?"

"Yes, my...Dominic."

"My Dominic?" The side of his mouth lifted in a playful smile. "You sound possessive already."

She wanted to tell him that she was. That she hated every woman that had stared at him last night, especially the ones she knew had a connection to him, either past mistresses, or perhaps current mistresses.

"What's the matter? You're frowning." She smiled as he kissed the tip of her nose. "Have you noticed it's quiet around here this evening?"

She nodded. "Yes, as a matter of fact, I have."

"And do you know why that is?"

When she shook her head, he said, "I've given the servants the night off, except Joseph. The place would fall apart without him."

She knew immediately why he'd let the servants have the night off. She would lose her maidenhead tonight. Tonight Dominic would take her in his arms, make love to her, and she would never be the same again.

Arlie clung to him, kissing his neck as he strode toward the stairs. At the top, he looked down the hallway toward her quarters, then in the opposite direction toward his own.

"A preference?"

"My bed," she said, the word so intimate, she could feel the blood rush to her cheeks.

Behind the closed door of her room, he set her on her feet. He removed his jacket, his blue eyes devouring her with a heat that sent her pulse racing. The moment the jacket hit the floor, his lips were on hers again, soft and tender. "You are so beautiful, Arlie," he murmured against her lips.

She had received the same compliment from other suitors, but it meant so much more coming from Dominic. To know he desired her made her bold, and she kissed him hard. He smiled against her lips while his fingers worked the buttons on the back of her gown, and in that moment Arlie realized what it meant. Panic rose within her, and she pushed against his chest. "Wait."

He stood back, his gaze searching hers. Her heart beat so loud it roared in her ears. *Regardless of what tomorrow would bring, you must make love to this man.* Her body and her soul demanded it. She had turned him away only to regret it. No longer. With her mind made up, Arlie took a steadying breath and pulled off the gown. It pooled around her feet. She felt naked wearing only her corset and chemise. When she stood before him completely naked, her self-confidence began to waver—especially when Dominic was fully clothed.

Slowly and seductively his gaze moved downward. Arlie thought she might die on the spot until a moment later his heated gaze met hers once more. "You take my breath away." An approving smile came quickly to his mouth, one that put her mind at ease. He wanted her, and she wanted him. Mutual desire—and every part of her being screamed for him to take her.

Before she could blink, his shirt had joined his jacket on the floor. When he slipped out of his pants, she swallowed past the lump in her throat. She had never seen a man naked, but she had read racy novels, and in her mind she had envisioned what a man looked like down there—but she hadn't expected him to be so large.

He pulled her into his arms, and she could feel the steely length of his penis against her belly, pressing into her. Excited, a little scared, and intensely curious, she reached between them and lightly touched him. He sucked in a deep breath and she smiled, intrigued that she should have such power over him.

Dominic moaned deep in his throat, trying to keep his desire in check, a feat in itself when her inexperienced hand held him, exploring him by running her fingers up the length of his cock, circling the head lightly. His breathing became labored as she squeezed him tight, her fingers wrapping around him. If she only knew how close he was to exploding. With a groan, he brought her down on the bed with him, and her hand slipped from his throbbing shaft to his back.

He smothered her face with kisses, raining them down her delicate neck, collar bone, then to her lovely young breasts. He kissed one, then the other; the nipples thrust out, turning as hard as diamonds. As her hands wove through his hair, her moans urged him on, making his kisses bolder. He moved down her soft belly, kissing the soft warm skin beneath his lips, and to the triangle of pale hair that beckoned him.

His entire body shook with a need that shocked him. Never had he needed a woman the way he needed Arlie.

* * * * *

Through a haze, Arlie opened her eyes to find Dominic positioned between her thighs, his breath stirring the curls at the very center of her womanhood. Her eyes widened in shock, a moment before his tongue stroked her slit. Instinctively she tried to clamp her legs together, sure that she would burn in hell for such an act. Dominic's hand smoothed along her thigh, then his mouth, kissing her, making her relax. With a calming breath, Arlie opened to him.

Letting her legs fall open, Arlie swore she saw him smile for a fleeting moment. Her hands fell from his hair, to the sheets at her sides, gripping the linen as the stirring in her body intensified with every stroke of his tongue. Liquid fire roared through her veins as she climbed toward an unbelievable pinnacle that once reached brought a feeling that was surely close to ecstasy. "Dominic," she cried, then closed her eyes and rode it out.

When she opened her eyes, he was rubbing one of her nipples with his forefinger and thumb, extending it, sending a wave of desire to the very core of her. Already desire and need started to stir deep within her.

"Dominic," she said again on a desperate whisper, wanting him to end this ache within her.

* * * * *

"Yes, my love," he said, meeting her satisfied stare with a sensual smile. She was so gorgeous, so innocent...a lethal combination. With every minute, she became less inhibited, and her response to his oral play made him yearn for the ultimate consummation.

As she stared up at him with those green eyes so full of passion, he wondered if in the morning she would regret giving herself to him. He put the unsavory thought from his mind and kissed her breast. He moved over her, his knees pushing hers aside as he settled between her thighs. He saw the pulse beating frantically in her neck. "Are you sure, Arlie?" he asked one last time, hoping her answer would be yes. He couldn't remember a time he had been so hard or so ready.

"Yes," she replied, lifting her face up to his, an invitation to kiss her. With a groan, he took what she offered, capturing her lips against his own, and sliding his tongue in at the same time he slipped inside her tight, wet sheath. Hitting the barrier of her maidenhead, he rejoiced in the knowledge that he would finally sample that which he'd been yearning for so long. His heart swelled as he stared down at her face, so trusting of him. "Relax, Arlie," he murmured against her lips, and then thrust home. She gasped against his mouth, her entire body tensing beneath him.

"I won't move, so you'll have time to get used to the feel of me inside of you." Her vagina hugged him so tight, he had to use every ounce of control not to spend himself.

He kissed her forehead, rained kisses along her nose, before taking possession of her mouth again. He deepened the kiss and she started to move her hips, just the slightest bit. Sensing she was ready, he slowly pulled out, then back in. She met each thrust with one of her own, her sheath hugging him tight. Sweat beaded his brow, and his entire body trembled. Her hands moved down his back over his buttocks, and when she squeezed with her fingers, he increased the rhythm.

* * * * *

Arlie marveled that she could accommodate Dominic's size. At first she thought she would split in two, but then the pain passed and yearning took its place. As he began to move, she opened her legs wide, wanting to feel all of him. Becoming bolder, she ran her fingers over the corded muscles of his back, and down the smooth skin of his firm buttocks. Lifting her hips she met him thrust for thrust. His cock swelled inside her, stretching her, filling her, the sensation making her want to scream in ecstasy. As his momentum increased, she felt an overwhelming pressure begin to build inside of her. Like she had experienced before, yet greater, more intense. A few more thrusts and she cried out, her vagina pulsing around his shaft. She held onto him, her breaths ragged as she rode out the orgasm.

A moment later he arched against her, groaning loud as he found release. He collapsed on her, his head resting on her breast and she took his weight happily. She wove her fingers through his hair, while another smoothed over his broad shoulders. She sighed. Never had she known such exultation.

* * * * *

Arlie woke to the rain pelting the bedroom window. She opened her eyes to a room cast in shadows. Instantly memories of the night before raced through her mind. She smiled recognizing the pain in her nether regions for what it was. Dominic had loved her well last night, taking her time and again, until she'd been so tired she could scarcely lift her head from the pillow. She glanced over and finding the space beside her empty, disappointment filled her.

"You finally getting up and about?"

Arlie jumped at the sound of Mary's voice. The maid stood in the sitting room, pouring oil into a steaming bathtub. "I was beginning to wonder if you had taken ill."

Pulling the sheet to her chin, Arlie sat up. "I feel fine, Mary." *Now go away*, she wanted to say, knowing she would not be able to get out of the bed and walk to the bath naked. Though Mary had seen her body before, it was different now. Her innocence was forever gone.

"I'm glad you're feeling well. His lordship wanted me to tell you that he had business to attend to this morning, but he will meet you for lunch." She glanced at the clock on the mantle. "He should be returning shortly."

"Then I'd best take my bath now."

"All right then, I'll leave you to it. Let me know when you're finished and I'll help you dress."

"That's all right, Mary. I don't need your help."

The older woman walked over to the bed, and with hands planted firmly on generous hips, said, "My dear girl, I know that you and the master passed a night in each other's arms. It's completely natural. The two of you are perfect for one another, and as you know, we here at Rochford manor love our master. We are a loyal bunch, and we would never hurt him, nor you."

Arlie's cheeks grew hot under her knowing stare.

"Now, with that said, I'll be back to help you dress."

The door closed behind Mary and Arlie jumped up out of bed, gasping as she looked down at the blood that stained the sheets and insides of her thighs. She rushed to the tub and slipped into the warm water, relaxing, closing her eyes, remembering the night just passed. Never had she imagined that making love could be so wonderful. Dominic had been a most gracious lover, bringing her to the heights of passion time and again. A smile tugged at her lips remembering how he'd made her body come to life.

By the time she got around to washing her hair, the water had grown tepid, but some of the soreness had left her body.

She stepped out of the tub, dried herself off with a towel, and stood before the roaring fire. Her mind raced, wondering what she would say when she saw Dominic.

* * * * *

Dominic leaned against the closed door.

Arlie's back was to him, her wet hair clinging to her body, covering her slender back and buttocks from his view. He heard her sigh as she turned her back to the fire, facing him. He smiled with appreciation. Her eyes were closed, her lips red and swollen from their night together.

His gaze moved down over her ripe young breasts, the nipples hard from the coolness of the room, down past her flat stomach to the triangle of pale curls between her legs. His cock stirred, hardening with every second. She was beauty personified, and she belonged to him.

He moved toward her quietly, wondering what her reaction would be when she saw him—joy or regret.

She didn't open her eyes until he was just steps from her, and when she did, the look in them took his breath away. She stared up at him with a devastating smile for a moment before she threw her arms around his neck and pressed her soft body against the length of him.

Overjoyed at her reaction, he kissed her long and hard, his hands encircling her small waist. "Glad to see me?" he asked.

"Very," she replied with a wicked grin as her fingers began unbuttoning his shirt.

"You're very adept at this for having just lost your virginity."

A tawny brow lifted. "I learned from the best."

He grinned at the compliment.

Once he was stripped of his clothing, he took her hand and led her to the bed. He saw the bloodstains that confirmed he was the first. Their eyes met. "You belong to me, Arlie. To me and me alone."

"Always," she said, going into his arms.

He pulled her close, his heart pounding hard against her. He had been unable to keep her out of his mind the entire day. Memories of her sweet surrender burned in his brain, causing a deep ache in his heart and in his groin. He had hoped she would be a wonderful lover, and last night she had proven she was — in spades. He had felt guilty each time he reached for her throughout the night, his body needing her, yet she went to him willingly, encouraging him with heated words.

"I missed you," she whispered, her lips leaving his to travel down his neck to his chest. She looked up at him with a wicked smile and flicked his nipple with her tongue. His cock reared and her smile widened.

"Little vixen," he said, as she made her way down his stomach.

His breath caught in his throat as she tasted his cock, her pink tongue swirling around the head. Her hands splayed on either one of his thighs and curled around to his buttocks, pulling him closer to her mouth.

She took him into her mouth, a little at a time, getting used to the feel of him. She sucked, first softly, then harder until his breath came in gasps.

He put her at arms length. He looked at the bed and with a smile she stood. He could not wait. He turned her around, kissed her smooth, slender back, and slipped into her soft recesses from behind. He groaned as he filled her to the womb.

She gasped out loud, from pain or pleasure he knew not which, but he did not move, wanting her to become accustomed to his body. He pressed his chest against her back, while his fingers teased her nipples into tight buds.

While he played with one nipple, the other hand roamed down her body, to her mons and the soft curls that hid her sex. His fingers wove through the soft hair, working the tiny pearl until she moaned low in her throat with her release.

Her vagina clamped tight around him, and he groaned her name as he exploded.

Chapter Ten

Dominic pretended to take great interest in the ledger before him, while the young couple sat on a nearby settee talking in low tones as not to disturb him. Which was ridiculous. It was as impossible to concentrate on his work as it was to keep from watching Arlie and Daniel's every move.

Not even a week had passed since he and Arlie had become lovers, and in that time she'd become like a drug to his senses. Every evening right after dinner Arlie went to her room, and shortly after he would join her there. In the joyous hours that followed, they would make love, rediscovering each other's bodies, showing and giving pleasure.

With Arlie his lust seemed to be unending. He sometimes took her three or four times in a night. She never complained, never turned him away. In fact she seemed to enjoy their lovemaking as much as he did. He should be exhausted he knew, but he wasn't. Even now he imagined her naked on his bed, her long legs wrapped around his waist, her smile soft as she stared up at him with passion-filled eyes.

Arlie's laughter filled the room and his eyes narrowed. She and Daniel had their backs to him, yet he could see her profile. The smile, bright white teeth, tiny and perfect. Her lips, so pink, turned up at the corners, and her green eyes sparkled as the young man whispered something in her ear. Dominic clenched his fist, yearning to knock the American's perfect teeth out.

Of all Arlie's suitors, the American was the most aggressive, but after days of turning him away, Dominic decided that he could not keep making excuses without making trouble. He didn't want anyone getting the idea that he and Arlie might be sharing a bed, although those who knew him best probably already placed wagers.

Dominic didn't want to think beyond the moment. He and Arlie were lovers—no more, no less. One day they would tire of each other and go their separate ways. *Like hell*, he thought in his heart, but his mind conjured up an image of another woman to whom he'd given his heart—one who had betrayed him.

He must accept that Arlie would be courted by others, and one day she would marry someone else. He dismissed the thought almost immediately, knowing that would never happen. At least, not while he felt this way—as close to out-of-control as he'd ever been. Certainly not as long as she satisfied the craving he felt for her and her alone.

"My lord?"

He glanced up to see the angel who had turned his life upside down watching him with wide-eyed innocence. At one time he had thought it an act, but now he knew her well enough to be certain it was no act. She *was* innocent—or had been until he'd taken her maidenhead, making her his. And already she was an accomplished lover. Before long, she would know every way to pleasure a man and to be pleasured in return.

"Mr. Butler has asked if we could take a stroll in the gardens."

Dominic stood abruptly, nearly toppling the chair over before he caught it. "Of course. Shall we," he said, motioning toward the door.

The two hesitated. Arlie bit her bottom lip, but it was Daniel who stepped forward. "Could Miss Whitman and I have a moment alone, Lord Rochford?"

Dominic stared at the young man, who in turn watched him with little apprehension. Daniel, so much like Dominic had been at his age, was wealthy, arrogant—and a man who knew a hot skirt when he saw it. The difference between them was Dominic had a bad reputation for chasing woman, and Daniel didn't. Dominic wasn't sure if the man was as true as he pretended to be, or if his conquests just didn't kiss and tell. Either way, he didn't like Daniel—not at all.

"I promise we will stay within your sights," Daniel said emphatically, taking Arlie's hand in his own.

"Very well," Dominic replied, glancing at their joined hands before looking directly at Arlie, whose expression was impossible to read. He knew she had been surprised by his insistence that she see Daniel and quite possibly enjoyed Dominic's discomfort at seeing her with another man.

"Thank you, my lord," Daniel said, already ushering Arlie out the door.

Dominic sat down, his gaze fastened on the window where the gardens lay beyond. He would watch every step they took. He even opened the window, hating himself for being so intrusive, yet he was glad when he clearly heard Daniel's voice.

"I've yearned to see you for days now, Miss Whitman. I've thought of you constantly since the ball. I had begun to think you had no interest in me."

Dominic closed his eyes, telling himself to quit eavesdropping on the pair; but instead he leaned forward in his chair, waiting for Arlie's response.

"I've been quite busy of late, but I'm glad you came. I've always enjoyed your company, Mr. Butler."

Their voices faded as they moved further down the pathway. It took every ounce of his restraint not to follow them. He tried unsuccessfully to read the ledger before him and finally began pacing the floor, watching the clock, forcing himself to have patience.

Just about the time he decided to track them down, he saw them rounding the corner, heading back up the path toward the manor. Relieved, he rolled back on his heels and folded his hands behind his back when the two bound through the door in youthful laughter. Dominic clenched his teeth together taking in Arlie's glowing cheeks and Daniel's. He smiled at her with a combination of lust and adoration.

"Lord Rochford, I want to thank you for your hospitality today. I would very much like to court Miss Whitman—with your permission, of course."

There. The words Dominic had been dreading for weeks now. He hadn't realized what an impact they would have on him until that moment. Many replies raced through his mind, but he knew none made sense, and he found himself replying, "You will have to ask Miss Whitman if she wishes to be courted."

Arlie blanched, yet she recovered quickly and turned to Daniel with a beguiling smile in place. "Well...certainly."

Dominic thought Daniel looked far too pleased with himself.

"You do me a great honor, Miss Whitman," he replied.

Dominic watched with a sinking heart as Daniel kissed her hands, lingering over them far longer than necessary. Walking to the door in long strides, Dominic opened it wide. "We will see you again...in a few days or so."

"Yes, in a few days," Daniel said, his disappointment evident at being told to stay away for at least three days. He'd probably anticipated coming back the following day. "Until we meet again, Miss Whitman."

Arlie walked him past the open door, and then with one final chaste kiss on the cheek, he left.

Dominic walked back into his study, waited for Arlie to follow, and shut the door behind her. He stood with his back against the hard surface, staring at Arlie, who watched him with a frown. *What was she thinking? Did she want the young man?* Daniel was handsome, and his family was well to do. He could give her a good life.

"So, do you like him?" he asked, trying to sound unaffected when he was seething with jealousy.

She shrugged. "He's a nice man."

"Nice," he repeated as he moved toward her slowly, watching the pulse in her neck race. He stopped a few feet away from her. Then he shifted his gaze to her breasts, displayed nicely in the yellow silk gown that accented her slim figure to perfection. "What do you mean when you say *nice*?"

She let out an exasperated breath, but remained silent.

He shouldn't be mad at her. After all, he had invited Daniel in. But he *was* annoyed with her. He hated the way she laughed with Daniel. The sparkle in her eyes, the way she smiled. How easily they conversed — as though the two were life-long friends, when in essence they'd only spent a few hours together.

"He's a nice man," she said, her voice weary. "What do you want me to say? That I hate him? Well, I don't. He's polite, kind…a true gentleman."

A true gentleman — unlike himself. She didn't have to say it, he saw the accusation in her eyes. Dominic knew he deserved it. He deserved worse. He had taken this innocent young woman and turned her into his lover. A woman who had been entrusted to him. Her father had chosen him over everyone he'd ever known to take care of her, and what had he done? Within a few months' time, he'd taken her virginity, and along with it, any chance of marrying well. The best she could hope for now was to be someone's mistress. That, or she'd have to be a damn convincing actress come her wedding night.

"What do you want me to say?" she asked, her eyes searching his face. "Tell me?"

He took the steps that separated them, his fingers moving to the soft skin of her throat. "I'm thinking how desperately I want you." His fingers trailed along opposite collarbones, then down to the swell of her breasts. Slipping his hands beneath the silk, he brought both perfect globes out of their confines, filling his palms with their lushness. Staring into her eyes as they darkened with passion, he whispered against her lips, "I want to taste every single inch of you until you can't stand it anymore and beg for me to take you."

"Take me, Dominic," she whispered against his lips.

He needed no more encouragement and pulled her into his arms, kissing her with all the frustration he felt—and all the desire. As she leaned into him, he lifted her skirts with his hand, smiling against her lips to find she wore nothing beneath, and was already wet for him.

"Do you want me?" he whispered, pressing his rock-hard cock against her.

"Always," she said on a breathless whisper.

He lifted her, wrapping her long legs around his hips. Carrying her, he walked over to the desk where he gently set her down. She leaned back on the desk, her legs spread wide. Dominic unbuttoned his breeches and thrust into her, burying himself to the hilt.

Hearing Arlie's soft sigh, he hooked her legs over his shoulders, and penetrated her harder.

He let out an unsteady breath. He wanted her now more than he ever had. She was in his blood and he knew he would never tire of her.

"Dominic," she moaned, her orgasm clenching his cock.

He closed his eyes, letting his head fall back on his shoulders as he came with an intensity that left him shaking.

* * * * *

Arlie felt like she was living a dream. For weeks she and Dominic had been lovers. Not a single night passed that he didn't make love to her. She wondered if the magic she felt would end one day, as all things ended.

"Penny for your thoughts."

She glanced across the carriage at Dominic, who watched her through those beautiful eyes, framed by impossibly long lashes. Dressed in a black suit, he looked deliciously handsome, and she wished more than anything they weren't going out. She knew it was terribly possessive of her, but their relationship was too new and she hated to share him with anyone.

"I was just thinking how happy I am."

He grinned boyishly. "Are you?"

"You know I am," she said, certain she would never tire of staring at him.

"Good. I want your happiness above all else," he replied in a sensual voice that sent shivers down her spine.

The carriage pulled in front of the theater, and Arlie took a deep breath. She would have to put on the act of a lifetime. When women fell all over Dominic, she would have to pretend indifference when inside she would be boiling with jealousy.

The secret of their relationship could never get out. If it did, it would destroy Dominic, and herself as well. Though she knew she could survive the scandal, she wondered how it would affect Dominic. These were his peers, not hers. She could always leave and disappear, but he would never be able to walk away from his title or vast wealth.

Why couldn't they just be lovers and leave it at that? Why did he believe she needed a husband? She tired of the endless men who came to the manor, and Daniel, though he was kind, grew bolder with each visit.

Each of the men who called thought her chaste and innocent. If they only knew that in the confines of the manor she behaved like a harlot, making love with Dominic, not caring who discovered them. She and Dominic had grown reckless, making love constantly: in the library, in the parlor, in the study, on his desk. Any given time someone could walk in on them, and the strange thing was, she didn't care. Dominic aroused her so—nothing else mattered except him and the joy that he brought her. Perhaps she was more like her mother than she knew…

"You're frowning and you haven't even seen the first act," he said with a forced smile. She knew he dreaded this outing as much as she did, but they couldn't forever stay closeted up in the manor without drawing attention to themselves.

At the theater, she and Dominic were stopped on the way to their seats by acquaintances, most of them aggressive women who obviously wanted to get into Dominic's bed.

Seeing Veronica on her husband's arm didn't help Arlie's sullen mood, nor did the knowing look the duchess threw her way. Did Veronica suspect what had happened between she and Dominic? In her heart, Arlie wanted to think that she was the only woman in his life, but could she be so sure? Her mind raced back over the last few weeks. Dominic had come home the same time every night, and always they made love. She refused to dwell on it, choosing instead to trust him.

Avoiding the woman's stare, Arlie looked away.

"Miss Whitman. Miss Whitman!"

Arlie turned to find Daniel making his way toward her. Dressed in a burgundy suit, he looked pleased to see her, and once again she felt uncomfortable knowing she was stringing him along. She knew it helped the pretense that she sought to marry, but the lie unsettled her, especially when she truly wondered what Dominic had in mind. Perhaps when he tired of her, he would unload her on Daniel.

"Miss Whitman, how nice it is to see you," Daniel said, his gaze moving to the décolletage of her gown, before he ripped his gaze back to her face. "I'm sorry I missed you yesterday. You left for your ride just moments before my arrival. I almost went in pursuit of you, but I have seen for myself what a superb horsewoman you are."

"Thank you," Arlie said with a small smile, wondering if she would burn in hell for all the sins she had committed of late. It truly horrified her how little she cared what others thought of her. Always she had done things people expected of her, and now that she was living life by her own terms, she was having the most fun—but she wondered what price she would pay in the end.

"Would you and your guardian like to sit with us?"

"No," Dominic said, before Arlie could respond. "Miss Whitman and I already have our seats."

"But thank you," she offered as Dominic pulled her along with him through the crowd.

"That was rude."

"I don't like the way he looks at you."

A thrill raced through her at his words. She knew he was jealous of the other man, but he seldom showed it.

They had prime seats, overlooking the stage. The air quickly took on a stifling quality, making Arlie whip open her fan.

During the intermission Daniel came by to talk with her, and though Dominic was there to act as chaperone, he talked animatedly to the group beside them.

What she wouldn't give to tell Daniel that nothing could ever happen between them. How difficult it was when he watched her with such hope and adoration in his dark eyes. She did not deserve his affection.

Daniel returned to his seat, but throughout the second half, she could feel his gaze on her. Relief raced through her when the final curtain fell and she and Dominic made it to their carriage without delay. Dominic told her they had been invited to a party, but Dominic had declined the invitation, making up yet another excuse.

Taking a seat in the carriage, across from Dominic, she leaned back against the velvet and stared out at the passing city. For a night that had started off rather well, she felt emotionally exhausted.

"You're quiet."

She glanced at Dominic who was busy untying his cravat. Oh, but he was dangerously handsome—and so unattainable. She had caught the look in many women's eyes this night as they watched him, their desire for her lover obvious. "I'm just tired."

"Liar."

Smiling softly, she glanced back out the window to keep from looking at him.

"Tell me what's bothering you." His voice was soft.

Her gaze returned to him, her humor fleeing as she weighed her words. "I hate the lies that I'm telling, especially with Daniel. He doesn't deserve to be deceived."

He frowned. "Would you have him know about us?"

She shrugged. "I honestly don't care anymore. I just know I hate myself for doing this to him."

"You underestimate Mr. Butler. Now, I don't want to speak of him any more."

She gasped when he grabbed her and pulled her onto his lap. With a flick of his wrist, he closed the carriage curtain. Before she knew what had happened, he was kissing her and pulling her gown down. His mouth left hers, raining kisses over her throat to the swell of her breasts. With a growl, he laved her nipple, sucking it greedily.

Her fingers wove through his thick hair, holding him tight against her breast, not wanting him to stop. He lifted her skirts up around her hips and fumbled with his breeches. A moment later she gasped when his hard shaft impaled her.

She knew the manor was not far from the theater, and that time was of the essence. She moved her hips, riding him, clinging to him, arching her back, offering her breasts to him. He did not disappoint, he stroked her pebble-hard nipples with his velvety-tongue, sucking one then the other until she cried out his name.

Enjoying the sensation of being in control, Arlie rode Dominic hungrily. The first flutters of her climax began, and she quickened her pace. His hands clenched at her waist, lifting her up, to where just the head of his shaft was within her. She looked down at him. He smiled mischievously. She pulled his hands from her waist and sat down hard, grinning as his hard length filled her completely. Her orgasm temporarily put on hold, she moved slowly, rocking her hips against him, circling around, feeling his long, hard shaft stretch her.

She smiled when he groaned against her neck. "Witch," he whispered, nipping at her ear, his teeth grazing the lobe.

She could not contain her excitement further, and picked up the pace, the urgency sending her into a frenzy. Dominic's breathing became harsh, matching her own frantic need. Arlie cried out, and seconds later he joined her.

The carriage stopped immediately. Arlie smiled against Dominic's lips and slowly got off him. He buttoned his breeches and she pulled down her skirt just as the door whipped open. Arlie patted her hair before stepping out of the carriage on wobbly legs, keeping her gaze averted from Joseph, and the footman who had no doubt heard her cries of pleasure scant seconds before.

She didn't wait for Dominic, and instead went straight to her room. The game she and Dominic played had become a dangerous one. Every day they took a new risk, making love wherever they chose, not caring if they were caught, yet knowing if they were, it would be ruin. But just like now, she gave in to him so easily. All he had to do was look at her in a certain way and she was his for the taking. She could not be within five feet of him without wanting to tear his clothes from his body. He had become an addiction, and she wondered if she would ever feel differently.

She hoped not.

Pulling off her gown and her underclothes, she caught a glimpse of her naked body in the cheval mirror. She stood before it, looking at herself critically, seeing what Dominic saw when he looked at her.

She had never thought of herself as beautiful, nor did she necessarily now. Her gaze shifted from her face to her body. Her breasts were not large, nor were they too small, her waist, on the other hand was little, her hips slender. No, she was not bad to look upon, but could she compare to Dominic's last mistress?

Veronica was voluptuous, her breasts huge in comparison to Arlie's, her hips more curved and womanly.

As the door opened, she started, but didn't move. Dominic's lifted brow told her she had been caught staring at herself. But instead of being embarrassed, it aroused her.

Without a word he came up behind her, his arms wrapping around her waist. She leaned her head back against his strong shoulder, watching their reflection as his hand trailed from her cheek, down her throat, over a breast. His large hand splayed against her stomach, and then to her already wet cleft. A finger slipped inside her, then another. She had never seen anything so erotic, and she found that as he continued to tease her, she couldn't look away, mesmerized by the sight of him pleasuring her.

"I want you again, already," he said against her ear. "You set a fire in my blood that cannot be quenched."

His fingers continued to stroke her, the pad of his thumb moving over the tiny pearl. Immediately the sweet twinges started deep inside her, squeezing his fingers that moved in and out of her cleft. She pressed her thighs together and he removed his hand.

She turned in his arms, helping him strip off his clothes until he stood as naked as she. Tall, dark, hard. A man like no other. And he was hers...at least for now.

He watched her through long, dark lashes, his smile wicked as he lifted her into his arms and strode toward her bed. He deposited her on the soft mattress as though she were made of the finest crystal.

Not once had he said he loved her, yet as she opened her arms to him, she knew it didn't matter — at least not now.

"You're such a treasure," he said, parting her legs with his knees. "Perfect in every way."

As he entered her, she felt complete, all her troubles slipping away. Unlike the quick mating in the carriage, they took their time. His strokes were slow, deliberate. He went up on his elbows and stared down at her. His beauty took her breath away. He kissed her lightly, his lips grazing her jaw then her ear. "You are in my blood," he said, his voice hoarse.

She smiled, her joy knowing no bounds. His lips met hers again, soft at first, then hard, like the pounding of his lower body against her. When she neared the very brink of climax, he withdrew completely, staring down at her. She lifted her hips, desperate to feel his hard shaft within her again, to take her to ecstasy. "Dominic — please."

With her whispered plea, he plunged within her, to her very womb, sending her to yet another pinnacle. Her body thrummed, every nerve ending aware of the power poised over her. With a groan, Dominic filled her with his seed and collapsed onto her. She ran her hands over the muscles of his strong back, marveling at his power and what a wonderful lover he was.

For a long time they lay in silence, neither saying a word. But when he sat up, the sheets draped around his loins, Arlie felt a stab of regret, wishing for once he could stay with her the entire night. Yet, he wouldn't. He never did, and he never would.

He kissed her, silencing any questions. And as he closed the door behind him, she fell back on the mattress, wishing for an end to her madness — yet dreading it all the same.

Chapter Eleven

"I'm sorry, I don't believe I heard you correctly?"

"Lord Rochford, I am asking Miss Whitman for her hand in marriage. I would have her for my bride, sir...with your approval, of course."

Dominic glanced past Daniel's shoulder, to Joseph, who stood as still as a statue. The only indication that he listened was the lifting of a gray brow, along with the slightest curve of his lip.

It was no secret to anyone in his household, particularly his most trusted butler, that he and Arlie were intimate, though he doubted many knew to what extent.

"Sir?"

Dominic returned his attention to the young man who looked uncommonly pale considering the heat of the day. Daniel, had been "courting" Arlie for weeks now. Those visits had always been chaperoned, and not once had Dominic thought the man would actually get around to asking for Arlie's hand. In fact, he'd had high hopes Daniel would return home to America.

"I don't know."

"I beg your pardon?"

Dominic shrugged. "I can't give you an answer right now. Perhaps after I speak with my ward, I'll have a better idea as to how she feels about it."

"Do I have your permission then?"

How could he give permission for Daniel to marry his lover?

Joseph coughed, though it sounded suspiciously like a laugh.

"I...would prefer to discuss this another time. I have matters—"

"Lord Rochford, please forgive me for my abruptness, but there are distressing rumors circulating about Miss Whitman, and I feel I must question you about them."

An unsettling silence fell over the room as Dominic stared at the younger man.

"Such as?"

"I mean no ill will, and I beg forgiveness for being so blunt, but they are saying she is the daughter of a fisherman and her mother was...a woman of ill repute."

Dominic knew *the ton* well. Any gossip, true or not, could ruin Arlie. Daniel shrugged indifferently, but Dominic knew otherwise. Her background made all the difference in the world. "I know not what to believe. I thought perhaps—"

Dominic sat back in his chair, the blood roaring in his ears. "Mr. Butler, I was under the impression that you *cared* for Arlie."

Daniel's hesitation said more than any answer could have, and Dominic knew he had been right about the young man all along—he expected a healthy dowry. "You are an American. Why should you care if your bride is of the gentry?"

"Well..."

"You were wanting a dowry?"

Daniel's cheeks turned red under Dominic's harsh stare. "I would have her without the money, though I have to say it is a nice enticement. But there are also rumors that the two of you..." Daniel shifted on his feet. "How can I say this as not to offend...that you and Miss Whitman are lovers," he blurted.

Dominic's stomach dropped to his toes.

"Rochford, I have told others that nothing could be further from the truth. Granted, you never allow us any time to ourselves, and you choose to serve as chaperone, rather than hire someone else, yet—"

"Enough," Dominic said with a calm he did not feel. "Though you say you don't believe these lies, there's something in your voice that tells me you're not certain."

Dominic knew he should feel relieved the rumor was out, but he wasn't. For so long he had tried to hide the affair. In the meantime, he had hoped everyone would forget about Arlie's history. A nerve in his jaw twitched. He knew exactly who to thank for the rumor. "And what do you believe?"

A bead of perspiration formed on Daniel's upper lip, and his hands trembled as he wiped it away. "Of course, I don't believe the gossip. I should have kept quiet. Forgive me for saying anything. I will not speak of it again."

"On the contrary I'm glad that you told me. Rumors can do horrible damage to a young lady's reputation, as you can see. If you, a true friend, think that the lies are true, then what must others think?" Dominic felt like an invisible vise tightened around his heart. "Perhaps it is time Arlie considers marriage. Maybe then it will put an end to these nasty rumors—which are completely absurd." Dominic carefully schooled his features and looked directly at Daniel. "I want you to know that there is nothing going on between my ward and myself. I suppose my reputation has done us both harm in this matter."

"I apologize, Lord Rochford."

Dominic sat down and stared at the young man. "Please sit." He motioned to a chair and Daniel sat on the very edge, looking ready to bolt. "You have my permission to ask for Miss Whitman's hand. In fact, of all the men who've been calling on my ward, I like you the most," Dominic lied, knowing damn well he hated Daniel most of all.

"Now, tell me who has started this ugly rumor."

Daniel blanched. "Lord Rochford, I cannot—"

"Come now, Daniel—we are practically family."

Although the words were meant to reassure Daniel, he looked increasingly uncomfortable. Loosening his cravat with a finger, he sat back in the chair, looking like a sheep being led to the slaughter.

"I heard it from an acquaintance, who in turn heard it from Duchess Banfield," he said, two bright spots appearing on his cheeks.

Dominic shook his head. "Well, there you see."

Daniel frowned. "See what?"

"The duchess—come, don't act surprised. You know Veronica and I were more than friends. I saw the disapproval in your eyes at the ball." Dominic cleared his throat. "I've had to make a lot of adjustments in my life since having a ward, Daniel, and breaking off my relationship with a married woman was one of them. I don't want my ward believing that's what married people do. So, you see, Veronica is simply trying to extract revenge—a silly lovers game, that I'm afraid has hurt my ward far more than myself, the intended target. I normally would not entrust you with this information, but I know that you will keep it in the strictest of confidence."

Comprehension slowly fell over Daniel's features. Immediately he looked more at ease. "Certainly…I understand completely and am most grateful to you for telling me the truth. I also think it's admirable of you to realize your behavior with the duchess could harm your ward—we wouldn't want Miss Whitman thinking it is the way of married people to take others to their bed. I mean no ill toward you, Rochford. But I could never stand for unfaithfulness in my marriage."

Dominic thought the man better think again—because Dominic wasn't about to give Arlie up.

A knock at the door stopped further conversation. A moment later Arlie stepped in looking irresistible in her breeches and white shirt. Her long hair flowed free down her back, curling at her slender hips accented perfectly by the tight pants. Dominic noticed Daniel's brows raised considerably as she came toward them.

"Mr. Butler, I didn't know you were here."

Daniel looked her up and down. "You are dressed...differently." His tone was clearly disapproving.

She lifted her chin. "These are my riding clothes."

"Do you not have proper riding attire?"

"I prefer breeches," she said matter-of-factly, as she straightened her spine. "I always have, and I always will."

The young man seemed to sense her mood, and sat up straighter. "Which is fine, Miss Whitman. I just...am not accustomed to seeing a woman dressed in such a way." He turned to Dominic. "May I have a word with Miss Whitman—alone?"

Dominic glanced at Arlie. She stood, her arms crossed over her chest watching him. He nodded, stood slowly and walked to the double doors.

His heart beat in double-time. All he would have to do is tell Daniel the truth.

Without looking back, Dominic walked out of the room, and closed the door. He wondered if he'd just made the biggest mistake of his life.

* * * * *

Dominic glanced at the auburn beauty at his side. Veronica had met him at the park shortly after he'd sent the message. He never doubted she would show. After all, it had been months since they'd last slept together. He knew she had another lover, but she had a voracious sexual appetite and by the expression on her face, she was counting on a rendezvous.

Leaning heavily against him, she smelled of expensive perfume—too strong, compared to the light scent of lavender that Arlie wore.

Veronica's fingers traced circles on his pant leg. "Dominic, don't tell me you've lost interest in your little ward already?"

He lifted a brow. "What has Arlie to do with anything?"

Her throaty laughter filled the carriage. "Oh, Dominic, you think I'm so naive. You forget I play this game as well as you, or any man. You've bedded her. It's obvious. But I don't care." Her hand moved to his cock. "I still want you."

Just last night he had experienced unparalleled passion in Arlie's arms. The thought of having sex with Veronica had lost all appeal. But he had some convincing to do, not just to Veronica, but to himself. Arlie had taken hold of his heart and as the days passed, he felt himself falling further under her spell. The knowledge unsettled him. He grabbed the bottle of port that Veronica always kept stuffed under the carriage seat, and took a long, steady drink.

When Daniel had asked for Arlie's hand, he had considered for a heart-stopping moment marrying her himself, but he knew far too well it would be impossible. His grandmother could and would cut him out of the family fortune immediately. He would be stripped of his title, his estates, his wealth…everything.

Plus, in time the novelty would wear off…it always did. Even as the thought entered his mind, his body renounced it. Arlie had set his blood on fire from the moment he'd met her, and from the first touch he had been consumed. Every time they made love he gave a little more of his heart.

Despite that knowledge, thirty minutes later Dominic was in a rented room, flat on his back, his naked ex-mistress kissing a trail from his chest, straight down to his cock. Try as he might to put Arlie from his mind, he found he could not. Sitting up abruptly, Dominic gently pushed Veronica aside.

"What is it?" she asked, falling back on the bed, irritation marring her features.

"I can't do it," he said, finding his pants and pulling them on, never so anxious to leave a naked woman than at that moment.

"I should have never come here."

"Don't be silly," she said, trying to pull him back down.

He stepped away, ripped his shirt off a nearby chair and quickly put it on. "I would ask that if you care for me at all, that you stop the rumors. Arlie doesn't deserve to be ruined by them," he said, knowing he said it for naught. Veronica would stop at nothing to have her revenge.

She glared at him. "You'll be back, Dominic. I know it, just as I know that it is impossible for you to be faithful to any one woman."

Having no desire to argue, he headed for the door.

"Dominic, please reconsider. She is, after all, a *whore's* daughter."

Dominic stepped dead in his tracks. His gut twisted in a knot as he heard Veronica's throaty laughter.

"Everyone knows the truth, Dominic. Everyone knows that she is *not* the daughter of a baron — or whatever pathetic fabricated tale the two of you came up with. I won't ask if you knew all along, because it's obvious that you did by your reaction."

He said nothing as he continued for the door. The minute he reached his carriage, self-loathing came over him in waves. He had very nearly made love to another woman. How could he have done this to Arlie?

When he walked into the manor, his self-loathing grew by leaps and bounds. Joseph took one look at him and frowned. "I'll draw a bath," he said, his voice a mixture of disgust and impatience. "You reek of perfume."

A bath was exactly what he needed. He wanted the scent of the other woman off him. He wanted nothing more than to take Arlie in his arms tonight. He wanted to tell her how much he cared for her, how much she meant to him, and then show her.

As he headed for the stairs he stopped short, seeing Arlie coming down, her hand resting on the banister.

Dressed in a cream silk robe, her hair fell around her like a veil. Her beauty stunned him and he realized he wanted her now, as always, perhaps even more, since he was terrified at the next words he would hear.

When would I ever get over her? He wondered. *Never* echoed in his mind. She took a few more steps then stopped, her gaze focused on his lips before slipping to his neck. Her eyes narrowed in suspicion. "You were with her, weren't you?"

His heart missed a beat. *How did she know?* He'd been discreet.

As though reading his mind, she replied in a solemn voice, "You smell of her perfume. Plus her rouge is on your jaw and neck."

He glanced down and saw the telltale signs of makeup on his white cravat. "I swear we did nothing," he said, desperate to have her in his arms again, needing to have her tell him she would never leave him.

Her mouth opened in disbelief. "You liar."

"Daniel knows about us. Everyone knows... Veronica started the rumor and I had to put an end to it."

"So you slept with her?"

"No, I didn't sleep with her. I swear it!"

"Yet you were with her. And you did more than talk," she accused, her voice unsteady.

There was nothing he could say. He had been with Veronica, and he'd had every intention of making love to her in the hopes that she would not only stop the rumors, but would help him prove to himself that what he felt for Arlie he could feel for anyone.

For a moment time stood still as she watched him. Her green eyes were stormy with anguish. Her pink lips trembled, before she bit down on her bottom one. Tears swam in her eyes and he reached for her, but she swatted his hand away. "Don't touch me. Don't *ever* touch me again!"

Without another word, she turned and ran back up the stairs. He flinched when her bedroom door slammed behind her. He closed his eyes and fought the yearning to go to her.

"My lord?"

"Yes, Joseph?

"Could I interest you in a glass of brandy?"

"Do me one better, will you? Get me the bottle."

* * * * *

Arlie pretended not to notice Dominic, who watched from his study. Smiling up at Daniel, she took his hand in her own, entwining her fingers with his strong ones. How she wished he could make her feel the same way Dominic did.

"Kiss me," she whispered.

"Pardon me?" Dominic asked, his eyes widened, obviously surprised by her question.

"I thought it was time we *truly* kissed."

His frown quickly turned into a grin. "Are you sure?"

"I've never been more certain."

His hands moved to either side of her face. Gently, he leaned forward, and touched his lips to hers. She lifted her chin a fraction to be more accommodating. "Again, Daniel. Kiss me again."

His eyes brightened. This time, he pulled her up against him, while his mouth covered hers. She parted her lips in invitation, hoping he would take the initiative and deepen the kiss. He slipped the tip of his tongue in, and Arlie waited for the fierce pounding she always experienced with Dominic to begin. After a few passion free moments, Arlie realized to her great disappointment, that "the tingle" wouldn't happen.

Not with Daniel anyway.

Unable to meet his gaze, she instead glanced at the button on his waistcoat. "It's time for my piano lesson," she said, hating herself for the lie. She wanted to get away from everyone and everything. It wasn't Daniel's fault. She liked him, and he would make someone a wonderful husband...but that someone wasn't her.

It was all Dominic's fault. Dominic had ruined everything.

"Until tomorrow," he said, giving her a kiss on the cheek.

"Until tomorrow," she repeated.

He left her standing in the garden. She kicked a pebble, lifting her face to the gray sky that matched her mood so perfectly. How dare Dominic give Daniel permission to marry her? She knew the only reason he had given permission was because he had tired of her and wanted Veronica back.

When she heard steps on the path behind her, she didn't have to turn to know who they belonged to.

"Did you enjoy it?"

She turned and met Dominic's cool stare. "You mean the kiss? Yes, as a matter of fact, I did."

The nerve in his jaw ticked double-time.

"I'm tired and I don't want to fight. I'm going to my room now."

"He's talking of putting an announcement in *The Times*, you know."

She shrugged. "So be it."

"Is that what you want? To be Mrs. Daniel Butler?"

"It does have a nice ring, doesn't it?"

He cleared his throat. "Do you want him?"

"What do you care?" she replied, barely above a whisper, finding it hard to believe he had finally got around to asking her how she felt.

He grabbed her wrist. She tried pulling away, but his hand was like a steel band. His eyes were piercing, staring all the way into her soul. "I want you now more than ever. It kills me to see you with him. Especially when you won't listen to me. I swear to you Veronica means nothing to me. When I'm with you I—"

"Stop it!" she yelled, pressing her free hand against her ear. "I won't listen to this anymore. She is your lover, as she was before I came here. You've made your decision and I would ask that you leave me alone—now and always."

The line of his mouth tightened a fraction more, and he released her.

It was the most difficult thing she'd ever done, but she left him standing there. Her willpower was slipping. It would have been so easy to give in to him. Even now, when she should hate him, she wanted him. Every time she closed her eyes she saw his face, remembered his touch, the feel of him inside her. The wicked things they did. The wonderful things that she missed desperately. God help her, but she loved him, despite his infidelities and the fact that he would never be faithful to her, and he would never love her in return.

Racing to her room, she flung herself on the bed, willing herself to sleep, but instead she lay staring at the ceiling, trying desperately not to cry. Finding rest impossible, she ordered a bath and stared out the window as the servants prepared it. When she was left alone, she stripped her clothes off and stepped into the steaming water.

Slipping deeper into the warm water, Arlie sighed. She could not stand another day in this house. To sit across from *him* at dinner was pure torture. His stare burned into her, daring her to meet it. Every time she looked at him she couldn't help but think of him with Veronica. Why? Why had he betrayed her? Had he grown tired of her so soon, or was he only trying to help by forcing the gossips to recant their stories? She shook her head, disgusted with herself. Why did she even try to rationalize his behavior? Had she slept with Daniel, he would have sent her packing, without giving her a chance to explain.

Hearing the door open, she turned, expecting to find Mary bringing her towels. But it wasn't Mary—it was Dominic. His shirt was open to the waist, exposing his hard chest and heavily-muscled stomach. His breeches and boots were covered in mud. His hair looked tousled, like he'd raked his fingers through it time and again. He looked dangerous...and so very masculine. She licked her dry lips. "What do you want?"

His steps echoed on the floor as he came toward her, his gaze not once leaving hers. When he reached the tub, he went down on his haunches, his fingers drifted lazily through the water, coming dangerously close to her breasts. Despite her attempts to not be affected by his presence, her body was responding to him against her will. Her nipples tightened, remembering the feel of his hands on them. Her stomach clenched, a deep ache that only he could relieve.

"Arlie, I never meant to hurt you. I only wanted to protect you from the gossip. Veronica has a lot of power, and she would destroy you if she could." He looked so tortured, she almost touched him, but she restrained herself. "It's true, she once meant something to me, but that was before I met you."

Trying to ignore his nearby fingers that rested on the bath's edge, she glanced at him again. His blue eyes were dark and tortured, dark circles appeared like bruises beneath them. She knew he hadn't slept last night. She'd heard him walking down the hall, his footsteps stopping outside her bedroom door. He knocked lightly. How tempted she'd been to let him in, but she couldn't. Knowing he'd been with another woman, just hours after she'd given herself to him, was gut-wrenching. To make matters worse, he had given Daniel permission to marry her.

"I did not sleep with her, I swear it. Forgive me, Arlie—please."

Watching him, she started to believe that maybe he had done it to protect her and that he was truly sorry. She closed her eyes, wondering how she could possibly be contemplating forgiving him such a thing.

"I know what I did wasn't right, and I know that no matter what I say, it won't change anything. I regret it deeply, but I swear to you, we did *not* have sex."

She turned from him, unable to look at him without thinking of he and Veronica entwined in each other's arms — just as they'd been the morning after the Banfield ball.

"I told myself I wouldn't care if you married Daniel, yet I do. The thought of the two of you together makes me crazy." She glanced at him, unable to help herself. His gaze moved to her lips. "When I think of you laying beneath him making love to him, I want to kill him...and you as well."

Her breath caught in her throat when his fingers pressed around her neck. Dear Lord, would he strangle her right here? His gaze softened, and his fingers splayed and slowly slid down to her breasts, palming one in his large hand, before running the tips of his fingers over a pebble-hard nipple.

"Be mine, Arlie. I want you to belong to me and no other."

For so long she had yearned to hear him speak those words. *But he's betrayed you*, her mind all but screamed. Meeting his stare, she whispered, "I want you, too." She needed him, wanted him more than anything and anyone, and apparently he felt the same. Yesterday didn't matter. Only now — this very moment.

Relief evident on his features, Dominic lifted her from the bath and walked across the room in long strides where he tossed her on her bed. She lounged on the silk comforter, loving the feel of her wet flesh against the smooth material, as she watched him undress. While he stripped off his shirt and pants, he watched her, his eyes dark and promising.

Joining her on the bed, he smiled wickedly then he kissed her lips, her throat, her breasts, then her stomach, and lower still. He kissed the insides of her thighs, then with a low groan he kissed her pleasure pearl. He stroked his tongue over her slick folds, lifting her pearl with the very tip of his tongue until she cried out. Her fingers weaved through his hair, pulling him closer to her, anchoring him there.

Her breath came in long surrendering moans as he continued his explorations. Her bones felt as soft as butter, and when she thought she could take no more, she was hurtled beyond the point of no return, as wave upon wave of pleasure pulsed through her body.

His hard body moved between her legs that quivered from her climax. Looking up into his handsome face, her pulse skittered seeing the desire there—the look of complete possession.

Again, her body began throbbing, needing him inside her to satisfy the craving. She arched her hips against him, prompting him to take her.

"Please...take me," she whispered against his mouth.

He entered her in one fluid motion. Her legs wrapped around his hips, taking all of him within her, pressing against him until she was sure he touched her womb.

"I love you," she whispered against his neck, meaning it with all her heart and soul.

He kissed her, hard and passionately, his tongue darting in and out of her mouth, matching the rhythm of his body. "You're mine, Arlie. My angel, my life." He groaned low in his throat. "Mine and only mine."

When they both lay sated, their limbs entwined, Arlie wondered if he meant any of the words he'd uttered. She knew she tortured herself, but then his words came back to her. *My angel — my life. Mine and only mine.*

Chapter Twelve

Arlie pretended to sleep as Dominic got up and dressed.

He kissed her forehead, walked to the door, then closed it softly behind him.

A hot tear ran down Arlie's cheek, followed by others.

Why had she been unable to resist him? In giving in to him she had failed herself. Was she no better than her mother? Why was she so willing to open her legs for a man who did not love her?

Dominic had proven the obvious...he would never be faithful. And worse still, she had told him that she loved him last night while in the throes of passion. He hadn't responded, so she'd told him again when they lay quiet in each other's arms. She remembered how he'd frozen and then been silent, saying nothing, except that she was his.

But *being his* didn't mean the same as love.

Her mind raced, wondering what alternatives she had. Knowing they were few, she decided the best thing to do was not let him touch her again, and to take Daniel's proposal seriously. Daniel was a good man, who could offer her a nice home and a good life. She could do far worse than the young American; perhaps one day she would desire him in the way she desired Dominic.

Yes, that's what she would do. She would give Daniel her answer today.

Arlie rose and took a hot bath, scrubbing away the traces of lovemaking. Never again would she know Dominic's touch — a fact that taunted her. Even now her body stirred, remembering the feel of his lips against hers, the touch of his fingertips on her breasts, the stroke of his tongue against her cleft, bringing her to heights she had never thought possible.

Putting Dominic from her mind, she took great pains with her appearance. She chose an emerald-green riding habit that complemented her eyes. Daniel would prefer the habit's conservative cut over her breeches.

Arlie walked to the stables and breathed a sigh of relief seeing Dominic was not around. She knew her behavior was improper since she had no chaperone, but she didn't want to give herself any more time to talk herself out of accepting Daniel's proposal. It was the only solution.

Riding into London, Arlie thankfully saw no one she knew, since stopping would give her time to change her mind. Having passed by Daniel's townhouse on an earlier occasion, she knew where it was. Now she glanced up at the building, wondering if it was too early to call on him. But if she didn't do this now, she would probably never return.

Climbing the steps, she took a steadying breath and grabbed the brass knocker, knocking several times against the heavy door. Her stomach clenched in a tight knot and her heart pounded nervously as she waited. She was about to leave when the door abruptly whipped open.

A young maid with cap askew looked at Arlie disapprovingly. "May I help you?"

A combination of relief and disappointment flooded Arlie as she looked at the maid. "Yes. May I speak to Mr. Butler?"

The woman glanced past Arlie's shoulder, obviously looking for her chaperone. She lifted a brow seeing she had none. "May I tell him who's calling?"

"Yes. Miss Whitman."

The woman's eyes instantly lit up at the mention of her name.

"Come in, come in, Miss Whitman. Please have a seat here in the parlor."

Dangerous Desires

The servant left her sitting in an old settee, the worn material dull and faded. Arlie's gaze moved over the room, taking in the sparse furnishings, worn carpet, yellowed drapes, and wallpaper that was ripped and torn in places. She had heard that Daniel came from a well-to-do family—yet the state of his townhouse made her wonder if his wealth hadn't been exaggerated.

The sound of boots outside the parlor door brought Arlie to her feet. A moment later Daniel entered, a wide smile on his face. He looked youthful, boyish, and very handsome in a brown suit that accented his dark good looks. "Miss Whitman, what a pleasure it is to see you." He took her hand and brought it to his lips. "I must say I'm pleasantly surprised. Can I hope this visit means you bring me good news?"

She managed a smile, even though she felt like crying. "I have come to tell you yes. I accept your proposal."

He pulled her into his arms, his hand brushing along her spine. She wanted desperately to feel the same excitement with Daniel as she did with Dominic, but as he pulled away, she knew it wasn't to be. She could only hope that in time she would feel differently.

"I will place an announcement in the paper immediately."

"Yes," she said, her mind reeling with all she had to do.

"We will decide on a day, though I think it best to wait perhaps a year."

Her heart sank. *A year!* That was not what she wanted to hear. She could not live in Rochford's house for a year and not want him. Nor could she stand having Dominic parade his mistresses in front of her. No, that would not do!

"I had hoped it could be sooner."

He grinned. "If only that was possible. My family must be able to attend, and they are away—oh, and I would like to marry in America. That is where we will be living. In Richmond, Virginia."

169

She shook her head. The thought of moving an ocean away was distressing to say the least.

"Don't fear, darling. But we will also have this townhouse, and we can visit London every summer. Don't mind its current state, soon things will change, and you will be able to decorate in whatever fashion you see fit."

She had a suspicion Daniel thought her wealthy. Could he possibly be marrying her for the money? If so, he would be disappointed. True, Dominic had secured a dowry for her, but it would not be a fortune. Perhaps she had best tell Daniel the truth.

But as it turned out she didn't mention her past at all. By the time she left Daniel's townhouse, her stomach had tied itself in knots. He'd been so excited, she hadn't been able to get a word in edgewise, as he talked endlessly about their life together, planning every detail down to when their first child would be conceived: on their wedding night—a night she already dreaded.

When Rochford Manor came into view, Arlie stopped at the iron gate, her fingers curling around the cool metal. The home had become her sanctuary these last few months, and in a way, her prison.

How could she possibly stay at the manor another twelve months, living with a man she could not resist? She would never be able to live in the same house and stay out of his bed. His touch made her feel so wanton, she scarcely knew herself anymore. It was impossible. She couldn't stay. But what could she do?

The gate creaked as she opened it. She stepped onto the stone pathway and closed the gate behind her—the sound imposing and somehow final. She had done this. She had let the affair happen, and now she must end it.

Arlie walked into the manor and down the long hall, remembering the first day she had come here, and how easily she had fallen under her guardian's spell. How eager she had been to please him, wanting nothing more than his approval.

She had got much more than that.

At the door to Dominic's study, Arlie stopped and took a deep breath, her hand poised to knock when the door swung open.

"You were up early this morning," Dominic said, meeting her with a kiss.

She closed her eyes, inhaling the masculine scent of him. Her heart began to beat unsteadily as he pulled her into his arms and deepened the kiss.

"I came to your room this morning," he said, his voice a husky whisper. "But you were gone." He kicked the study door closed with his foot and to her distress, she felt herself falling under his spell once again.

"Mmmm, you smell so good." His hands went to her hair, pulling the ribbon out, weaving the thick strands through his fingers. Next, he pulled at the buttons at the back of her gown, but she stilled his hand.

"We need to talk."

One dark brow lifted. "Can't it wait?" he asked, flicking his tongue over the sensitive flesh of her ear.

She shook her head and took a step back, jumping when she ran into the door. "No, we must talk now."

All humor left his face as he watched her warily. "All right, you have my full attention."

He motioned for her to take a seat and with every step she took toward the couch, she felt a sense of impending doom. How would he take her news? Would he be happy, relieved, or angry?

Sitting stiffly on the couch, she cleared her throat. "As you know, Daniel has asked for my hand."

He nodded. "Of course, I am aware."

"I've given it much thought…and I believe it is for the best that I accept his offer."

Dominic's eyes narrowed dangerously as he sat forward in his chair. "What!?"

"I believe it is for the best. You have to admit that we have carried on this thing between us for far too long. We have been found out, and in order to keep people from speculating further, I think it wise that I marry Daniel."

He stood so quickly, the chair he'd been sitting in crashed to the floor. His eyes flashed with rage as he raked his hands through his hair. Silence fell over them like a heavy mist, but still she said nothing, waiting, watching.

He walked to the window, looked out for a few moments, the nerve in his jaw twitching. He was furious. When he stopped in front of her, his expression was lethal. "Do you mean to tell me that you will go through with this marriage?" His voice was full of disbelief.

Arlie nodded.

"Do you love him?"

"Of course not, but I see no other choice."

His jaw hardened. "I would give you a choice."

Hope momentarily flared in her breast. "What choice?"

"Be my mistress."

The words were like a hard slap. "Mistress?" she choked.

"Yes. I will give you a good life, Arlie. You will have the best of everything."

Not a wife, but a mistress. After leaving her father, her mother had given up everything for a man of privilege. Yet only months into their relationship, he found another more to his liking and kicked her out of the apartment, took away the jewels, the gowns, and the carriage, leaving her with nothing. Penniless, she had gone back to work as a prostitute and died within a year. Many believed she drank herself to death trying to nurse her broken heart. Arlie would not repeat the same mistake.

"Arlie?"

She stared at him, wanting desperately to remember him as he was now — tall, dark, sinfully handsome, and so unattainable. She shook her head. "I cannot accept."

"Why?" he said between clenched teeth.

"You would tire of me soon."

"I would *never* tire of you."

"I want marriage."

"You know I cannot offer you that."

She didn't bother to ask why. She knew why. Because of who she was. It didn't matter that she had been accepted by *the ton*. It only mattered that she hadn't a single drop of blue blood in her veins, and therefore, wasn't good enough for him. "I know that you have a country estate, *my lord*. I would ask that I stay there. I think it only right, especially in order to let things die down."

* * * * *

Dominic stared at Arlie, finding it hard to believe they were even having this discussion. Just last night she had professed her love for him over and over again. He in return had told her how much he cared for her. He had thought that she had forgiven him for having met with Veronica. He had hoped that they could continue their relationship as though the entire incident had never happened. Apparently, it was not to be.

"I have already told Daniel that I will marry him," she whispered.

He closed his eyes, then ran a trembling hand down his face. He could not believe his ears. He stared at her, hoping she would tell him she did not mean what she said. Yet as the seconds ticked by in silence, he realized she was intent on going through with it. She *would* marry Daniel. Fury quickly replaced the disbelief.

Unable to look at her a minute longer, he strode for the door, but stopped short of it. "I'll see that your things are packed. You'll be on your way to Whitley within the hour."

* * * * *

Dominic's country home, Whitley, was a gorgeous, extravagant Gothic manor, made of large gray stones. The manor's whimsical towers and turrets reminded Arlie of a French Chateau in a much-loved book.

Although the manor was lovely, the moment Arlie stepped foot into the marble foyer, she knew it missed one very important element—Dominic.

The ride to Dominic's country estate had been agonizing. She cried for the first few hours, then finally fell into a fitful sleep where she envisioned her life with Daniel. She knew she could do far worse than the handsome American, yet she had a hard time convincing herself that she would ever stop loving her guardian.

Dominic's grandmother had become a great friend, doing her part to keep Arlie's mind off of Dominic. They both liked to garden, and often times would spend the better part of the day tending to the roses and rare flowers.

The dowager talked often of the family that once lived together at the old manor. Her eyes would twinkle with laughter at the mention of a young Dominic's antics, but then she would grow sullen once she brought up her son. Arlie wondered what regrets the older woman had being estranged from the family she loved—yet resented at the same time.

Late one evening Arlie was resting in her room when the dowager entered without knocking and announced they had a guest.

In her heart of hearts, Arlie secretly hoped the guest would be Dominic, but to her chagrin, it was Lord Malfrey, coming to offer congratulations on her upcoming nuptials. The dowager sat in the same room during the visit, working on her needlepoint, though Arlie could feel her gaze upon them.

The moment Lord Malfrey left, the dowager set her needlepoint aside and plainly remarked, "That man has every intention of making you his lover. You must be wary of men like him, for they wait until you have a ring on your finger, and then charm you until you cannot say no."

"I will never be unfaithful to my husband," Arlie replied, meaning it.

The dowager smiled. "Do you love Mr. Butler?"

Arlie could feel her cheeks burn as the older woman stared at her. "I care for him."

"But do you love him?"

Arlie shook her head. "No, I don't."

The dowager let out an unsteady breath. "It is as I thought. Perhaps you should reconsider his offer then."

How could Arlie tell the dowager that she loved Dominic? That she would never be happy with anyone, save him? And that she could never have him, because she was a lowly commoner and that because of the dowager herself and the rest of *the ton's* rules they could never be together, bound in marriage at least.

And Arlie would never be happy with less.

* * * * *

Dominic sat back in his chair and motioned for Joseph to refill his glass.

"My lord, you have had much to drink. Perhaps you would prefer—"

"I would prefer you keep your mouth shut and do as you're asked."

Joseph lifted his chin and poured the brandy. "You will get no sympathy from me come morning when you are so sick you can scarcely stand." Setting the glass decanter down on the corner of the table with more force than necessary, the butler let out an exasperated breath and headed for the door, but just short of getting there he turned. "My lord, if I might—"

"Say it!"

Joseph flinched as though he'd been slapped. "Why don't you visit her? It has been four weeks and two days, and you are plainly miserable. Perhaps if you just visited her—"

"What good would it do?"

He shrugged. "Maybe she feels as you do. Perhaps together you can come by a solution."

"I have already asked her to be my mistress."

Joseph sighed dramatically. "And you are surprised she left you?"

"What more can I do?"

"May I suggest marriage? After all, the way you two have been behaving, she deserves as much."

Dominic drained the brandy and slammed the glass on the table. "I have no desire to marry. Plus, you know as well as I do that my grandmother would never stand for it. No, Joseph, I cannot marry. Not now, perhaps never."

"Well then, what do you expect her to do—stay underfoot until you are ready? I think not, my lord. She is a woman who has much to offer a man. She has a combination of youthful innocence and a sweet spirit that can capture the heart of any man. She made you laugh, my lord, a feat unto itself. And her beauty surpasses any I have seen in a—"

"Enough!"

"As you wish, my lord."

As Joseph shut the door behind him, Dominic thought how long the weeks had been without Arlie. How he missed the sound of her voice, her laughter, her anger, her kisses...her body. He had even gone so far as to visit a brothel with Langley, hoping a warm body would make him forget about Arlie, but instead he'd ended up getting drunk and sleeping it off on a couch.

More than once he had dreamt of Arlie's wedding. She looked so beautiful in her flowing white gown as young Daniel took her hand in his. Then they were dancing, laughing...so in love. The image shifted to the two of them making love. Arlie's cries of passion, the look in her green eyes as she stared up at her husband.

A knock at the door brought him abruptly out of his unwanted thoughts.

"My lord, Mr. Butler is here," Joseph announced from the doorway.

The name of his rival pushed his anger up a notch. "Send him in," he replied, taking a deep breath just as the young man came in.

"Rochford," Daniel said with a triumphant grin—one Dominic yearned to wipe from his face. "I have come to ask a favor of you."

Dominic lifted a brow.

"I would like to visit Miss Whitman at Whitley."

Dominic opened his mouth, but Daniel held up his hand.

"Before you answer, I would request your presence there as well. In my letters from Miss Whitman, I get the distinct impression that she misses you. I would like to surprise her."

It disappointed him that Arlie had written to the young man and not himself, yet he couldn't help be delighted she had mentioned him in correspondence to her fiancé.

"Does she write you often?"

"Only twice."

"And does she fare well?"

Daniel smiled. "Yes. She says your grandmother is a most gracious hostess. They take long walks together, and Miss Whitman rides every day. Oh, and she particularly enjoys gardening. You made an excellent choice by sending her there.

Already the gossips have ceased their chatter." Daniel clapped him on the back as though they were life-long friends. "So what do you say—will you go?"

Dominic needed little time to think about it. He'd been wanting to go to Whitley for weeks now, and up to that moment had no legitimate reason to visit. Now he had reason: he'd been invited to visit, and he would also serve as chaperone...since Dominic knew his grandmother favored the match, she would do little to deter Daniel.

"When will you be leaving?" Dominic asked.

"Saturday. I plan on staying until the following Monday— unless I'm called back on business before then."

"I'll leave tomorrow and give the servants time to prepare for your stay."

Daniel nodded. "Excellent! I'm hoping this will give us all an opportunity to get closer. I've a lot to be sorry about. I know now that I've judged you unfairly."

* * * * *

It took the better part of the day for Dominic to get to his country home by horseback, and it gave him the time he needed to prepare himself to see Arlie again.

It had been years since he'd last been to Whitley, and though he'd yearned to return, always he found an excuse to stay away. Now as he entered his country estate, memories of his childhood, particularly times with his mother, came rushing to the forefront.

His mother had been a beauty. A woman devoted to her husband, who had in turn, been a philanderer of the worst sort. The poor woman tried to keep him from straying by always looking her best and making herself accessible for his short visits. Unfortunately, he proved he was beyond control. He bedded the servants and even Dominic's fiancée.

He flinched at the memories still as strong now as they had been in the first weeks after the events. Never would he forget the sight that greeted him when he opened the door to his father's chamber, a place he had always stayed away from until that fateful day.

Having been unable to find his beloved fiancée, Dominic raced through the manor in the hopes to surprise her with the bouquet of flowers he'd hand-picked to celebrate their upcoming marriage. Hearing the unmistakable sound of lovemaking coming from his father's quarters, he'd ground to a halt. His mother was gone, which meant his father was with another.

Dominic walked silently to the door and pushed it open to find his father having sex with his betrothed, his grunts filling the room along with her soft sighs of surrender. Numb with shock, Dominic had been torn between ripping his father off her, or slamming the door, alerting them to his presence—yet he did neither. He stood watching until they finished and his father rolled off her, his chest heaving from the exertion. His fiancée saw him first, her horror-filled gasp burning in his ears as his father turned to the door. Never in his life would he forget the look on his father's face—the surprise, then the triumphant smile.

From that moment both his father and his fiancée were dead to him.

He never thought much of his father's philandering, until as a young man himself, he began to use women in the same manner. He figured if he didn't give them his heart, then what damage could it do? Two people coming together for sexual gratification couldn't hurt anyone. Yet when one person loved more than the other, the results were disastrous. In the end it had killed his mother. And his father, though saddened by his wife's death, took no responsibility. He believed she killed herself because of a mental disorder.

But in truth, she died from unhappiness, knowing she would never be enough woman for a man like her husband, no matter what lengths she went to. Hell, the bastard had had a passion for making others miserable.

Shaking his mind of the unwanted memories, Dominic walked down the hallway, passing rooms he had chosen to forget. Despite his effort not to feel any emotion, a wave of sadness and melancholy washed over him.

"My lord, what an unexpected surprise," a booming voice said from behind him, nearly startling him out of his skin.

He turned to find his housekeeper, Mrs. Mitchell, watching him with a delighted smile on her face.

"Mrs. Mitchell, how are you?"

"I am very well. Thank you, my lord, for asking. I dare say, your grandmother will be most pleased to see you."

Dominic managed a smile. "I'm sure she will be," he replied, doubting very much that his grandmother would ever be happy to see him. Particularly in "her" home where she reigned supreme. "Is Miss Whitman at home?"

The woman's round face split into a wide smile. "Aye, my lord. She is in the garden. How she loves it there. Such a love for flowers I haven't seen since your dear mother, of course. And she's such a lovely young lady, so kind and courteous. You've done a superior job, my lord, if I should say so myself. And the dowager is quite grateful for her company. She gets so lonely at times, my lord. I wish that you would come more often."

"I shall certainly try. Now, I would like to see Miss Whitman. Thank you for your help, Mrs. Mitchell."

Dominic walked through the kitchens, saying hello to the staff before stepping out the back door, wanting to take Arlie by surprise.

For a moment he didn't see her, then he caught a glimpse of pale blonde hair swept up in an untidy bun. A current of excitement raced through him at the sight of her. Dressed in a plain cotton dress with no corset beneath, she knelt. A streak of dirt ran across her cheek and nose. She had never looked more adorable, digging in the dirt while humming a song, her voice as light as an angel's.

She glanced up abruptly, and dropped the spade at her side.

"Hello, Arlie," he said, walking toward her, and as he did, she slowly came to her feet, brushing the dirt from her skirts.

"I did not know —"

"I thought I'd surprise you."

"You did," she tried to smile, but her lips trembled, and he wished above all else to know what she was thinking.

"Daniel asked that I come. He will be here in a few days. He thought it wise that I play chaperone."

She nodded. "You look well."

He smiled. "As do you. How do you like it here at Whitley?"

She grinned and he realized how much he'd missed that smile — how desperately he'd missed her.

"Your grandmother has been most kind to me. I've enjoyed her company immensely. You have a beautiful estate, and I ride most every day. It is a splendid home you have."

He was glad she liked it, but a part of him wanted to hear that she hated it and wanted to come back with him. Only then would Rochford Manor be a home again. "I'm glad you like it."

"I wished I had known you were coming. I would have changed," she said, her cheeks turning pink under his stare.

"You've lost weight," he said, noticing the stark planes of her face, and the protruding bones at her hips. "Is my grandmother starving you?"

"On the contrary, she all but feeds me herself, but I find that I have no appetite."

"Are you ill?"

Arlie shook her head. "No." I miss you desperately, she wanted to say. I want you so badly that I lay awake at night and think back on the nights we made love. And every time I think

I'm over you, visions of you with another woman fill my mind, and they drive me crazy to where I can't eat or even sleep.

"Then what plagues you?"

As if you didn't know... Oh, but he was a sight for sore eyes. For weeks now she had yearned to see him, but settled with feasting on the family portraits in the hall. Even as a boy he had been handsome, with a look of arrogance and self-assuredness others lacked. Every time she passed one of those pictures, she found it hard to resist the urge to touch it, wishing that it was he in the flesh, rather than oils and canvas. Yet now he stood before her, flesh and blood.

"Lord, how I have missed you," she whispered, surprising even herself.

His eyes instantly softened and as he took the few steps that separated them, she felt compelled to step back. Why did he have to look so wonderful when she looked haggard? And why had she expected differently?

"I hate how we ended things between us," he said, his eyes warm. "I want you to know that I have accepted your engagement to Daniel. He is a nice young man and I think he'll make you very happy."

Not the words she had been hoping for.

Finding it hard to smile, she simply nodded, her gaze falling to his shoulder, not wanting him to see the hurt in her eyes. Their time apart had done nothing but confirm her as just another one of his lovers—nothing more. "I am glad that you approve of him. He will make me happy." This time she forced a smile, hoping it looked genuine.

Chapter Thirteen

The two days that followed were hell for Arlie, namely because Dominic was her constant companion. They rode together, ate together, she played the piano for him, and once they even danced while the dowager played for them. Dancing had been the most difficult—standing in his arms, smelling the heady scent of him, so masculine and sexual, remembering the ecstasy she'd felt in his arms...an ecstasy that would no longer be, especially with Daniel on his way to Whitley.

The morning of Daniel's arrival, Arlie had tea with the dowager. The older woman talked about the upcoming nuptials as though it was her own wedding. Since Dominic's arrival, the dowager appeared younger, and more at ease. From time to time Arlie would glance over at the older woman and see her watching them, a strange expression on her face. Did she guess what had happened between the two of them? Arlie certainly hoped not.

With every day that passed, it had grown more difficult to hide her feelings for Dominic. Arlie wanted Dominic as much as she always did. Now that they'd had time by themselves, far away from London and *the ton*, her feelings were even stronger. The knowledge that soon she would be married to a man she didn't love unsettled her so. She wanted to run far away from everyone and everything.

Arlie closed her eyes. What she wouldn't give to have her father here now, to hear his advice on what to do.

Lifting her chin, she let out a deep breath. Now she would show Dominic that she could be impartial as well. When Daniel came she would be attentive, loving, kind, and perhaps a little passionate. Maybe she hadn't given Daniel the chance to stir her desire. She'd been so caught up with Dominic, she had no desire to try. But now — now she was ready.

Hearing a horse approach, Arlie stared out the window, her mouth splitting into a smile as she recognized Daniel. He raced toward the house on the back of a white palfrey. Arlie ran down the steps, anxious to see him again, and hoping to put her fears to rest.

He dismounted and she ran toward him and into his open arms. She needed to know that marrying him was the right thing to do.

"Arlie, it seems like an eternity since last I looked upon your beauty."

"Daniel," she said, hugging him close, waiting for the stirring she so desperately needed to feel.

"I am most anxious to spend some time with you." His gaze scanned the immaculate grounds. "Is Rochford here?"

Always it was Rochford. But perhaps he had been wise in requesting her guardian's presence. Now she knew where she stood with both of these men: this one before her cared for her enough to marry her. "No, but he should be returning shortly."

The dowager walked out, her face devoid of emotion as she met Daniel. She followed them, not asking to be invited along, but playing the bit of chaperone to the extreme, and Arlie was thankful. Daniel was obviously miffed that the older woman stayed close by and even interrupted him from time to time. But the interruptions pleased Arlie, and she even encouraged the dowager to stroll with them in the gardens.

The dowager was just telling a story about Dominic hanging from one particular tree, when they were interrupted by a peal of loud feminine laughter. Arlie turned to find Dominic walking toward her, a beautiful brunette on his arm.

Arlie's heart turned to ice. The gorgeous woman had alabaster skin, blue eyes, and hair as dark as Dominic's. She had wrapped one of her arms around Dominic's waist, while he had slung one of his casually over her shoulders. They quite apparently knew each other...intimately.

Arlie heard the dowager gasp, and could see the disapproval in the older woman's eyes. How dare he bring a woman to Whitley, in front of them, and especially his grandmother, who openly opposed such behavior? What was he trying to prove—that he was still every bit the rake she knew him to be?

Hell, she needed no confirmation of that.

He'd betrayed her just weeks into their relationship, and now she was having to put the pieces of her heart back together.

He didn't bother to look in their direction as he and the women headed up the front steps. The door slammed behind them a second later. Arlie's heart felt like it had been ripped out and stepped on.

"It seems he has changed little," the dowager said, her voice clearly disappointed. "I think I shall go rest." Without another word, she left Arlie and Daniel alone in the garden.

"I'm sorry I told him to come. I thought he would be different, especially around you, my dear," Daniel said, shaking his head.

"Don't let him bother you," Arlie replied, forcing a smile, when she actually felt like crying. "What matters is that you're here with me now. I've missed you so much."

She knew he wanted to kiss her and probably only waited for her to say he could do so. Lifting her chin, she parted her lips in open invitation, waiting for him to take what she willingly offered.

Though it seemed an eternity, a moment later Daniel touched his dry lips to hers. Closing her eyes, Arlie slid her arms around his neck, pressing herself against the length of him. She swallowed a gasp, feeling his arousal against her stomach. As the kiss deepened, it was all she could do not to pull away.

But she didn't, instead she imagined it was Dominic she was kissing and clinging to. Opening up to him, her tongue grazed his, flicking against it, teasing him. All the memories of being held in Dominic's arms came back to her tenfold, and as she pressed herself against Daniel, she tried to wipe out the image of her previous lover, but to no avail. Her body knew it wasn't Dominic.

Daniel put her from him abruptly, his mouth open as he stared at her. "I did not mean for things to go so far," he said, concern all over his face. He glanced over her shoulder, searching the grounds to see if anyone had borne witness to the encounter.

"I did," she said, almost smiling at the shocked expression on his face. The worry left his brow, and a moment later, he smiled again.

* * * * *

From his room, Dominic could see the garden perfectly. As the woman with him began to strip off her gown, he caught sight of his ward and her fiancé kissing, their bodies pressed together, their tongues mating feverishly.

The blood roared in his ears.

"Do not undress," he said, glancing at the woman, a previous lover of his, who had been more than happy to reinstate their 'relationship'. "I was wrong to invite you here," he said walking over to help her button her dress. "Please accept my apology. Perhaps another time."

He could tell that she thought it a joke at first, but moments later she stormed out of the house and into the waiting coach. Dominic sank down on the bed, his hands covering his face. What a mockery he had made of his life. How sad he was.

The woman he longed for was in the arms of another man, and it was of his own doing. He could go down there, tell them both how he felt, but would it matter? From all appearances Arlie was lost to him. He knew that now. To see her in the young man's arms only confirmed it. He would do well to leave her alone. His grandmother would be here to play chaperone for the young lovers. He shook his head, remembering himself as a young man, outwitting the most competent of chaperones, his grandmother included. But Daniel would not seduce Arlie. No, he would wait until their wedding night as any gentleman would.

He strode for the door, stopping just long enough to explain to Mrs. Mitchell that he had business in London. Her skeptical expression said she didn't believe a word, but to her credit, she didn't say a thing.

He whipped open the front door and came face to face with Arlie and Daniel. The younger man's expression condemned him. What a hypocrite! Dominic had heard from Langley that Daniel had a favorite prostitute he visited every Monday night in London's east side. No wonder he only planned to stay at Whitley until Sunday.

"My lord, are you going somewhere?" she asked, her gaze moving to the bag in his hand.

"I'm returning to London."

She said nothing, refusing to meet his stare. It was apparent that he had hurt her yet again.

"I wish you godspeed," Daniel cut in, obviously relieved to have him out from underfoot.

He knew a moment longer under the same roof with Daniel and Arlie together would drive him insane. But leaving the two by themselves would be even worse, especially after witnessing that kiss.

"On second thought, I think I'll stay," he said, turning on his heel, striding down the long hallway before slamming the parlor door behind him.

Arlie had been surprised to see the brunette leave as quickly as she arrived, but she had not been sorry to see her go.

"Daniel, would you mind giving me a few minutes with my guardian?" Arlie asked.

"No, please take as long as you need. It is obvious he is unwell. Take your time. I will go walk among your beautiful blossoms." He kissed her cheek. "My mother will absolutely adore you. She loves gardening as well."

Arlie walked slowly down the hall, wondering why she was so concerned about Dominic, when he had done nothing but hurt her. She knocked on the door, and when he didn't answer, she entered. She shut the door behind her, and before she could draw a breath Dominic stood before her. He braced his hands on either side of her face, and stared down at her, his mouth tight and grim. "Tell me, does he make you feel the way I do?"

Nervously, she moistened her dry lips. "Don't do this, Dominic. You know it's not what you want."

"Oh, but it is. For all that I've told myself differently, it's exactly what I want. I've sat in this house for days, knowing that you slept nearby, wanting you so desperately I thought I would explode."

"But you have acted—"

"Yes, I've acted, and apparently pretty well." He kissed her softly, his lips barely grazing hers. Immediately she leaned into him.

"I want you, Arlie. I want you so much it hurts. I've been miserable without you. Though I've tried to block you from my thoughts, I find I cannot." He pressed his thick erection against her. "See what you do to me?"

Her blood sang in her veins as his mouth claimed hers in a kiss that would have brought her to her knees had he not been holding onto her. His hands cupped her face, his thumbs running up along her cheekbones. "Do you want me, Arlie?"

"Desperately," she whispered, not caring about anything but being in his arms, the feel and smell of him overpowering all her senses.

His hand moved up her bare thigh to the slit in her drawers, his fingers stroking her soft folds that had immediately grown damp for him. "Dominic, I feel powerless against you," she whispered against his chest.

He slipped a finger inside her. "It has been too long."

His hot breath fanned her neck as he lifted her in his arms. Her back pressed against the hard door. Dominic smiled devilishly as he pulled her legs up around his hips and rubbed his long, thick shaft against her. The only barrier between them was the material of his breeches. She shifted against him, her breath coming in short pants as the first waves of pleasure began to grow within her.

Dominic's cock throbbed with unspent need. He steeled himself as she pressed against him, her body tensing in release. He caught her cries with his mouth, kissing her. He wanted desperately to bury himself in her hot warmth, but he wouldn't. No, when they made love again, they would take their time.

It took all his restraint, but he kissed her neck and whispered in her ear, "Tonight, my angel. Let's wait until tonight. It will make the waiting that much sweeter."

"I cannot wait," she said in an agonized whisper. "My body aches for you."

He kissed her nose, then put her back on her unsteady feet. "Do you want to tell Daniel?" he asked.

Her brow furrowed into a frown, but reality came crashing down when she heard the front door open and close. "Yes," she whispered against his lips. "I'd actually forgotten about him."

Dominic grinned triumphantly before kissing her again. He stepped away from her just as the door opened. Daniel stood in the doorway, his hands folded before him, looking from one to the other. His eyes narrowed suspiciously. "Are you finished talking?"

The question hung precariously between them. It was so quiet she could hear his breathing. Or perhaps it was her own.

"Yes, we're done talking," Dominic said, sidestepping him. "I will see you later." He made it a point to look directly at Arlie.

"My, his mood has suddenly changed for the better. Whatever you said, it must have been convincing," Daniel said, his gaze slipping once more to her lips.

She wondered if he guessed what had happened between them. Or perhaps her guilty conscience just made her feel that way. Running her hands down the skirt of her gown, she smiled shakily. "Daniel, I need to speak with you in all honesty."

"Please do."

Taking a deep breath, she blurted, "Daniel, I can not marry you."

He frowned. "What?"

"I can't marry you."

Taking her hand in his, he pulled her to the nearest settee. "I don't understand? The kiss that we shared. I didn't mean to take such liberties. I thought you wanted—"

She put a finger to his lips. "I did want to kiss you. And please know this much, Daniel. I truly wanted to marry you, but I can't. You see…" She closed her eyes and took a deep breath before she said, "There is no easy way to say this, so I will simply come out with it. I'm in love with someone else."

His brows furrowed into a frown. His hands slipped from hers as though she burned him. "Who? Who are you in love with? I don't understand. You have made me believe that I—"

"Dominic."

He blanched. "I beg your pardon?"

"I'm in love with Dominic."

His eyes widened in disbelief, then he closed them while expelling an unsteady breath. When he opened them again, they were cold, matching the sardonic smile that tugged at his mouth. "That son of a bitch. He's been sleeping with you the whole time, hasn't he?"

She couldn't deny it and she wouldn't. She would give him that much. "I'm sorry, Daniel."

"All the rumors were true then. I should have known he wouldn't be able to keep his hands off you. But when Rochford told me himself that there was nothing going on, I believed him. And you truly acted like an innocent. Yet I had a suspicion when you kissed me that you were not chaste. Why did you do it? To make him jealous?"

Shame and regret washed over her. "I didn't mean to hurt you. I wanted to tell you before now, but I couldn't."

"That's all well and good now, isn't it? I've already placed a wedding announcement in the paper. I believed you were who you claimed to be! Tell me, are you the daughter of a baron as the dowager and Rochford claim, or are you really the daughter of a commoner and a whore as rumored?"

Her cheeks turned crimson under his accusing glare. When she said nothing, he swore under his breath. "You have made me look a fool."

There was little she could say to make him feel better, she knew that. He had trusted her and she had set him up, knowing all along that things would come to this.

"Is he putting you up in a townhouse like he does his other women? Or will you continue to live like this, hiding away in the country while he beds everything in London?"

He may as well have slapped her—but she deserved it. He curled his lip in disgust; his usually kind eyes narrowed as though the sight of her repulsed him.

"I will be his wife one day," she said, lifting her chin.

His harsh laughter vibrated throughout the room. "If you think he'll marry you, you're even more a fool than I thought. Do you realize how many women have thought they would be the next countess of Rochford, only to be discarded within a few months' time? One came close...within the week of the wedding actually. The wedding was canceled and the intended bride was never heard from again.

"And think about this. Why would he marry a whore's offspring when he could have any number of blue-blooded women at his disposal?"

Biting down hard on her lower lip, she avoided further confrontation and simply stated in a calm voice, "I think we've said enough. It would be best if you leave now."

"I'll put a retraction in the paper at once."

She nodded, jumping when the door slammed behind him.

For long minutes she sat alone, feeling sick to her stomach. He would tell everyone who would listen about her relationship with Dominic.

She might never marry Dominic, but did it matter? She would never wear a wedding ring, and never could she be anything more than his lover, always kept away in a private home, never to share his name. Nor would their children bear his name.

The door opened and closed. A moment later Dominic stood behind her. "Well, he certainly didn't waste any time leaving, now did he? I was cleaning my pistols, certain I would be called out. In fact, I was almost looking forward to it."

Dominic's dismissive manner irritated her. But at the same time she wished she could be so casual when it came to others' feelings.

"It seems I wasn't worth his trouble."

"How can you say that?"

"Because that is the way I feel. I hurt him."

Dominic sighed. "Do you think he is all that he pretended to be? I'm not going to go into it, but suffice it to say, he counted on your dowry to get out from under his father's thumb...the boy detests work of any kind. You would have tired of him before you crossed the Atlantic."

The words made her wince. Daniel didn't want her for the person she was, but rather for what her dowry could bring him. The entire relationship had been based on lies. Daniel would waste no time in telling everyone about she and Dominic. She would be an outcast, banished from Society.

"Don't get me wrong, love. You are the kind of woman that all men desire. But he wouldn't have made you happy."

He embraced her, kissing the top of her head. The masculine scent of him enveloped her and she closed her eyes, wanting to forget about everything but him.

His hands moved over her breasts, his fingers playing with her nipples through the fabric of her gown and for a moment she savored the sensation. Yet she was reminded again of the lies that stood between them, and she pulled his hands out of her gown. Kissing each hand, she turned to meet his guarded stare.

"You asked me once if I would be your mistress."

His eyes lit up instantly. "Yes." His voice was low and sensual.

"Tell me again what it would be like."

He smiled before he kissed her slowly, then passionately. "I'll treat you like a princess. I'll buy you a townhouse with a wonderful view of the Thames, or Hyde Park—anywhere you want, it doesn't matter. I'll come to you every evening and we'll spend our nights, the *entire* night, together. We can go to the ballet, to the opera, anything and anywhere you want to go."

"I want to marry you," she blurted before she could stop herself.

His eyes searched hers, but he said nothing.

"You won't, will you? Tell me, Dominic, is it because I'm the daughter of a whore?"

Her ice-cold hands trembled while she waited for his response. Long minutes passed with his face a mask that showed no emotion. Would he leave her?

"Arlie, don't ask that of me. Not now. I can offer you no more than what I have. It is up to you to take it, or no."

She sighed dejectedly. "Then the answer is yes."

He watched her intently. "Yes...what?"

She brushed her fingers against his lips. "You will have me say it just to hear it from my lips, won't you? Well, fine. Yes, Dominic, I will be your mistress...for as long as that is." It didn't matter that he wouldn't marry her. She just knew life without him would be unbearable.

"You sound so certain things will end between us," he said, kissing her shoulder.

She shook her head. "I'll never leave you, Dominic. Not unless you ask me to."

He smiled triumphantly, pulling her close to him, his lips soft against her own. "There's not a chance in this world that I'll ask you to leave," he whispered, before claiming her mouth once again.

Chapter Fourteen

Dominic's grandmother did not take the news of Arlie's broken engagement very well, or Dominic's declaration that he and Arlie had been and would remain lovers, no matter what she or anyone else said.

After calling Dominic every conceivable name in the book, the dowager countess ordered Dominic and Arlie from Whitley manor.

Visibly shaken by his grandmother's tirade, Arlie had agreed to accompany Dominic to Rochford Manor. He told her that she would stay at the manor until he could find a townhouse—which proved to be far easier than originally anticipated. Knowing that gossip was spreading fast, Dominic toured vacant properties, accompanied by his solicitor, who wrote up the papers on a nice townhouse near Hyde Park and conveniently close to his own.

Dominic ordered Philip MaQuie, a decorator who was all the rage in Paris, to redecorate the townhouse in all the latest styles—and to spare no expense.

Dominic felt that Arlie deserved the luxury. She had given him a happiness he'd thought unattainable until then. He had never known such passion for another person, and if he could, he'd give her the stars.

* * * * *

Arlie was nothing short of stunned at her first glimpse of the townhouse Dominic had bought for her. The brick three-story townhouse with wrought-iron balcony and handrails, sat on a quiet street near Hyde Park. Newly decorated in her favorite shades, the home was everything Arlie could have asked for. She would only be sharing it with Mary, the maid she'd stolen from Rochford Manor, and three servants who would see to her every need. Of course, she would also be sharing the home with Dominic — when he came to visit, which he swore would be often.

Her bedroom, larger than the one at Rochford Manor, had been filled with feminine touches and lots of flowers. The furniture was of a rich mahogany. Arlie opened a drawer and found them stuffed with new underclothes in a variety of lace and silks. She smiled, finding four pairs of breeches and shirts, all in different styles and colors.

On the vanity sat a small velvet box. With trembling hands, Arlie opened the box and gasped at the tear-drop diamond earrings that twinkled back at her.

Arlie spun in circles, finding it hard to believe this would be her home now. Falling back on the soft mattress of the four-poster bed, she ran her hands over the snow-white comforter, and gasped when she caught sight of her reflection in the mirrors above her.

She laughed out loud. Dominic was truly sinful.

When four days had gone by without so much as a letter from Dominic, Arlie grew restless. The separation was pure torture on Arlie, and once she'd even been tempted to ride to Rochford Manor to talk to him herself, but she resisted, knowing how desperate it would appear. She would simply have to wait to hear from him.

It was a Friday morning when she finally received a message that he would be coming to her that night. Taking a long hot bath, she dried her hair by the fire, her body racing with excitement and trepidation as she took great care in her dress.

Arlie realized that being Dominic's mistress would not be so horrible. The hardest thing would be not sharing the same house with him, or just having the knowledge that she would see him every day…if even just in passing.

Now they lived under different roofs, and *both* of them had to trust each other explicitly. Everyone in her household was employed by Dominic, and Arlie knew if she took one wrong step, that the servants, loyal to him, would tell him everything. But she had no desire to stray. Her lover satisfied her in every way. She prayed Dominic felt the same.

Yet, what if he didn't? What if he tired of her, or started seeing Veronica again? She shook her head. She must let go of her fears and trust Dominic, she told herself as she paced the plush carpet of her chamber. Dressed in a short black Chinese robe, one of the many gifts he'd bought for her, her hands moved to her stomach.

She was certain she was pregnant. It had been two months since her last period. At times her menses had been late, but never this late. Although at first she had tried to avoid seeing the signs, she could no longer. Keeping her breakfast down had proven impossible, and her breasts were very sensitive.

What would Dominic say when she told him he would be a father? Would he be upset, or would he be happy? So many thoughts scrambled in her mind that her head hurt.

Her heart jolted hearing the voice of the butler...and Dominic's voice, and then the sound of his boots as he took the stairs two at a time. She willed her heart to cease its pounding, but it was impossible — she was too excited to see him.

Dominic opened the door, then closed it, and leaned back against the dark mahogany. His mouth softened into an irresistibly devastating grin, and his gaze moved slowly down her body, coming to a stop at the tops of her thighs where the skimpy robe stopped. The wicked tilt of his brow said more than words ever could.

Standing before the fire, she slowly untied the robe and let it slide down her body to pool at her feet. His eyes lit up instantly, and he pushed away from the door, walking toward her like a panther stalking its prey.

He took her into his arms, pulling her flush against his hard body, holding her so tight, she could scarcely breathe. "God, how I've missed you."

His words filled Arlie with relief and joy. "I've missed you, too."

He smiled against her mouth before kissing her, his lips first soft and exploring, then harder when she thrust her tongue into his mouth.

Arlie groaned as his hands cupped her sensitive breasts. He rolled the nipple of one between his thumb and forefinger, sending a wave of pleasure straight between her legs.

Needing to feel his skin beneath her fingers, Arlie sank down on her knees, unbuttoned his breeches, and took his already rigid shaft into her mouth. Dominic's hands clasped her shoulders. She could hear his heavy breathing, feel his body tighten as she grew more relaxed, taking him deeper into her mouth.

He groaned low in his throat, his hands moving to her head, anchoring her there. She smiled to herself, while running her fingertips up the backs of his thighs, over his firm buttocks where she squeezed and pulled him tighter to her and took him deeper still. She ran her tongue along the ridge of his penis, sucking hard on the head.

Always it seemed Dominic worried about her pleasure, but tonight would be different—Arlie wanted to give him all that she could.

Her thoughts were cut short as with a growl, he lifted her up into his arms, and tossed her onto the bed. "There will be time later for slow pleasure." He pushed his boots and pants off, then made quick work with his shirt. "But for now I have a great need to be inside you."

She opened up to him and he entered her with a hard thrust. She gasped with elation, the feel of his shaft like heaven. He kissed her, his mouth hard and unrelenting. His smooth thrusts took on a rapid pace, and Arlie wrapped her legs around his waist, taking him further into her body. Her lips traveled over his strong jaw to his ear. Her tongue darted out, laving his earlobe, encircling it. He groaned and drove into her. She gasped as the steady flutters began deep within her, and continued like waves slamming on the shore. He followed close behind.

He looked up at her, grinning. "Can you tell that I've missed you?"

"Yes," she whispered, kissing his cheek. "And I missed you just as much."

He stayed with her until the early morning hours, and as promised, they took it slow. All along Arlie thought she should tell him of the baby, but her new station in his life made her pause. Would he want her still if she grew fat with child, or would he take another lover?

Misgivings began to grow, until finally she put them out of her mind, knowing they served no purpose.

When Arlie opened her eyes again, the blinding sun met her. Immediately she turned to the space beside her to find it empty. Dominic had already left, the only sign he'd been there, the indentation of his body in the sheets and the soreness between her thighs.

She smiled dreamily, remembering every detail of the night just spent. Time and again Dominic had taken her to the heights of passion, and when she thought he was too exhausted, he would surprise her yet again and make love to her. Her lover pleased her in every way.

A knock at the door brought Arlie out of her musings and she sat up, running fingers through her tousled hair. "Come in, Mary," she said, gripping the sheet up under her chin.

"Hello, my lady," Mary said with a wide smile. "His lordship asked me to bring you a hearty breakfast this morning. Did you sleep well?"

"Very well," Arlie replied, not at all embarrassed in front of the maid she had stolen from Dominic's manor. The woman was a bona fide saint—loyal to the end, and she acted more like a mother to Arlie than her own had been.

"He left you a note," Mary said, handing her the ivory parchment.

Like a child at Christmas, Arlie opened the parchment, chewing her lower lip as she read the neat penmanship of her lover.

"Is it good news?" Mary inquired.

"He's taking me to a wedding."

"You don't sound very happy about it."

Glancing out the window, Arlie let the note fall to her lap. "Mary, have you ever loved someone so much, it literally hurt?"

Mary smiled serenely and patted Arlie's hand. "Indeed, I know what you mean. My dearest Johnny was the love of my life. He had pale blonde hair like yours, and marvelous hazel eyes that sparkled with life. He stole my heart when we both worked for the same employer, he as a footman, and myself as a lowly scullery maid. We were engaged to be married, then two days before our wedding day, he was killed."

"Oh, Mary, I'm so sorry," Arlie replied, feeling wretched for having broached the subject.

"You had no way of knowing, my dear. There was a time I couldn't talk about it without crying, but now I can. Time has eased the pain a bit. I loved him so completely, I was sure that when he died, I would too."

"How did you go on?"

She shrugged. "You just do. The first few months were horrible, but as time went by, it became easier. I try to remember the good times. There's not a single day that goes by when I don't think of him." She sighed heavily. "Anyway...about love. I know I'm prejudiced where your lordship is concerned, but you know he'd marry you if he could. And speaking of marriage, we'd best get you ready for the wedding. What time will his lordship be here to pick you up?"

"Four o'clock," Arlie replied, both dreading and looking forward to venturing outside her townhouse, which had served as her sanctuary since becoming Dominic's mistress. Now the time had come and she must face the gossipmongers. Best to get it over with.

"I'll get your bath ready then."

The entire day Arlie spent preparing for the wedding. She took sips of wine to help calm her tattered nerves. As she paced a path in the bedroom, she wondered if she should tell him about the baby? No, that would be all wrong. Especially at a wedding. He would obviously think she was trying to pressure him into marriage.

An hour later she decided to wait for him downstairs. Reading couldn't hold her attention, so tossing the book aside, she sat at the piano and pounded out a minuet.

This morning she had gotten sick again. Within weeks she would be showing. Last night she had been tempted to tell Dominic of the child, but every time she opened her mouth to tell him, she found she could not. Would he think she was trying to trap him? What happened to mistresses who became pregnant? A vision of Dominic parading a new mistress around under her nose came to mind. It turned her stomach.

She closed her eyes, letting the music fill her, soothe her. Why did she have to be so desperately in love with him? He, and he alone had the power to break her. She sighed heavily knowing she was becoming more like her mother every day.

* * * * *

Dominic heard Arlie playing the piano the moment he entered the townhouse. He smiled as he strode toward the double doors of the parlor. The music grew louder, almost thunderous. He sobered. She was in a mood it would seem. Quietly opening the door, he closed it behind him and watched, entranced by the sight.

As always when she played, her eyes were closed, her head moving in time to the music as though it took over her body. Her diamond earrings stirred with the movement. His smile quickly disappeared, however, when he saw the stream of tears running down her cheeks. His heart lurched. What had made her so upset, he wondered as he walked toward her, feeling the urge to comfort her—and do serious damage to the person who caused her this grief.

He was but a few feet away and still she did not see him. An angel, her perfect features so fragile...and she was his. He reached out to her, the backs of his fingers lightly grazing her smooth cheek, wiping the tears from them.

Startled, she jumped and the notes ended abruptly. She pressed her hands to her heart. "Dominic, you startled me!"

"I didn't mean to," he said wiping the rest of the tears from her cheeks. "Why are you crying?"

"I was thinking of my father and my mother, of you...of me."

"And this makes you sad?"

She shook her head. "No, you make me very happy."

He smiled, surprised at how relieved he was to hear those words. "Good...now enough tears. Come, let me see you." Helping her up, he stared appreciatively at the ice blue gown which had cost him a small fortune, but was worth every shilling.

Her smile was a combination of innocence and practiced seduction, and he was hard-pressed to find the reasons to make his friend's wedding.

"My dear, I would take you to bed right now, but I fear Langley would be knocking down our door, and we shouldn't cause so much scandal in one week, now should we?"

She smiled at his jest, and he was thankful she could handle the rumors that had been circulating. As he helped her into the carriage, he knew firsthand that some mistresses became nearly inconsolable when gossipmongers started their abuse. Yet Arlie had not asked him for a single thing. Everything he bought her was on a whim, and it seemed no matter where he went, something made him think of her. He enjoyed seeing the raw pleasure on her face as she opened his gifts. She was so unspoiled.

Since she moved into the townhouse, his fears had been eased knowing she truly belonged to him. He'd intentionally waited days before visiting her that first time, mainly because his duties required his full attention, but also to see how much control she had over him. He intended to wait even longer, but he couldn't stay away from the woman who had imprisoned his heart and mind.

Everyone knew of their relationship now, yet he couldn't help but yearn for the days when they lived under the same roof, when he only had to walk down the hall to see her. Now he had to venture into London daily, and there were always people watching. But he only had himself to blame. His own indiscretion had got to them, and the games they had played with Mr. Butler, who had informed anyone who would listen about their heated affair. As to be expected, he and his mistress were now all the rage.

In the carriage, Dominic noticed Arlie was preoccupied, spending the majority of the time staring out the window, and answering his vain attempt at conversation with a quick reply. The night past had been heavenly, but perhaps she suffered from lack of sleep. Or perhaps she had tired of her position as mistress already? Granted, it wasn't a difficult life, yet at the same time it could be lonely. Though she had been invited to a few tea parties by his closest friends, Mary told him that Arlie never went out, instead she chose to stay within the sanctuary of the townhouse reading, writing, or playing the piano, always waiting for his arrival.

As they entered the tree-lined drive of Langley's estate, Dominic put all negative thoughts from his mind, telling himself he would enjoy this day.

"It looks like a carnival with those huge white tents," Arlie said, a sudden smile on her face easing his fears.

"Indeed, it does. And what fun it shall be."

She flashed him a skeptical smile, obviously catching his forced enthusiasm.

As Dominic entered the hall with Arlie on his arm, he could literally feel the excitement of the hundreds of guests that milled about. Arlie's hand tensed within his and he patted it, and smiled reassuringly. "All will be fine," he said, a moment before he spotted his grandmother in the corner, her piercing gaze riveting him. Her expression was not friendly in the least. He knew how she felt about his and Arlie's relationship. He also knew that she would hold this "family scandal" over his head for the rest of his life.

Dominic let out a defeated sigh, and led Arlie over to his grandmother — feeling as though he was leading a lamb to slaughter.

"Dom, it's good to see you."

Dominic could feel Arlie stiffen at his side. He glanced at her and saw two bright spots of color on her cheeks.

"Miss Whitman, how are you faring?" the dowager asked, her brow lifted high.

"I'm well, thank you for asking," Arlie replied.

"I thought that I might come visit you at Rochford Manor, Dominic," his grandmother said, surprising him. Not once since his father's death had his grandmother bothered to visit, and the thought that she wanted to now made him suspicious.

"You are always welcome to visit," he said, hoping he at least sounded sincere. "Well, I'm certain Langley is wondering where I am. We must be going now, Grandmother. I will speak to you later, I'm sure."

"You can count on it," she replied with a thin smile.

"She hates me," Arlie whispered, fanning herself vigorously. "It's distressing, because I'm so fond of her.

And…everyone is staring at us, Dominic. I think perhaps it was a mistake that I came with you. Maybe I should leave."

He stopped abruptly. Lifting her chin with gentle fingers, he kissed her softly and hid a smile when he heard the gasps all around them, his grandmother's leading the way. "My grandmother dislikes most everyone, and the only reason she's angry is because we've scandalized the Rochford name. She must forget that my father has done more to disgrace the family name than I ever could. Perhaps that in itself is the reason she cannot stand me.

"If they don't like it, then the hell with them. Now, my best friend is about to get married, and I have the bride's ring. I would like you to be here, but if you feel you cannot bear it, then I will walk you to the carriage, and I can meet you at the townhouse later."

Dominic saw a mixture of hesitation and determination in her eyes. She smiled softly. "I love weddings. And since I am fond of Langley —"

"You are *fond* of him?" He frowned. "How fond?"

She lifted a delicate brow. "Fond enough. Now come, or we'll be late."

He knew she toyed with him, yet he hated the jealousy he felt from something meant to be a joke. What if Arlie did become *fond* of another man? Sure, he had bought her clothes, bought her a townhouse, and kept her in jewels, but was that enough? Any man of means could do the same, a few could do one better and even marry her — like Daniel, who just so happened to be staring at he and Arlie. Standing with a striking brunette, the younger man's smile faded as their gazes locked. Despite his effort to forget the occasion, Dominic remembered the American and Arlie kissing in the garden at Whitley.

Dominic pushed the image away and seated Arlie beside Langley's family. Langley's aunt welcomed her with open arms, but the rest ignored her.

Arlie watched Dominic head toward the bridegroom and the rest of the wedding party. She ignored the stares directed at her, focusing instead on the beauty around her; the flowers, the music...the bride who looked splendid in cream silk and lace. Langley's wife, Rose, though no slim beauty, had a riot of auburn curls, a charming smile and a wonderful Irish accent that was easy on the ears. When she laughed, it sounded like music.

While the couple spoke their vows, Arlie watched Dominic. How handsome he was in his black tailcoat and Cossack trousers, the white of his shirt emphasizing his dark good looks. Not a woman around didn't covet the man, and Arlie felt a rush of sheer pleasure knowing she held a special place in his life.

For a brief moment Arlie envisioned herself up at the altar, Dominic at her side, exchanging vows that would bind them together forever. How wonderful it would be to know he was hers until the end of time. Her hand instinctively moved to her still flat stomach. At least she'd always have a part of him, no matter what happened.

Putting all negative thoughts aside, she instead let her mind drift to the baby. What would he or she look like? Would the baby have dark hair and blue eyes, or blonde hair and green eyes, or perhaps a combination? She realized she truly didn't care—just as long as the baby was healthy.

When the priest pronounced Langley and Rose man and wife, the couple kissed and a cheer rang out over the vast hall. Finally, when the hall had cleared, she made her way out just in time to catch sight of Dominic, looking tall and splendid, and far too cozy, as he lifted a beautiful redhead's hand to his lips.

"Miss Whitman."

Arlie turned to find Dominic's grandmother standing behind her, leaning heavily on her cane. "Could I have a word with you?" she queried. Before Arlie could reply, the dowager was already walking toward an adjoining room.

Glancing over her shoulder, Arlie saw Dominic still heavy in conversation with the pretty redhead. Seeing she would get no help from that quarter, she followed the dowager and sat down.

"I understand my grandson has set you up in style." Her brow lifted, her voice condescending, as though she and Arlie hadn't shared a rare friendship just weeks before. "I will not mince words. I thought you were different, Arlie. I thought that you would want a man who would, at the very least, marry you. Dom will never marry you. I know him as well as I know myself. He is just like his father, and the only reason he married was because I forced him to. Dominic's mother was a good woman, and she truly did love my son. Unfortunately, he could never be faithful to her and in the end it killed her. I would hate to see the same happen to you."

Arlie's cheeks burned. "I know you're disappointed in us, but I love your grandson with all of my heart."

The dowager shook her head. "What happened to that girl with dreams of a wonderful future? You promised me a day not so long ago that you would never let a man use you, but look at you, Arlie. That is exactly what you have done. You have let him have his way with you, and where will you be when he tires of you?"

"He will not leave me."

The dowager laughed cruelly. "You are so young, Arlie. You know nothing of the world. Dominic is content at the moment, but how long will that last? How long do any of his relationships last? And when it is over and he is no longer paying your bills, where will you be? I'll tell you where. You'll be out on the streets, looking for another man of means that will take you in and pay your bills. I dare say Miss Whitman, you will end up just as your mother did."

Arlie flinched. She didn't like the reference to her mother. Arlie loved Dominic deeply. Her mother didn't know what the word love meant, and had looked for it in the arms of many men. But with Dominic, Arlie knew what she felt was true love. The dowager smiled sadly. "One day he will marry, Arlie, and there will be nothing that you can do about it. You will be his mistress for a time, but you will *never* experience what it is to walk down the aisle with him, or to wake up in his bed every morning."

Feeling light-headed under the onslaught, Arlie asked, "Why are you saying this?"

"Because you deserve much more than what you've settled for. You are a good woman and deserving of a man who will marry you and give you sons and daughters. But that man is not my grandson. I know him too well. And I know you as well. Will you truly be happy being the other woman? Will you be complete just sitting by waiting for him to come to you, waiting while he is doing his duty to his family?"

Arlie knew exactly what the dowager implied, and the image hurt terribly, especially now that Arlie was pregnant with Dominic's child. It was on the tip of her tongue to tell the dowager that she carried the Rochford heir, but she couldn't bring herself to say the words, for fear of what the response may be.

"Leave him, Arlie. Release him."

Leave him? "I will never leave him...not ever. I don't care if he's married to the Queen, I will still be in my townhouse every night, waiting for him to come to me. And when he does, I will love him so completely that he will be hard-pressed not to stay with me."

"Grandmother, what are you doing, or need I ask?" Dominic asked, taking Arlie's hand in his own.

"I was just asking how things were going for Miss Whitman. It sounds as though you've taken good care of her — as you take care of all your women."

"Grandmother, you are ever the charming one, and as much as I'd like to prolong our visit, we need to take our leave now. I bid you good day."

They spent the next few hours in light-hearted conversation, and Arlie tried in earnest to have a good time. But try as she might, the dowager's taunting words came back to haunt her time and again. She began to feel as though this was the beginning of the end.

Seeing Daniel made her wonder what would have happened had she took a different course and not broken off the engagement. She would still be engaged to Daniel, but living under Dominic's roof and sharing his bed. In all, it was better this way. At least she was being honest with herself and not hurting anyone else in the process.

Daniel had been pleasant enough, speaking with her briefly, trying to make it look to everyone that all was well, even though she sensed an underlying resentment. But she couldn't very well blame him. His pleasant manner was more than she could have hoped for.

Once they were back at the townhouse, Arlie let Dominic lead her to the silk-covered bed. As Arlie undressed slowly, Dominic lay on the bed and devoured her with his heated gaze. She loved the power she had over him, and realized with a pang it was the only time she had control of their relationship. She was a puppet on a string when it came to the rest, and in that she was content because she loved him.

She crawled onto the bed, and with a wicked smile, slowly pulled the pants off of him. Kissing first his toes, then his knee, then his thigh. His penis was engorged, pulsing and throbbing. She took the glorious length into her mouth, rolling her tongue over the smooth head, loving the feel of him, the taste of him. His shaft jerked beneath her ministrations and she took him further into her mouth, moving up and down his length until he panted.

Her stomach that had been in knots all day began to relax as another emotion took hold, making her warm all over. She pressed her legs together so great was the need to feel him inside her. But she wanted to satisfy him, knowing one day soon he would be sharing his bed with another.

She kissed his stomach, his chest, and then straddled him, his huge shaft rearing between their bodies. His hands cupped her breasts while his gaze shifted to his penis, then back to her face. She knew what he wanted, and she wanted it too. She leaned over him, pressing her mons over his erection. He sucked in his breath and she kissed him. His hips came up off the bed, and she impaled herself upon him. He sat up enough to take a nipple into his mouth, teasing it with teeth and tongue. She increased the pace, riding him until her body clenched around him, bringing them both to climax.

Chapter Fifteen

Dominic knew his grandmother would not lose a battle with finesse. On the contrary, rumor had it that she would go to any length to get what she wanted.

That thought was uppermost in his mind when he arrived that morning at her townhouse having read her urgent request. The last time he'd received such a message, his father had been killed in a hunting accident. Now, he wondered if his grandmother had fallen ill. But as he entered the parlor, he found her in perfect health.

"Grandmother, what is this about?" he asked, holding onto what little control of his temper he had left.

She took a deep breath, then with a smile replied, "It is time for you to produce an heir."

Dominic headed back toward the door, when her voice stopped him. "I know you have never looked upon the union of marriage with glee, but you must procure an heir for the Rochford dynasty. You yourself know that if something happened to you, those nitwit cousins of yours would take over, and Lord knows every ancestor of ours would be rolling over in their graves."

Dominic turned to face her. He retraced his steps until he stood before her. "All my life I have strived to please you, to no avail. As a young man I told you my wishes were to simply be left alone."

"And I have done that."

"To a point," he replied, taking a deep breath. "I understand that you wish me to take a wife in order for me to have sons who will inherit, but I must ask you to stop this nonsense. If I must find a wife, let me do it. I alone will pick, not you. I will ask that you leave me to make my own judgments. After all, I keep the family business running, and I do my fair share in the name of Rochford. In fact, I would ask that you relieve yourself of this silly idea of me marrying and let us continue our relationship as things have always been. Let nature takes its course, and in time I will marry."

She shrugged. "I simply want an heir—a legitimate one."

"I wonder, Grandmother, if you do this only because you know that I have never been happier than I am now."

Her immediate smile proved he was right.

"You're in love, aren't you, Dom?" she laughed loudly. "You love Arlie and you would do anything for her, save marry her. And you know deep in your heart that you would love to marry her, even though you don't trust yourself enough to. You know you could never be faithful, because you are just like that bastard who sired you." She tapped her fingernails against the wood of the chair and stared at him without blinking.

When he didn't reply, she shook her head. "Well, dear boy, it matters not, because you have no choice. The deed is done and I have helped you in your quest. Lady Katerina is expecting you at her Paris estate the first of next week. I'm not saying that you have to marry her; I'm just asking you to consider her. She is the daughter of a duke and very sought after."

As his grandmother continued her rambling, Dominic knew that she would stop at nothing to see him married off. His insides churned at the thought of taking a wife, especially when his heart belonged to Arlie.

* * * * *

Just a few days before Christmas there came a knock at Arlie's front door. Dominic had left for Paris on business just that morning, Mary was out, and the few servants left in the house were busy working in the kitchen.

Opening the door, Arlie tried to hide her surprise seeing Daniel standing on the steps, shivering from the cold. She hesitated, uncertain why he would come visit.

"Miss Whitman," he said, brushing snow off his jacket. "It is rather brisk out here."

"Do come in," she replied, taking his coat and hat.

"I realize I should have sent word first, but I came on a whim."

"I am delighted to see you," she said, ushering him toward the parlor. She lifted the bell to order tea, when Daniel stopped her, his hand squeezing hers.

"I've come as a friend, Miss Whitman."

The urgent tone of his voice alone made the breath catch in her throat. He quickly removed his hand from hers and took a seat. "There is a rumor spreading fast, and I dare say it is quite shocking...and I suppose I wanted confirmation."

She was past the point of letting idle gossip get her down, but he had piqued her interest. "Certainly. What is it, Daniel?"

"Well, I've heard it on good authority that Rochford is engaged."

Arlie laughed halfheartedly. "That is ridiculous."

He frowned. "Is it really?"

"It's absurd," she said, her voice dropping to a mere whisper, when she saw the knowing look in his eye. Her stomach instantly clenched in a knot, but she told herself to not take anything to heart.

"You don't know, do you? That bastard! Rochford is engaged to Katerina Derpeu the daughter of a duke. She is a classic beauty, and most sought after in her homeland. I've heard that he is with her now, at Katerina's Paris home, going over the wedding details."

Arlie felt the blood drain from her face. That very morning Dominic had left, saying he had "business" in Paris. Now she knew what her mother must have felt when the same had happened to her. "I didn't know," she said, feeling stupid and defeated.

Daniel took her hand in his and squeezed it tight. "Dearest Arlie, how could you? He keeps you locked up day in and day out, while he's out cavorting with his fiancée, and Lord knows who else."

Disbelief washed over her, imagining Dominic with his lovely French fiancée. She was no doubt as stunning as Daniel said, probably even more so. And very sought after. Leave it to Dominic to snatch a woman that every man wanted.

No wonder he had been so quiet these last few days, talking about unsavory business he must attend to. Each night he would take her with an urgency she had thought was love. Soon he would be sharing his bed with another woman, and he would have no use for her. And what of her child? Still she had not told him…and now it was too late.

"You look unwell."

She glanced up to find Daniel watching her with a quizzical, almost satisfied expression. No doubt he was enjoying himself immensely, probably feeling it was exact revenge on her for humiliating him. Anger rippled along her spine.

"I do feel unwell."

"Can I do anything?"

"No, you have done enough by telling me. Thank you for your friendship," she managed to reply. "I know I'm undeserving of it, especially after all I've done to you. I hope that I can repay you someday."

"You can," she thought she heard him say, but wasn't sure when he cleared his throat a moment later and excused himself.

Hours later she still sat in the same seat, staring out the window as night descended. Where was Dominic now, she wondered? With his fiancée, preparing for a long night of social functions, balls, soirees, where they would mingle arm in arm among the other blue-bloods of society?

Yet, what if Daniel had lied? What if Dominic really wasn't engaged and Daniel had only told her this to get back at her? But, how could she know for sure?

She straightened. There was only one way to find out.

* * * * *

As Arlie approached Langley's estate, she sat forward in the carriage seat, her nails biting into her palms. Twice already she'd almost asked the footman to turn the coach around, but instead she'd strengthened her resolve and walked into Langley's home with a false smile on her face.

Arlie noticed instantly how happy Langley appeared. His contentment with Rose surprised her, especially since he had told her he planned on taking a mistress. Did he have a woman on the side, she wondered. He sat there looking happy and content with Rose, but was there another woman waiting for him?

Dominic had once mentioned that Langley did not look kindly on marriage and had done it only for the money, yet as she watched Langley watching his wife, Arlie wondered if he'd found love. Would the same thing happen to Dominic? Would he fall in love with his beautiful bride?

The thought made her feel like someone had stuck a blade between her ribs.

"Arlie, what a pleasure. Dominic stopped by this morning on his way to Paris and said you were unwell. I would hope that is no longer the case."

Dominic had noticed her morning sickness, which had worsened since last week. "I am fine," she replied, feeling suddenly foolish for being there, but needing to know the truth. Before she lost her courage, she blurted, "I came to ask a question, and despite your friendship with Dominic, I would hope you can answer me truthfully."

He sat up straight, his expression all business. "Certainly."

Arlie took a deep breath. "Is Dominic engaged to be married?"

She had her answer the moment Langley quickly glanced in his wife's direction. "Darling, would you mind if Miss Whitman and I had a moment alone?"

Rose nodded and left the room.

"Arlie, you know Dominic would never hurt you."

"So...it *is* true."

"I cannot deny it."

The pain was so acute, she felt she would die from it. Swallowing past the tears that clogged her throat, she asked, "Why wouldn't he tell me, Langley? Why would he have me find out this way?"

Langley shook his head. "It has all happened so very fast for him. I know he has planned to tell you, but he probably could not find the right moment. He adores you, Arlie. I've never seen him so happy."

"So he leaves for Paris to be with his fiancée, while his mistress stays behind in London having no idea what is happening." She ran trembling hands down her face, her gaze moving to the liquor cabinet just beyond Langley's shoulder. What she wouldn't give to get blissfully drunk, yet she had the baby to think about. The baby...a constant reminder of Dominic.

"What will you do?"

She saw the pity in his eyes and hated it. This is what happened to all kept women eventually. It was just coming sooner for her than expected.

"What can I do? I told him I would never leave, and I have no desire to, yet I have no desire to share him either."

Langley lifted both brows, but said nothing. She would receive no sympathy from anyone. This simply happened to her kind. Her kind...she *had* become her mother.

She let out an exasperated breath. "Why does love have to hurt so much, Langley? I love Dominic desperately, yet I cannot have him. Someone else will get to share his bed, his life, his name. She will get the acknowledgement, and I will get whatever is left over. And I will take it like scraps from a noonday meal, and be happy for it."

He lifted her chin with his fingers. "Dearest Arlie, Dom loves you. You know that as much as I do. And though he may take a wife, it will be in name only. Certainly he will do his duty, but you are his wife in his heart. If he could, it would be you he takes to the altar and not Katerina."

Katerina. Unwanted images came to mind. Different faces, body features, all of them beautiful. Arlie stood abruptly, the room spinning for a moment as a wave of dizziness washed over her.

Langley was there to steady her. "Are you all right? Perhaps you should stay over."

Arlie shook her head, feeling the urge to run. "I must go. I thank you for being honest with me."

His brow furrowed with concern. "You deserve honesty, at the very least."

Arlie left Langley's in even worse spirits than she had arrived.

The following morning, she woke from a fitful sleep resolved to move on. After all, despite what Langley said, Dominic didn't love her. *How could he?*

As the week continued, rather than go into mourning, Arlie decided the best course of action would be to do the opposite of what everyone expected her to. She rode every day despite the cold temperatures. She visited friends, mostly Langley and his lovely wife, Rose, who became a good confidante to her. Feeling daring, she'd even ridden to Rochford Manor. She stood outside the iron gates, remembering when she had arrived not so long ago, a young girl with fanciful dreams. Never in her worst nightmare could she have imagined this ending.

Staring at the manor, she recalled the days she and Dominic had slept, lived and loved under the same roof. Now someone else would be there, snug in his bed, while she was in London, hoping he'd come to her.

She knew she could leave and save herself the misery of having to confront him. Always she could return to Wales and raise her child. There would be any number of men who would take her to wife and raise the baby as their own. But the thought left her sick at heart, knowing she would be miserable, and it would be unfair to the man when she was so in love with another.

She chose to stay in London for now, even though Dominic had hurt her more in a shorter space of time than anyone in her entire life.

* * * * *

Having received Langley's urgent letter about Arlie's visit, Dominic's heart raced as he bounded up the steps of her townhouse.

Langley had gone into full account of their meeting, saying Arlie had been terribly distraught by the news he was to marry. In fact, she nearly had fainted, something Arlie did not do.

Mary jumped seeing him standing in the hall, brushing the snow from his lapel.

"Where is she?" Dominic asked, letting her take his jacket and hat.

"Well, my lord, she went to the theater, I believe."

He lifted a brow. "The theater? She went alone?"

Mary looked hesitant to say anything further, but with a dejected sigh, she replied, "No, my lord. She went with Mr. Butler."

The name he hated most of all. That single name conjured up unwanted images of Arlie and the young man standing hand in hand, her sweet laughter, adoring smiles, and passionate kiss as the two clung together in the garden at Whitley. The blood roared in his ears. Had she slept with Daniel after having heard of his engagement to Katerina? "When did they leave?" he asked, his voice clipped despite his effort to remain calm.

"Some time ago. In fact, I would think she'd be home any time."

"Then I will wait," he said with a forced smile. "Could you get me a brandy? I'll be in the study. Oh, and Mary, please let me know immediately when your mistress has arrived."

"Indeed, I will, my lord," she said with a quick smile, making him wonder how much the woman really knew.

The minutes ticked away, seeming more like hours, and with it visions of Arlie and the good-looking American kept coming to mind. What was she doing with the man? Hadn't he made it clear to her in the beginning that she belonged to him and no other?

He took another drink from the bottle, having foregone the glass some time ago. The liquor warmed his stomach and fired his already burning temper. By the time Dominic heard the front door open, he was furious.

But he was unprepared for the sight of her. With drops of snow clinging to her beautiful pale hair, her cheeks pink, and her green eyes twinkling, he almost forgot about his anger.

"Dominic?" she gasped, her smile faltering for a moment. "I thought you were in Paris."

He let out the breath he'd been holding. "Obviously. Is that why you went out with Mr. Butler?"

He saw it then. Her brows lifted, as did her chin. She was ready to fight. "I went out with Mr. Butler...as a friend."

"And I've no doubt Mr. Butler acted as a friend."

"Despite your sarcasm, Daniel was a true gentleman...as always."

Dominic walked toward her, stopping mere inches from her. She stared up at him, her eyes holding a challenge.

"I don't want you seeing him."

"Well, there are some things that can't be helped."

"Such as?"

"You getting married…and me seeing other men."

He saw the fury in her eyes and knew she wasn't bluffing. Never in his life had he been so enraged. Clenching his fists at his sides, he said in a steady voice, "I should have told you about Katerina, I know that, yet at the time I couldn't. I knew how devastating it would be. I wanted to save you the pain."

"So hearing you're going to be married rumored about town wasn't supposed to hurt me? God, Dominic, you can't know the hell I went through when I heard. How would you have me feel? I hate it! I hate the fact that another woman will share your name, your home, your bed, your children. I hate everything about her and I don't even know her. You have no idea how much it hurts!"

She blinked back tears and his anger instantly evaporated. "That's where you're wrong, Arlie. I *do* know. I felt that way when you were engaged to Daniel. I felt it when I heard you were with him tonight. Arlie, don't you know how much I love you?"

Her brows furrowed into a frown as she looked up at him, her mouth slightly open. "What did you say?"

He smiled as he claimed her lips, kissing her softly at first, then urgently with all the passion, fear and love that had been pent-up for far too long. "I love you, Arlie," he said, never so sure of anything in his life.

Instantly she rewarded him with a smile. "Dominic, I love you, too."

Lifting her in his arms, he took the stairs two at a time, and coming to her room kicked open the door, uncaring that it splintered the wood.

When he had her on the bed, he stripped her of her clothes and stood staring at her. Blood filled his cock, knowing soon he would be within her tight warmth.

Ripping off his clothes, he settled between her legs, too desperate to be inside her to seek slow pleasure. He kissed her, his hands straying to her breasts, the tight nipples thrusting against his palms. It suddenly occurred to him that her breasts were larger, more than the handful they usually were. A nagging began in the back of his mind, and he let his hand wander lower over her ribs, to the soft swell of her stomach that was firm, but obviously round with child. His heart missed a beat as he rolled off her for a moment, staring down at her face, then letting his gaze move down her body and up again. "You're pregnant, aren't you?"

Her eyes widened in alarm, but she didn't deny it.

Oddly, the news was not at all unpleasant to him, a man who never gave much thought to children—except on how to prevent them. "How long have you known?" he asked, resting his head on his elbow.

"Four weeks now," she whispered, her voice wary.

He bent and kissed her breast, his tongue swirling around the hard nipple before trailing down her stomach where his tongue circled her navel. "And why didn't you tell me?"

"Because...because I was worried."

He went lower still. Smelling the musky scent of her, he spread her legs open and kissed her there, licking her soft folds and teasing her pleasure pearl until she writhed beneath him. A moment later he felt the beginning of her climax and left her just shy of fulfillment. He worked his way back up, wanting her to need him as desperately as he needed her. "Why were you so worried?" he asked before taking a nipple into his mouth.

She arched against him. "I thought you wouldn't want me any more. I worried that you would find another."

"You don't know me very well then."

"But..."

He placed a finger to her lips, then replaced it with his mouth. Unable to restrain himself any longer, he thrust within her. He groaned, holding himself steady as he savored the feel of being inside her honeyed warmth.

Their mating was fast and furious, like lovers kept away from each other for far too long. On the brink of climax he looked at her. Her eyes were dark with passion, her mouth open as he thrust in her time and again. "Come for me, Arlie."

He lifted her hips and ground into her hard, and she cried out his name on a sob as her sheath clenched him tight. With another thrust, he came with a ferocity that left him trembling.

And afterward, she lay beside him, her eyes closed, her head on his shoulder, looking the very picture of contentment. He pulled her closer and smiled as she threw her leg over his.

"I was certain you had left me," he said, putting a stray lock of pale blonde hair behind her ear.

She opened her eyes, her brows furrowed into a frown. "Why would you think that?"

"Langley wrote me and said you came to him the other night and were quite distraught. I imagined all sorts of terrible things."

"I *am* terribly distraught."

"So distraught you went out with Daniel?"

"Dominic, you are to marry another. Certainly me going to the theater with another man cannot compare with marriage? It's not like I am marrying Daniel."

His finger moved over her eyelids, down her pert little nose, to her full lips. "No, my love—and you will never marry him."

She sat up, leaning on her elbow. "Are you telling me I may never marry, yet you can?"

He smiled, seeing he'd hit a nerve. "You can marry…"

Her brows furrowed. "But you just said—"

He kissed her, cutting her off. "You can marry me…but only me."

She pulled away, her mouth open as she searched his face, obviously looking for signs that he was joking.

He'd known when he'd left for Paris that he had no intention of marrying Katerina. When he'd received Langley's message that Arlie had come seeking the truth of his rumored engagement, he'd just given his betrothed the bad news. Katerina had cried her eyes out, while his grandmother remained uncharacteristically silent.

Never had he felt lighter than when he'd walked away, not caring if he had his title, his lands, or his inheritance. He only cared that he had Arlie.

"Well?"

"Well, what?" she asked, beaming with happiness.

"Will you marry me?"

She laughed with delight. "Yes, I will marry you."

"We will be poor."

She kissed him passionately, surprising him more. "Dominic, I don't care, just as long as I have you."

For a man who had been coveted for his title and money, the words meant more to him than she would ever know.

Epilogue

Dressed in her mother's simple cream-colored wedding gown, Arlie marched down the aisle in front of a group of twenty friends and family, including Dominic's grandmother, who smiled radiantly. The dowager Countess had been ecstatic from the time she learned the news that Dominic and Arlie were to marry. Though she never confessed to it, Arlie had the distinct impression that it had been the dowager's intention to bring them together all along.

Knowing a Rochford heir was on the way only added to the dowager's glee. Arlie and Dominic's grandmother spent hours talking about the future, and even the past. Arlie hoped that one day the dowager would be able to bury her disappointment in her son once and for all. The dowager also apologized to Dominic for having treated him so horribly over the years. She had told him she had let her resentment of her son affect her judgment.

Dominic had readily forgiven his grandmother, and even asked her for forgiveness for not being the type of grandson he should have been. They planned to spend much more time together, to repair the damage that had been done throughout the long years of estrangement.

Word of the marriage leaked. Though many gossiped about them behind fans and parlor doors, Arlie knew by the barrage of invitations they had received that society wasn't about to let them become outcasts just yet.

Arlie's heart beat an unsteady rhythm as she stared at Dominic, who looked devastatingly handsome dressed in black, save for the white shirt that matched his smile.

Her black prince. Her husband.

Langley handed her over to Dominic, placing a chaste kiss on her cheek. "Keep him in line," he said with a devil-may-care smile.

"You can count on it," she replied, before taking Dominic's hand.

"You look lovely," Dominic whispered.

"As do you," she replied, feeling the heat of his stare clear to her toes. This sinfully handsome man would be her husband. She would share his name, his home, his child, his life. This was the happiest moment of her life.

As she spoke her vows, Arlie wished her father were here to see her happiness. Though he wasn't alive to share this day, she had a feeling he watched from heaven, pleased that his ultimate plan had worked so well. After all, why else would he have entrusted her to a complete stranger, other than the hope of having him see to her future? And Dominic had seen to her future — firsthand.

They held the reception at a private hotel, rather than the manor which already swarmed with well-wishers. Dancing with Langley, Arlie caught sight of her husband talking with a gorgeous brunette. Seeing her watching him, he smiled deviously.

"Now you see what you've gotten yourself into?" Langley asked, his smile playful as he winked at his friend while pulling Arlie close against him. "Does he think he is the only one who can play such games?"

"It appears so, since he's coming this way," she said, a second before Dominic tapped none-to-gently on Langley's shoulder.

"Excuse me, sir, but you're looking a little too comfortable with my wife."

Langley looked at him with mock surprise. "It seems we've been found out." Kissing Arlie's cheek, he left them.

"When do you want to leave?" Dominic asked, his blue eyes sparkling devilishly.

She lifted a brow. "How about now?"

"Now I know why I love you so much," he said, sweeping her up into his arms, leaving their shocked guests looking after them.

That evening as Arlie lay in her husband's arms, having been loved well, she realized how perfect her life had become.

"I love you, Lady Rochford," Dominic said, kissing her already swollen lips.

She smiled against his mouth. "I love you, too, my husband."

"I can hardly wait until our son is born."

"Who says it is to be a son?" she asked, sitting up on her elbow.

He played with a lock of her hair, twisting it around his finger. "If it is a girl, I have this vision of a lovely young woman with blonde hair and green eyes, who wears breeches and rides astride, and who has every man in town—" He stopped abruptly and frowned. "On second thought, I don't want to think about it."

"And what of a son? I'm sure you don't mind if he is a rakehell of the worse sort, just like his father." She smiled, but it faded as she saw the playfulness leave his features.

He grew quiet, making her want to take back her words, but when he looked into her eyes again, he smiled softly. "Yes, he will be like his father. He will find a woman he loves more than life itself and make her a wonderful, *faithful* husband."

KIERAN THE BLACK

Preview

Prologue

Kieran the Black was a notorious Norman Knight, who rumor has it, decapitated the heads of three Saxon soldiers with a single swipe of his sword — a sword that measured six and a half feet in size — the very height of the great warrior himself.

Six and a half feet! Lizzie smiled to herself and turned up the volume on the "audio tour" she had rented at the exhibition's front desk.

She, along with a dozen other journalists, had gained entrance into the coveted William the Conqueror exhibition two days before its scheduled opening to the public. Because she was a lover of all things medieval, and a member of the Society of Creative Anachronism (SCA), this assignment had been right up Lizzie's alley, and she'd jumped at the chance to attend.

Now, standing before the relics of the ultimate warrior, Kieran the Black, Lizzie's heart gave a jolt. What would it have been like to be alive in the days of men like Kieran D'Arcy — when men were six and a half feet tall, and built like brick shithouses?

"Born 1036. Died 1067. You were only thirty-one," Lizzie

said aloud, resisting the urge to run a finger over the fine gothic carving of the warrior's name on the marble plaque. Something about the Norman knight stirred her soul. Perhaps because at the age of seven he had left his impoverished family to serve as page to a ruthless knight who had physically and verbally abused him. Maybe that abuse had turned Kieran's heart black, earning him the name Kieran the Black. Maybe it had given him a warrior's mentality — kill or be killed.

"Would you like to see it?"

Startled, Lizzie turned to find an old woman with frizzy white hair and enormous blue eyes standing at her side. She took off the earphones. "Sorry?"

"Would you like to see it?" The old woman nodded toward the sword encased in one-inch thick glass. "The Black One's sword."

Lizzie glanced over her shoulder. Seeing no one else about, she turned back to the woman who wore a somber black suit and crisp white blouse — similar to the employee uniforms of the exhibit hall. "Do you work here?"

The woman smiled and pushed on the glass. The side popped open on invisible hinges. Lizzie lifted her brows but remained silent as the tiny woman lifted the battle-scarred sword with little effort and put it into her suddenly damp hands.

Lizzie faltered, but held fast. The sword was heavy. So heavy, it nearly brought her to her knees, and she stood five feet, six inches tall. The woman beside her couldn't be five foot even and she had managed the sword with one hand.

Lizzie could not believe her good fortune. She wanted more

than anything to have the woman take a picture of her with the treasured piece, but didn't dare ask for fear of someone seeing the flash of the camera. With her luck the exhibit hall would somehow get a hold of the photo and she and her magazine would be banned from the UK.

The woman looked directly at Lizzie, her expression serious. "The Black One was not the bad man they make him out to be."

Lizzie nodded. "I know he wasn't bad. He couldn't help what he became."

"He was a product of his time. A mercenary who lived and died by the sword."

"That's so odd that you say that. I was just thinking the same thing. He was very much a product of his time. Oh, and then to be betrayed by his best friend. Now that is wrong on so many levels." The sword felt warm in Lizzie's hands, and with every passing second grew warmer.

The woman laughed lightly. "You know of The Black One then?"

Lizzie grinned, excited to have found someone who shared her enthusiasm for the knight. "Yeah, he fascinates me. I can't explain it, but—"

"There is a rumor that if you hold the sword in your hands

like so," the woman placed her hands over Lizzie's, "And rest

the point of the sword on the edge of any version of Kieran's

crest—see the ridge that runs right down the middle? Set the point of the sword right there—and you will be able to experience life as you've never known it."

Okay, now she was getting freaked out. Lizzie turned to the woman, who watched her expectantly. She was about to ask if she was on Candid Camera when the woman nudged her. "Go ahead…give it a try."

Lizzie glanced over both shoulders and seeing the way clear, she did as the woman asked. She set the tip of the sword on the crest, right into the ridge.

"And now?" Lizzie asked, brows lifted high, waiting for a camera crew to jump out and shout "surprise".

The woman smiled, took a step back and said, "Have a nice trip…"

About the author:

Julia Templeton has written contemporary, historical and time-travel romances for magazines and book publishers and, most recently, romantica for Ellora's Cave Publishing. She also pens novels under the pseudonym Anastasia Black with writing partner and fellow Ellora's Cave author Tracy Cooper-Posey. Aside from her passion for writing, Julia also enjoys reading, listening to music, collecting research books, traveling and spending time with family.

Julia Templeton welcomes mail from readers. You can write to her c/o Ellora's Cave Publishing at 1337 Commerce Drive, Suite 13, Stow OH 44224.

Also by Julia Templeton:

Now and Forever

Kieran the Black

Why an electronic book?

We live in the Information Age—an exciting time in the history of human civilization in which technology rules supreme and continues to progress in leaps and bounds every minute of every hour of every day. For a multitude of reasons, more and more avid literary fans are opting to purchase e-books instead of paperbacks. The question to those not yet initiated to the world of electronic reading is simply: *why?*

1. *Price.* An electronic title at Ellora's Cave Publishing runs anywhere from 40-75% less than the cover price of the <u>exact same title</u> in paperback format. Why? Cold mathematics. It is less expensive to publish an e-book than it is to publish a paperback, so the savings are passed along to the consumer.

2. *Space.* Running out of room to house your paperback books? That is one worry you will never have with electronic novels. For a low one-time cost, you can purchase a handheld computer designed specifically for e-reading purposes. Many e-readers are larger than the average handheld, giving you plenty of screen room. Better yet, hundreds of titles can be stored within your new library—a single microchip. (Please note that Ellora's Cave does not endorse any specific brands. You can check our website at www.ellorascave.com for customer

recommendations we make available to new consumers.)

3. *Mobility.* Because your new library now consists of only a microchip, your entire cache of books can be taken with you wherever you go.

4. *Personal preferences are accounted for.* Are the words you are currently reading too small? Too large? Too...**ANNOYING**? Paperback books cannot be modified according to personal preferences, but e-books can.

5. *Innovation.* The way you read a book is not the only advancement the Information Age has gifted the literary community with. There is also the factor of what you can read. Ellora's Cave Publishing will be introducing a new line of interactive titles that are available in e-book format only.

6. *Instant gratification.* Is it the middle of the night and all the bookstores are closed? Are you tired of waiting days—sometimes weeks—for online and offline bookstores to ship the novels you bought? Ellora's Cave Publishing sells instantaneous downloads 24 hours a day, 7 days a week, 365 days a year. Our e-book delivery system is 100% automated, meaning your order is filled as soon as you pay for it.

Those are a few of the top reasons why electronic novels are displacing paperbacks for many an avid reader. As always, Ellora's Cave Publishing welcomes your questions and comments. We invite you to email us at service@ellorascave.com or write to us directly at: 1337 Commerce Drive, Suite 13, Stow OH 44224.